P9-CFW-958

None to Comfort Me

ANNE MALLARD DAVIS

None to Comfort Me

CARNEGIE LIBRARY
LIVINGSTONE COLLEGE
SALISBURY, N. C. 28144

JOHN F. BLAIR, Publisher
Winston-Salem, North Carolina

122045

Copyright © 1978 by Anne Mallard Davis
Library of Congress Catalog Card Number: 78-21963
ISBN 0-89587-005-3
Printed in the United States of America
by Heritage Printers, Inc.
Charlotte, North Carolina
All rights reserved

Library of Congress Cataloging in Publication Data

Davis, Anne Mallard.
    None to comfort me.
PZ4.D2587No   [PS3554.A9315] 813'.5'4   78-21963
    I. Title.
ISBN 0-89587-005-3

For my two best friends

HARRY E. DAVIS
who also happened to be my husband

CARRIEMAE OSTERHOUT
who also happens to be my mother

None
to
Comfort
Me

NOBODY told me I'd have to go to a school painted baby pink. It . . . it's *stupid* and vulgar!"

Celia's mother looked up from the pile of linen she was unpacking from a trunk and meticulously storing in the cedar chest. "Don't whine and stamp your feet at me, young lady. It hasn't been a dream retirement for any of us."

"I shan't go. I'd rather attend another private school. Or have a tutor."

The child's crisp British accent, now so out of place, underlined Evelyn's growing discomfort, and she lost her temper. "No more private schools. And no more tutors. Ever. You're going to that damn public school tomorrow if it's painted circus stripes with polka dots, and that's final. Now go on outside and play."

"Nobody'll play with me."

"Then go climb some trees. Or something."

"Very well, if you insist." Celia went into the hallway, running her fingers dejectedly along the banisters enclosing the steep stairwell. Evelyn sat back against the cedar chest, not caring that her sweaty shirt would mar the antique wax finish. She was listening to Celia going down the steps, one resentful thump after another. The simple truth was that the child was something of a freak in the town of her birth. " 'Town of her birth,' indeed," Evelyn muttered, angrily mopping perspiration and tears from her eyes. The old family community meant nothing whatsoever to the ten-year-old child, who had been whisked away from it at the age of two months. In fact, Evelyn thought bitterly, it meant nothing much now to George and herself, either.

They had come home in August, 1939, fulfilling Evelyn's fervent hopes that when George retired from the Marine Corps, they would live in Beldon, the small South Carolina coastal town where Evelyn had grown up. George had yearned for Atlanta, with its obvious cultural and educational advantages. Evelyn never argued the point. But every time George mentioned the city, Evelyn somehow managed to recall her own happy childhood in a small town. George was engulfed by Evelyn's wistful expression, by her oblique references to the importance of close family roots for their only child. For George, standing up to Evelyn had always been like boxing with fog, cause for an aggravated chuckle. But, as Evelyn constantly reminded him, it would certainly be cheaper to live in Beldon. And Atlanta was close enough for time-to-time excursions. Small-town life would probably be more fun. One sunny morning, George quietly capitulated. "Hell, why not?" he said, grinning at Evelyn's tear-brimmed smile over Celia's exuberant excitement.

And it had seemed ideal. Evelyn would have her family and her childhood friends. There was a Marine Base a scant twelve miles away, where George could find the companionship of military men and have the privilege of using the Post's golf course. Above all, Beldon would fulfill the many promises to Celia through the ten constricted years of her life in foreign stations. They had said again and again that they would eventually live where she would be able to climb trees and go barefooted, eat fresh fruit, play with her friends unchaperoned. Best of all, Evelyn pointed out, there were six first cousins in two neighboring houses, and Celia could invite them over any time she wished. And the Sound was only a block away, with all its fun of swimming, boating, and fishing.

Of all the promises, the one that had most profoundly excited Celia was the decision to rent the top half of her grandmother's house. There was a newly installed kitchen with a glassed-in porch and four gigantic high-ceilinged rooms, each with its own fireplace. George and Evelyn were puzzled by Celia's squeals of joy when they told her. But for all her life, she had stared from the windows of cars and trains, from portholes of ships, filled with wonder at what it could be like to come home each day to the same house, to the same friends. And now she was to have a real home, complete with a resident grandmother known to Celia only by disembodied handmade presents and endearing letters.

Yet now, for Celia, the town was merely another foreign country, stranger even than their last apartment dwelling in Shanghai's French Concession. Or on any of the other far-flung Marine Corps bases where Celia had been raised a closely sheltered child. In Beldon, Celia's British accent made her unintelligible to her cousins. Yankee-bred George was still considered as "the outlander with that funny last name, Sturdevent." "What sort of name is that?" people inevitably commented, and just as inevitably mispronounced it. On the nearby base, George discovered that active officers had little interest in the friendship of a retiree, and golf was not much fun alone. Evelyn's childhood friends were reserved and withdrawn, curious at her return after thirty years of a mysterious life spent in unknown places with exotic names. "Why settle back here?" they would ask, and Evelyn could no longer answer.

Their first problem with Beldon had been simply trying to get there. Passenger train service had been discontinued "due to lack of demand." There was no bus line into town, and no airfield. They finally arranged to fly to Centerville, where Evelyn's mother would meet them. The only available plane reservations were on a local flight making a stop-start, zigzagging route along the eastern seaboard. The day they arrived, their plane was four hours late because of a violent thunderstorm, and both Celia and Evelyn were air-sick when they finally landed at the barren little airport. They stepped from the cool cabin to be slammed across the head with noonday August sun

3

and the dank smell of marsh enfolding the city in moist, wet-quilt heat.

"God!" George loosened his tie, but his shirt was soaked with sweat before he could cross the short distance to the garish red-brick terminal.

"Mother!" Heedless of the milling crowd and the weather, Evelyn dropped her overnight bag and sprinted across the field to embrace the slender, gray-haired woman she had not seen for ten years.

George picked up her bag, still struggling with his tie. "That's your grandmother, Celia."

Celia took his hand and cowered against him, tongue-tied with shyness and embarrassment at the sight of the two women's tear-streaked joy. More fragile than her photographs, her grandmother was shorter than her mother and smartly dressed in a simple voile dress, high heels, and a tiny hat. Her gray hair, naturally wavy, was cut short to frame delicate high cheekbones and blue-gray eyes. Celia had envisioned her as stout, somehow, and in the kitchen, wearing an apron. Or maybe rocking on the front porch, knitting.

"Let me look at you!" she was saying, stepping back to regard Evelyn lovingly. She smoothed the beginning strands of gray in Evelyn's chestnut hair and embraced her again. Celia averted her eyes, uneasy at the sudden vision of little girl where her mother ought to be. "Where's my grandchild?"

Celia clamped George's arm tighter, and he squirmed under the added heat of her body. "Run along and speak to your grand-mother." She shook her head, not releasing her hold. "For pete's sake, Celia . . ."

She was swept from his arm into a soft embrace, pressed to a soft bosom smelling of sweet talcum, showered with soft tears. "Not really! This grown-up young lady can't be my missing grandchild!" Her speech, too, was soft with its heavy southern slur.

Celia struggled free, straightening the front of her dress, ad-justing her straw hat. "How-do-you-do." She curtsied primly.

4

"George!" She swept past Celia to embrace him. Her hat veil caught over his pipe, and they laughed loudly, disentangling it. To Celia's horror, there were tears in her father's eyes.

"Sallie—you haven't changed a bit."

"Nonsense. 'Course I have. And look at you—all gray."

"But not bald yet, thank God."

The three of them hugged each other, while Celia fidgeted, digging her toe into a pocket of soft tar at the runway's edge.

"You're really here. I don't believe it yet."

George grinned down at them. "What say we get out of this heat."

They walked to the parking lot with Celia trailing behind, hoping bypassers would think she was alone. Sallie led the way to a new, light-blue Plymouth, handing a set of keys to George.

"This isn't the car I ordered."

"Yes and no. There was a delay on the bigger maroon model, and under the circumstances, with delivery so slow, Bob—our agent—thought you'd rather have this than none at all. Besides, he says blue stands up better in this sun."

"Well . . ."

"I'm sorry, George. I didn't know what to do." Sallie looked up at him, anxiously apologetic.

He knocked his pipe out and rubbed the bowl against his nose, massaging oil from his skin into the burled wood as he fought back his irritation.

"You know how cussed independent small-town dealers are. I thought I'd best take it."

"You were absolutely right, Sallie. Nothing else you could have done."

Knowing his hatred for pastel cars, "candied almonds" as he called them, Evelyn squeezed his arm. "We can swap it in later. At least we're home."

"Or will be in another two hours—if this damn thing runs." He slammed their luggage into the trunk, cutting his forehead on the raised lid. "Dammit all."

"George—please."

5

"Sorry. It's the heat."

Beyond tangled city streets, the single highway to Beldon took them across a narrow, rusting metal bridge. The flow of traffic vanished and George relaxed behind the wheel, marveling at the steady chatter of the two women, both talking at the same time about different things, but answering each other without pause.

From the instant she climbed into the back seat beside her grandmother, Celia had ceased listening. She dug her fingers into the upholstery, pressed her face to the window, and prayed for their long journey to come to an end. The ribbon of cement shimmered and wavered endlessly, a single spider's filament flung across a fragile causeway that spanned endless marsh and diminutive sand spits of islands. Occasional pine trees loomed from the roadside, stark thin branches without substance enough for shade. A slimy odor of mud permeated the car. Sky, sand, and endless horizon appeared to drop away from the roadway, leaving them spinning along the top of an endless glass dome. Celia squeezed her eyes shut against the dizzying sensation and clutched tighter at the edge of the seat.

Still talking, Sallie had been watching Celia closely, eager to know the reality of the many snapshots she treasured. It was hard now to trace the strong family resemblance. The child's face was damp, her light brown hair plastered across her forehead by the wide-brimmed straw hat. Celia's knees were concealed by the hand-embroidered hem of her silk dress. Only her hands were clearly visible, working nervously at the upholstery. With surprise, Sallie saw that they were miniature replicas of her own. Smiling, she took her perfumed handkerchief and leaned over tenderly to dab perspiration from Celia's face.

The soft scent gagged Celia, and she yanked away. "D-Daddy . . . I-I'm going to throw up."

"Figures." George eased the car to the shoulder, and Evelyn climbed out with Celia. "It's the heat," George said again, somewhat gagged himself by the heavy marsh odors.

6

Sallie fanned gnats from her face and gently touched his shoulder. "I want to thank you, George."

"For what?"

"Coming home to live. Ever since Charles died—well, it's been downright lonesome."

George tipped his head in hearty laughter. "With two daughters living alongside? And all those grandchildren?"

Sallie laughed with him. "That does sound silly. Agnes and Annie are real good to me—but, tell you the truth, it's Evelyn who's always been my friend-child. Know what I mean? Agnes —she's not a very happy person, and she takes it all out on her children. She won't even let them play in her new living room, so they spend all their time over at Annie's. Annie is so scatter-brained she doesn't notice what gets busted up, and—"

George twisted his damp shirt collar away from his neck. Family gossip had always made him uneasy, and this time, there would be no escape to a new assignment.

An hour later, outside Beldon, the road was cooler, winding beneath a tunnel of live-oak branches. The final approach to town, which Evelyn remembered fondly, was marred by a trailer housing development, fifty metallic shoe boxes on a treeless plain that had once been a shady park. "Are they for sale?"

"Oh, my, no!" Sallie laughed. "Who in this town would buy one of those ugly things? They're for rent. Construction folk mostly. Outlanders from the new bridge. Mighty rough bunch— we don't have much to do with them."

"God. Not even home yet, and already we're getting—" He was silenced by Evelyn's hand on his leg, the gentle pressure of her fingertips. George did not finish his sarcastic comment on Beldon's notorious snobbishness toward strangers, "outlanders," as they were called.

"What did you say?" Sallie repeated.

"Nothing. I—I was surprised to see a stoplight."

"Oh, my—those things. They're all over town now. Why, you can't go two blocks without having to stop. Usually for no reason at all. I don't see why you can't go right on through if nothing's coming. But you can't. Harlan—he's Sheriff now, you know—he's your second cousin, Celia—well, Harlan gave me a ticket for doing that. But I still do it! Only now I make sure Harlan's not behind me."

Evelyn stifled dismay as they turned into a gaudy new boulevard. Live oaks and magnolias had been stripped and razed to make way for a sleazy line of sun-baked commercial buildings. Garages, grease-larded restaurants, seedy motels, secondhand car lots, a fortune-teller. The unique quality of the entrance to the island town had been completely obliterated. Evelyn reflected bitterly that they could have been entering Jersey City, or any other grubby industrial area. At length, the street ran along a row of tall palmettos interspersed with heavy green pom-poms of oleander bushes. To their right was a sandy marsh and the first inlet of the Sound, sparkling salt water that scalloped in and out around town. Sallie pointed to a new building on the other side of the inlet. "That's the new Negro school."

Celia showed her first real interest, bobbing up to peer at the neat brick building. "Why do they call it Negro School?"

Sallie looked at her in astonishment. "Because that's where the colored children go."

"Will I go there?"

"Good gracious, child. Of course not."

"Why not?"

George coughed with a meaningful glance to Evelyn. "Here we go." In a louder tone, he tipped his head back toward Celia. "Why don't we talk about it a little later, when we get unpacked?"

Celia settled back in disgruntled silence. Ask questions, her mother and father always said; how else do you expect to learn? But try asking a few and see how far you get.

The car made a sharp left turn onto Main Street, and Evelyn sat forward with a happy shout. "Look!" This part of town, at least, had not changed. The street topped a sharp thirty-foot slope of grassy bluff and wound through giant live-oak trees festooned

8

with swaying Spanish moss. To their left was a row of stately nineteenth century two-storied homes set in manicured gardens of azaleas and magnolias. Built as town houses for wealthy plantation owners, they boasted graceful soaring pillars of varying design that gave shade and shelter to enormous verandahs and high-windowed front rooms. In a dignified row, the houses were all identically angled on their lawns, skillfully canted away from the street to catch the maximum amount of breeze and the best view of the distant ocean. Below the bluff, the whole panorama of the Sound stretched out from the foot of the seawall. Evelyn was disappointed that Celia's first view would be of the low tide, which left a stenching tableland of mud banks and oyster beds with spindly boat docks spearing out from the shore to service an assortment of beached rowboats and sailboats. The water line was still creeping out toward the deep-dredged shipping channel of the Inland Waterway, a twisting course that curved around a buoy, snaking through a network of marshy islands to the ocean eight miles beyond.

At the end of the bluff, the street dropped down gently, and they were plunged into the shopping center. Four blocks of cramped buildings supplied a minimal choice of household and clothing necessities. On the Sound side of the street, the stores were built on piers extending out to the channel's edge, and every building had an open dock at its rear with a fuel pump and mooring facilities for yachts and shrimp boats. The stores were low and sagging, each one propped and huddled into place by its neighbor. Beneath a constant insinuation of sea air and salt spray, paint and bricks were faded to a sad mélange of pastels.

At the end of the first block, Sallie pointed out the family store to Celia. "See? That's your grandfather's name," Sallie murmured huskily, still mourning the man who had died twenty years before. "Charles Villiers" was dimly visible in old-fashioned lettering across the windowless second-floor façade of crumbling brick. Built from the street to the waterside, Villiers was the largest building downtown, and the best hardware store in the county. It also housed the town's only funeral home, with a single hearse that, by necessity, was regularly pressed into service as an ambulance. "Villiers" was a byword in the community. "Cradle to grave," as the townspeople sardonically phrased it. And when Charles Villiers died and his two sons-in-law bought the store from Sallie, they had wisely decided to continue their new management under the well-established Villiers name.

Sallie waved vigorously to a short man lounging in the store's shady entrance door. "There's Alan—loafing as usual. I suppose poor old Fred is inside with the customers."

"Want to stop?" George asked unenthusiastically.

"No, no. They're planning to come over, soon as they know for sure you're here."

The stores ended at the foot of a bridge leading to the smaller islands between Beldon and the ocean, and George turned left for the final two-block drive to Sallie's house.

The great hallway was cool after their long ordeal of travel. Celia stood just inside the doorway, staring up the steep stairwell, inhaling the fragile odor of freshly cut roses.

The telephone rang. A sudden, cacophonous jangling split through the dusky hall. It receded momentarily, then began again, a shrill, impatient insistence for attention. "Drat!" Sallie trotted toward the base of the stairwell. "It's Miss Effie."

Celia narrowed her eyes in the dusky light, searching along the diagonal wall space below the steps for an old hand-crank phone. "Look, Mother. You were wrong. It's still there."

"For heaven sakes." Evelyn went to touch it fondly. "You don't have the dial system yet?"

"No." Sallie sighed. "They've been trying to put it in, but we just told them they'd have to wait until Miss Effie passed away."

"She's not still the operator!"

"Oh, my—yes—still. Kind of hard on all of us, because she's getting pretty deaf. But how on earth could anyone expect Miss Effie to learn a new job at her age? So we just remember to shout." She demonstrated her statement by snatching down the receiver and shrieking into the wall speaker. "Yes, Miss Effie, what is it . . . Oh ? . . ." Sallie cupped her hand over the mouth-piece. "Says she saw us go by her corner . . . What ? . . . No, you can speak to Evelyn later . . . Oh, good lord, Miss Effie—give the poor things time enough to go to the bathroom!" Sallie slammed down the receiver and hurried into her room to fling her hat on the bed. "I have to find my keys, and I'll be right with you."

One of Celia's favorite stories about Beldon was that of Sallie and her keys. A strange collection of them bristled from a loop of red grosgrain ribbon with two long ends intended to be tied to her belt. Instead, Sallie inevitably set the keys down absent-mindedly in some unlikely spot, and when it became necessary to open one of the myriad pantries or cupboards, the entire household had to be pressed into the search.

"Now, where can they be . . ." Sallie looked vaguely around the potted plants she had watered that morning.

Oddly reassured, Celia smiled for the first time, pulling off the straw hat and rubbing her matted hair.

Sallie was delighted by the change in Celia's solemn expression. "That's right! You make yourself at home." She darted over to give her another quick hug. "I've got some fresh cookies for you, soon as I find those dratted keys."

"Here they are, Mother," Evelyn called from the living room. "They're here in your sewing box."

"Now how on earth did they get in there? Thank you, dear." Sallie took the ring and went briskly into the kitchen, her stiff arthritic gait rattling the windows. "Ethel . . . oh, Ethel. We're home. I'm going to call in the others." She slammed through the kitchen to the back porch. "Jim! Cynthia . . . Mary . . . all of you . . . come on in here and meet my long-lost lamb." Celia tensed, hearing shrill giggles. Her cousins came racing in from the back yard, a tousle of brownish-blond heads, bright inquisitive blue eyes, their voices a soft babble of slurring sounds. They had been playing ball in the back yard, and in the assortment of dirty blue jeans and shorts, it was difficult at first glance to distinguish girls from boys. "This is Cynthia, and Little Sally." Her grandmother tapped two of the heads. "Sally's named for me, of course. And this is Jim, and—no, wait. Best do this by families." She moved through the group, accompanying her introductions. "Here's Jim and Cynthia. They're your Aunt Agnes's and Uncle Fred's children and they live right next door. Aunt Annie and Uncle Alan's house is over the back fence with Mary, here—Little Sally, Charles Two—named for your grandfather—and Louisa, our baby."

More giggles.

She drew Celia close, turning her to face the others. "You children just don't know how I've longed for this moment. Now you're all together, like you belong."

The six cousins ranged in age from five to twelve. Their common blood ties stamped a strong family resemblance on all of them and, recognizing her mirror image in their staring faces, Celia felt for the first time a deep stirring of identity in a so-far alien homeland. She stood, waiting and hopeful, her hands twitching at her embroidered silk dress.

An extra cousin was no novelty to them. Celia was, above all else, a stranger. They were distrustful of her luxurious dress, suspicious of her short, continental haircut, jealous of the legendary tales of her travels. "H'lo," they mumbled guardedly.

"How do you do it's a very great pleasure." Celia's nervousness gave the words a crisp staccato.

There were snickers and giggles, and one fuzzy attempt at imitation. "Howchdew!"

"Now, children," Sallie warned. "You know what I told you."

"Yes'm."

Sallie led them into the sunny dining room, where a powerful Gullah Negro was pouring lemonade. "And here's Ethel."

Ethel was six feet seven inches tall. She was jet black, with hands so large they appeared hinged at her elbows. Setting down the silver pitcher with a crash when she saw Celia, she bent over and clutched her in a clumsy hug. "Our chile done come home, Miss Sallie! I'd know her any place, yes, I surely would. Welcome home, honey. Welcome home." With its origins of African and

12

Elizabethan English, the backwater accent made her words meaningless to Celia. She looked from Ethel to the table to Sallie, uncertain as to how she was expected to answer.

"Looka them silk knee socks," someone whispered in the silence, and there was another outbreak of giggling.

"Children."

In an agony of self-consciousness, Celia found the first treats tasteless. She set hers aside and followed the cousins out to the front porch. George and Evelyn were sipping iced tea, sitting in high-backed wooden rockers and talking to the four additional strangers who were Celia's aunts and uncles. They looked at her curiously, shoppers studying a cut of meat they might decide to purchase.

"What a shame," Agnes commented. "She's going to be dumpy, like my Cynthia." Agnes was the oldest of the sisters, a long-faced woman of stuffed-link-sausage proportions. She was stiffly combed, her long braids clamped in a tight bun. Calculating, icy blue eyes swept up and down Celia's person. Fred Mark, her husband, was even taller, and his thin frame was elongated by the white suit he was wearing. "Come, now," he said. "This is hardly the time to discuss it."

"Oh, hush up, Fred." Annie laughed. "You're always spoiling our conversation." Only two years older than Evelyn, Annie was usually mistaken for Sallie's sister. She had thin gray hair, and blowzy flesh hung from her small frame in loose waves of fat that bulged over her corset and from under her sleeves. She smiled at Celia, her features as flaccid as those painted on a leaky balloon. "She looks to me like she takes after George more than Evelyn. Not as pretty."

Alan Taylor leaned back in his chair and threw one leg over the arm, hitching his dungarees looser, pushing a jaunty straw cap to the back of his head. "She looks to me like a girl who looks like herself, and a mighty pretty little self, too."

"Oh, thanks awfully!" Celia edged nearer to him.

"Thenks arhfully . . ." More giggles.

"Children!" Sallie smiled them into silence.

Voices eddied and swirled across the porch. George had never mastered Evelyn's knack for conducting three or four conversations simultaneously. He nodded politely and winked at Celia, who was equally as bewildered by the hubbub. The cousins started playing some kind of finger-fist game, with much squealing and slapping. Agnes began detailing her household redecorating; Annie outlined a new devil's food cake recipe; Alan touted his new boat; Sallie was describing their plane's arrival. Evelyn's face was radiant with excitement as she somehow managed to answer everybody. George relaxed stiff shoulders against the chair back. If Evelyn was happy, that was all that really mattered. Slowly he became aware of Fred's sad, immobile face. The man was also silent and withdrawn, his fingers drumming idly on the chair arm. Another outlander, George thought sardonically, and rose to lean against the banister beside Fred's chair. "How's it going, Fred?" He was embarrassed by Fred's eager response to his casual remark, and bitterly regretted the question when Fred launched into a heated monologue concerning the hardware store and the funeral home. George knew nothing about either business and could only nod sympathetically. Eventually, Fred recognized George's boredom, and his words wound down to an embarrassed silence.

"Well . . ." Fred stood up, opening a pocket watch hanging from his belt on a thin gold chain. "Speaking of the store, I better get back."

"Nobody's speaking about the store, Fred. I was talking about my boat." Alan's sarcasm oozed around a cigarette hanging from his lips, and he grinned at the laughter he drew from Annie.

"Oh, my goodness. There they go again." Annie dabbed at the constant perspiration on her forehead.

Agnes lifted her chin in stern rebuff to Alan. "Somebody better speak about the store, and it always winds up being my Fred. Like last night, Alan. You were supposed to be on ambulance run, but where were you when they had to call Fred instead? Least he knows his responsibility."

14

Blushing, Fred hushed her nervously and turned to Evelyn. "I hate to run off, but I left the boy in charge, and he's the only one down there. There's a funeral tomorrow, and the ambulance calls to worry about, besides a new shipment of hardware stock."

Alan poured himself another glass of tea. "Hell, Fred. Sit back down. You got nothing to worry about. Thomas is the smartest black boy in town."

"Thomas Berry?" Evelyn asked. "He's still with you?"

"Sure as hell is. Finished at State College for niggers last year, and he's smarter than any white man we've had in the store. More dependable, too. Right, Fred?"

"Yes, yes, Alan—right. As always. Right, right, right."

Everybody laughed, but George noticed the tremor in Agnes's lips, the nervous fingers plucking at her temples. She started to say something, but looked to Fred and remained silent.

Fred returned his watch to his pocket and patted his dry lips with a napkin. "If you left it to Alan, he'd let Thomas run the whole store and just show up to count the till."

"Well, Fred, I don't believe in spending twenty-four hours out of twelve down there, especially in this heat."

"Yes. Well, see you later." Fred paused to pat Jim on the head.

Embarrassed by Fred's tender hand, Jim doubled up his fist and pretended to sling a hard blow at his father's stomach. "Ah, Pop. You never remember."

"Uh—what? What—remember what?"

Alan snorted cheerfully. "Why, Jim, you can't expect your dad to play games with you. He's a high-class businessman." Alan rose from his chair and Jim pranced at him, shadow-boxing and grinning. "Owww . . ." Alan bent double, pretending his breath had been knocked out.

Annie beamed proudly. "You know, Evelyn, Alan's a regular Pied Piper with children. But I swear to goodness, sometimes I think we must have mixed up our broods at the hospital. My Mary and Little Sally—why, they're so quiet! Not like Jim and Cynthia."

15

"Hmf." Agnes sniffed and chewed hard on an ice cube, a sound she knew Annie detested. "They're certainly not so noisy at home."

"That's because they're never there." Annie shifted uneasily, glaring at Agnes's masticating mouth. "You know, Evelyn, Agnes went and fixed her house up so fancy nobody wants to set foot in the place. All Victorian, if you please. Why, a body's scared to move around for fear of breaking something. Now, my furniture may be old, but I have a home where children are welcome to romp and play."

"If you want to see your couch used as a trampoline, that's your business." Agnes chewed louder.

"Will you stop that!" Annie's hand went to her forehead. "You know perfectly well it gives me a headache, and—"

"Girls," Sallie said gently, momentarily ending the argument.

Evelyn set her glass on the floor, bending over to hide her quick smile. It seemed impossible that ten years could have passed and that Agnes and Annie were still carrying on their endless petty bickering.

Cynthia slid from her perch on the banister rail. "We gotta finish our ball game."

There was a quick stampede for the doorway.

"Children . . ." Sallie murmured.

Cynthia halted reluctantly at the screen door. "Oh, yeh." She looked at the floor to one side of Celia's feet. One year older than Celia, Cynthia was beginning to balloon with adolescent fat. "Don' s'pose you wanna come."

"No—no. Thanks awfully."

"No thenks, arhfullllllllly!" Two of the smaller cousins ran tittering down the steps.

"Now you all just wait a minute." Sallie shook her head indignantly. "What kind of invitation is that. Take Celia with you and show her around. You hear me, Jim?"

"Yes'm."

"I'd rather stay. Truly."

Evelyn pointed to the door. "And I'd rather you went. Now

stop behaving like a four-year-old and go play with your cousins."

The seven of them went slowly, sullenly, down the steps and across the lawn to the driveway that divided Sallie's sprawling yard from Agnes's. Celia blinked, squinting against the eye-watering glare of white houses and white sand. The sand was almost ankle deep and silky underfoot, but she winced as she felt it sifting into her shoes, a searing talcum in the afternoon sun.

"Well? What'll we show her?" Charles Two asked.

Jim shrugged. "You heard Gramma. Around." He flung out his skinny, sun-dark arms. "This here's the back yard—it's in the back of the front yard which is in front."

Cynthia was quick to copy him. "Over yonder is the pecan tree. It grows pecans."

The others took up the joke with shouts of laughter. "Yeah, and then we have the back steps that go in the back ..." "... and the garage, for cars, in case you didn't know ..." "... and the rose garden for roses ..." "... and the see-der cedar tree which comes from cedar seeds ..." Jim ran ahead to strike the side of a rickety tin-roofed shed. "And this here is the storage shed where Gramma stores things."

Celia folded her hands together, counting freckles on the backs of her fingers. It should be different, she thought, not like meeting any new group of strangers.

Jim sank to his haunches in the thin strip of shade by the shed. "O.K. We've shown her around. What'll we do now?"

"Don't s'pose you play ball?" Cynthia's tone made it a con-demnatory statement rather than a question.

Celia's temper began to take over her anxiety to please. "I do, too. I play cricket."

"Tha's a bug."

"It's a far more difficult sport than your asinine baseball."

"Oh, yeah?" It came from several indignant basemen and pitchers.

"Yes. Quite. I'd offer to teach you, but you're probably too slow to learn."

17

"Ha-ha, la-deedah!" chubby little Charles Two screeched, and stuck out his tongue.

The back door opened and Ethel came down the steps. "Your Grandma say to hush all that fussing."

They were momentarily silenced, and the cousins sprawled in the shade of the cedar tree, pulling up wisps of grass and thrusting them into an ants' nest, absorbed by the milling insects. Celia trailed after Ethel, grateful for an adult's presence and delighted for any excuse to leave the other children. "Where you going?"

"Fix some chicken for your supper."

"Can't I help?"

"No, you run along and play, honey."

The chicken coop was at the far side of the shed, where the pecan tree afforded some shade through baking afternoons. Celia gagged at the malodorous stink of feathers and manure, but Ethel nonchalantly stepped through the wire gate into the heavily soiled area. There was a silly medley of clucking as yellow chicks and older birds of all sizes ran toward her expecting to be fed, but the clucks rose to wild squawks when Ethel grabbed one bird up by its feet. There were two fryers she had personally fattened for this occasion, and she sought out the second one swiftly, grabbing it up and holding both birds by the legs while she fastened the gate. Celia watched in idle curiosity. The chickens twisted their long necks with chattering clucks over the indignity of their situation, their feathers gleaming iridescent browns in the sunshine. Ethel strode to the clear space beyond the tree. Her great strong hand clamped over the head of the first bird and she began to wring its neck, spinning the body as if cranking a car, letting the chicken's carefully tended weight become its own executioner. With a quick snap, she tore away the head, and the severed parts dropped to the sand. Wings flapping, blood spurting from its ruptured neck, the headless bird ran in a faltering, aimless circle, fighting desperately for the life it no longer had.

"Hey—looka him go!" Jim shouted in surprise.

"Oh, no . . ." Celia reached weakly for the side of the shed.

18

It was sticky with globules of fresh blood, and Ethel was already swinging the second bird. The head parted with another snap, and there were two carcasses flapping on their backs in the bloodied yard. Celia's scream was strangled by violent nausea, and Ethel hurried toward her. "Miss Celia, honey! What's the matter, child?" Celia screamed again, backing away from Ethel's red-stained hand and the spattering of gore on the hem of her starched apron.

"Hey—what's the matter?" Jim and Cynthia ran to her side.

Celia covered her mouth, watching the second chicken fluttering its last terrible moments.

"They're only old chickens!" Jim exclaimed, and Cynthia put her hands on her hips, echoing, "Yeah. Just chickens."

The eyes in the second head twitched, seeming to stare into Celia's, and she vomited again.

Cynthia sighed in exasperation. "She musta been behind the door when the brains was passed out . . ."

"Bastards!" Celia's face was streaked with convulsive sweat, and her voice rose to a shrill rasp. "You're nothing but a pack of dirty little provincial bastards. All of you." She ran for the back steps.

After a startled instant, Jim pranced after her, slapping his chest in glee. "Hey, looka me! I been promoted to a pro-venchal bah-stahd!" The others took up his cry, flinging Celia's words after her, until Sallie came into the kitchen and sent them home.

Celia fled to her room and refused to come downstairs again the rest of the day. She was thrown into another fit of vomiting at the mere sight of the crisp pieces of fried chicken on the tray Sallie brought her and flatly rejected the dish Sallie had been promising her across the years.

19

2

A S ONE SLOW, hot day faded into another, Celia and the cousins went out of their way to avoid each other. On the rare occasions Celia had to go out of the house alone, she walked quickly, apparently deaf to inevitable taunts of "Provenchal Bahstahd."

Evelyn's recollections of the graciousness of oversized rooms and high ceilings had faded to grim realization of the weeks of redecorating she faced. The plaster ceilings were cracked and patched, and she shuddered, remembering the powdered filth of redoing them, the clinging dust that penetrated every closet, cupboard, and drawer. "Heaven help us—they start doing the ceilings tomorrow morning."

"Hell," George said. "It'll give me something to do, cleaning up afterwards."

"Oh, George—dear George." Evelyn mopped her forehead—a futile gesture, her handkerchief was already so damp. "You swore to me you wouldn't mind being retired in Beldon."

"Oh, I don't. Not really." He unfolded the newspaper he'd already read. "It's just that I don't have anything to do. Yet, I mean. I'll find some hobby. Take up woodcarving, maybe. Don't worry. I'll be fine."

Nevertheless, after the twenty-second day, he quit keeping his line-a-day diary, the tiny journal he had begun as a boy and maintained through World War I and a minor war in Shanghai. He had gone to his desk early that morning, leaning against it and staring along the two blocks to the shimmering blue of the Sound. The tide was coming in, and a gentle breeze fluted the curtains, drifting them across his face. George stood long moments, enjoying the temporary coolness, thinking of— He realized with a start that he was thinking of absolutely nothing and hastily unlocked the top-right drawer, where he kept his diaries. There were twelve palm-sized, wafer-thin volumes with gold-leaf pages bound in black calf. Each book spanned four years. Oil-stained, blood-stained, tea-stained, tear-stained, they bore mute evidence that he had lived their cryptic comments. One was almost illegible because of salt water that had seeped into its waterproof container when George's ship was torpedoed and he had floated six hours on a raft in the Atlantic without hope of rescue. "Picked up in spite of heavy odds," he had written. "Temp. 78. Calm seas. Thanks to God." On impulse, George pulled out the earliest volume and thumbed through it. The very first entry read: "Tree house completed. Climbed up and read two chapters "Count of Monte Cristo." Fell asleep. Fell out. Left arm fractured. Temp. 59. Sunny." At the bottom of the page, four years later on the comparable day: "Received West Point appt. Report in Aug. Temp. 61. Windy & rain." Remembering his terror of those days away from home, he chuckled and pulled out another volume, reading at random. His marriage. His Guam service. Births and deaths of his two infant sons. Promotion. Celia's birth. He had kept his journal faithfully until this morning, when he uncapped his pen and wrote without premeditation: "Temp. 88. Humidity 93%. This concludes my entries. There is nothing more to say." He stood straighter to reread the last page, his stocky frame at ramrod attention, his gray hair neatly brushed and combed. With a quick look around the room to be sure no one had come in, he snapped a sharp salute and locked the half-completed diary back in the drawer with the others. He filled his pipe, giving infinite care to each grain of tobacco. Cars were beginning to move along the street, and there was a hoarse blast from a yacht signaling the drawbridge to open. George stared down at the street, rubbing his pipe bowl, taking no satisfaction from the sheen of the wood. Perhaps, he thought, he would buy a boat.

Later that morning, he was playing his fifth game of solitaire when Evelyn came back from registering Celia for school. He saw tears brimming in her eyes and put down the deck of cards. "Well? What's gone wrong now?"

Celia's years of private schools and tutoring during their travels abroad had combined to give her placement tests the rating of a high school sophomore in an academic system geared to the slowest children in a rural community. George yawned. "Nothing wrong with that. She's a smart kid, that's all."

"But—but you can't put a ten-year-old in high school."

"Why not?"

"She'd miss all the fun. All the parties, and dates, and—"

George slammed the top of the coffee table, scattering cards in every direction. "What the hell difference does it make if she does, or does not, date one of these local clods?"

"George!"

"I did not work thirty years for my only child to go picnicking, or dancing, with the son of some goddamn farmer, and—"

"George, what is it? What's the matter?"

He stood staring down at the shambles of his solitaire game. "Maybe we should take her out of school—travel for a year or two."

Evelyn stooped, picking up the cards one by one, straightening them meticulously in the damp palm of her hand. "We could. But that won't give her the 'normal' childhood we talked about."

"No. I suppose not." He rubbed his forehead, feeling the beginning of a recurrent headache sweeping over him in direct proportion to the heat of the day. "What—uh—what did the school suggest?"

"They want to put her in the seventh grade."

"Hold her back that much?"

"She'd be in the same class with Cynthia and Jim. He was a late starter, you know." Evelyn riffled the cards. "Celia—she—she had the lowest rating for her age in emotional tests."

22

George snorted. "As opposed to these local nitwits who don't know their ass from a book in the hand? What the hell does that mean? Celia was right—they're nothing but a bunch of little provincial bastards."

Tears rolled down Evelyn's cheeks. "It's all my fault. Oh, George . . . I thought you two would be so happy here . . . but . . . but nothing's working out like we planned. Maybe we should think about Atlanta, after all."

"No, no. We're here—we'll stay. I . . . I guess it's going to take more settling in than we figured, that's all. But it'll be all right, honey. I'm sure it will. In time." He moved toward the door.

"Don't you want your cards?"

"No. I'm going for a walk." Midway down the shadowy stairwell he almost fell over Celia. She was lying on her back, head on the lower steps, feet twined through the banisters. "What are you doing?"

"Lying here on the steps."

George's irritation aggravated his pounding headache. "I can see that. But why?"

"I just feel like it."

"You may just feel like a good swat on the behind." Looking closer, his eyes accustomed to the soft light, he could see her swollen eyes, her mouth pinched tight with the effort of self-control. He sighed in weary speculation as to why females cried so damn much, but gentled his tone. "Want to go for a walk?"

"No, no! . . . Thanks awfully."

He stepped cautiously over her head and went on down the steps, through the hall to the screened-in porch. There he stopped with his hand on the door, trying to decide which way to go. With a wry smile for his own foolishness, he fished into his pocket and pulled out a coin. "Two out of three," he muttered, flipping it. "And if it's Main Street, I'll go look at some boats." The coin spun three times. "Main Street and boats it is." He set out briskly.

Celia, fearful that he was going to insist on her walking with him, was relieved to hear the screen door squeak shut. She covered her eyes with her arm, listening to the faint shouts of her cousins at play. "Foreigner," they had taunted her at registration, when tests showed how fluently she spoke French. "Filthy foreigner," Jim had snickered behind her back. Thinking again of their first meeting, Celia pressed her arm down hard across her eyes, letting hot tears flow. "Oh, Lord," she prayed silently. "It's all your fault, actually. How could you let me down like that—letting me call them provincial bastards? It's too late now, but why didn't you let me call them 'damn fools,' or maybe even 'goddamn fools'?"

The next morning, Celia insisted on walking alone the five short blocks to school, feeling half nude in new short socks. She wore her favorite blazer, dark blue, with gold lettering embroidered on the pocket around an elaborate shield of rich colors depicting books, lanterns of knowledge, a library window, and a diploma. It was the emblem of the last private school she had attended, and Celia wished fervently that she were on her way back there now as, halfway to school, she became aware that all the other girls were wearing light-colored cotton dresses. When Celia reached the school yard, she was the focus of giggling clumps of children. Pretending not to notice, she stood still and looked around to get her bearings. Covering a full block, the grounds were a sweep of white sand with patches of grass that somehow survived constant trampling and scampering. The school building stood at the precise center of the block. A two-story rectangle, it had an auditorium added at the front, entered by wide steps leading up to a small verandah with oversized pillars of concrete. The entire structure was painted the shocking baby pink that Celia detested. A bell rang, its tones as sharp as the garish verandah that housed it.

All right, Celia decided. She'd show them. She began striding briskly toward the auditorium. She was quick to notice the other lone figure, a slender girl with limp, silky brown hair. She passed Celia with lowered head, apparently unaware of the stares and whispers that followed her. As far as Celia could see, she was the only girl not wearing new clothes. Her jumper was immaculately starched and pressed, but the plaid print had faded to dim tones of pink and burnt orange, sad contrast to the bright band of newly lowered hem. Her brown oxfords were scuffed and run down at the heel, and the lunch box she carried was dented under its fresh coat of red enamel.

To Celia's delight, they ended up in the same classroom.

At lunch time, Celia sought her out, anxiously circling and re-circling the grounds until she found her. She had gone across a driveway to the kindergarten playground and was sitting behind a wire fence in one of the low-slung swings. It was shady and cool, with a whisper of breeze from the water. Celia came to a halt, stuttering with shyness. "Hello—my—my name's Celia."

"Yes I know." She had enormous, sad brown eyes and a some-what sensuous mouth.

"C-can I eat w-with you?"

"If you really want."

"Oh, thank you. Thanks awfully." Celia sat down in the neigh-boring swing and fumbled at the catch of her new lunch box.

"Your cousins won't like it—you talking to me."

"The hell with them. I hate all of them, and I'll talk to who-ever I please."

"Well . . . O.K. My name's Martha."

They swayed gently in the long sweep of swings, eating, searching for conversation, until the tinny bell summoned them back to class. By then Celia had discovered that Martha lived two blocks away on her own route home, and they agreed to walk that far together. "I can't ask you in, though," Martha cautioned quickly.

"That's quite all right. I promised to go straight home any-how."

Martha's home was a rickety cottage with flaking whitewash finish. It was set squarely on the sidewalk with two steep steps giving access to the sagging porch. A disheveled woman with overbleached hair was sitting in a hanging porch swing, leaning against a young Marine Corps Sergeant as they drank from a shared beer can. "Hey, darling," she called to Martha.

"Hi." Martha waved a reluctant good-bye to Celia and went into the house.

Through the next few days Martha's and Celia's friendship flourished, fed by their mutually outcast condition. While Martha accepted her exile with stoic docility, Celia became increasingly sassy and outspoken. She flaunted her travels in classroom recitation. Whatever the literary assignment, she had read it "simply years ago." And she flatly refused to answer the teacher "ma'am" on the grounds that " 'ma'am' is for servants and other inferiors."

At the end of the week, when Martha admired her treasured blazer, Celia gave it to her, insisting over Martha's protests that she take it.

"Honest?"

"Honest. Because you're my best friend, and if you give your best friend something you truly like yourself, then you'll stay best friends forever."

Martha's laugh was a dubious one. "Sometimes you're just a baby. You know? But thanks anyway for the jacket." She began a detailed description of a boy who had followed her home from the movies, begging her for a date, but in spite of his wealth, her mother had insisted that she stay home and study. Celia masked a puzzled sense of disappointment, pretending eager attention.

There was a different man in the porch swing when they walked home that afternoon, a balding, heavyset civilian in dirty coveralls. His face was slashed by a scar that twisted his upper lip into a wet, lurid grin. He lurched to his feet when Martha came up the steps and crossed to her unsteadily. "Hey! There she is! How's things at the pink prison?"

"O.K."

His voice was suggestive innuendo. Dirty hands fondled at Martha's back, her thighs; caressed her shoulders beneath Celia's blazer. Celia shivered, feeling degraded to see his sweating

26

fingers fumbling at the embroidered emblem on the blazer pocket over Martha's breast. He was soiling the lettering. "You gonna be my girl, ain't you?"

"No. Never." Martha shied away and bolted for the door while the blonde woman and the fat man roared with laughter.

"Give her another six months," the woman said.

"I'll give her six weeks." He grabbed for the beer can, drained it with loud gulps, belched, and wiped at his mouth with his sleeve.

Celia hurried along the sidewalk, bitterly regretful at having parted so lightly with her blazer.

"Who was that awful man?" she demanded the next day over lunch.

"Mr. Brown. From the bridge crew. A—a friend of my mother's." Martha split a heavy piece of chocolate cake, extending the larger portion to Celia. "My mama runs a—sorta—sorta social club—where Marine fellows from the Post can come and play cards, and be with their friends, and you know—just have fun. And Mr. Brown helps her. He brings his friends—new fellows. To meet Mama, and—and to show them around her club. Some folks say my mama's not nice."

"She looks nice to me," Celia lied.

"Anyway, it's the best paying work Mama can find. See, she never went through school, so she wants me to go in the worst way. I'm going to college and major in Home Economics and teach. Before I get married, I mean. I'm gonna marry young, and—"

"For pete's sake. How come you're always talking about boys and getting married?"

Martha snickered. "Told you you were just a baby. I bet you don't even menstruate yet." She snickered again at Celia's blush. "I do. So I have to be thinking ahead." Her voice droned on in one of her increasingly lengthy expositions of how hard she planned to study, of the handsome man she would marry. She glanced up to find Celia absorbed in watching a rough-and-tumble version of crack-the-whip going on in the sunny school yard. It was an excuse for much jostling and horseplay, with shrieking girls and teasing boys, and Celia's eyes glistened with envy.

"Hey, Martha—maybe they'll ask us to play today."

Martha snapped her lunch box shut and stood up to shake cake crumbs from her dress. "Them and their dumb games. Kid stuff. Lousy little kid stuff. I'm thirteen-and-a-half, and I'm going to be something someday. I don't have time for their stupid games. But you go ahead and play with them—little baby."

"Not unless you want to. Honest, Martha."

Placated by the fudge Celia thrust into her hands, Martha sat down again and began to swing, and Celia promptly imitated her.

"Hey, Celia . . ."

"Hunh?" She averted her eyes quickly from the new game beginning across the road. Cynthia and Jim had not joined in, but were glancing in their direction, talking with their heads close together.

Martha leaned back with the swing's arc, pumping it gently. "Is it true you talk foreign?"

Celia hooted contempt. " 'Talk foreign'—how dumb can you get? You'll be some college student."

"Well, can you?"

"I speak French, if that's what you mean."

"Really and truly?"

"Yes. Of course."

"Say something. Please."

"What?"

"Anything."

"Well . . . *Écoutez-moi, s'il vous plaît.*"

"My."

"Hunh. That's nothing. That's for children who are learning."

Martha dragged her feet in the sand to halt the swing's swaying. "Would you teach me?"

"Gosh, I don't know. With your mushy kind of speech, it's—"

"Oh, I don't mean the whole language. Just some little something so I could say I speak French.

28

"Well . . ."

For two days Celia struggled to teach Martha first one simple phrase and then another. Her initial sense of superiority gave way to irritation with Martha's inability to grasp sound or grammar. Instead of an involved paragraph about the desk in Martha's room, they finally settled for *"Bon voyage, cheri,"* and still Martha could not remember the three words correctly or master the accent.

"It's terrible difficult, isn't it?" Martha begged anxiously.

"No it is not! I learned that much the first hour."

There was a brief flash of expression in Martha's great brown eyes. "You probably had a good teacher."

Notes had begun to flow between Celia's teacher and Evelyn, and Evelyn consulted George late one night in anxious conference.

He picked up his new Leica camera and began fiddling with the lens. "I don't know what to do about it, hon. As far as classwork goes, we all knew she was too far ahead of the others, and I think that's the teacher's problem. As for little what's-her-name, we've made a point of teaching Celia to choose friends for themselves, not their family. What are you going to do now? Turn around and tell her she can't play with this little girl because people think her mother's a whore?"

"But suppose she is?"

"Oh my god. Drinking a can of beer on the porch with enlisted men doesn't make the poor woman a whore. You sound like everybody else in town."

"You've been asking around?"

"Hell, yes. And that's all anybody has to say about her. That, and she's Catholic. Around here that's even a worse offense than prostitution."

Evelyn giggled.

"I'll give Celia a good talking to about her classroom manners, and I recommend we let it go at that. For now."

Evelyn kissed him on the cheek, and her face relaxed into such a happy smile that George decided against mentioning the military investigation he had launched just that afternoon with a phone call to an old friend who was now in command of the Marine Corps base.

Monday was a drizzly day with the first gray overtones of winter chill. Celia was secretly hoping the rain would continue through lunch hour so she might escape the torturous French session with Martha, but the sun came out at the last instant, and rather than face the loneliness of eating by herself, Celia trailed Martha across the yard to their regular swings.

"I brought pound cake," Martha announced, "so don't get snippy again or I won't give you any."

Celia shivered as she felt the damp wood of the seat, the sharp cold of wet metal chains against her arm.

"Boon vuyarge, cherry." Martha flipped her long hair free from her sweater and waited expectantly. "How's that?"

Celia sighed. "No good."

"I remembered all the words, didn't I?"

"Yes, but they're no good without the right accent. Start with '*bon.*'" They went back and forth over the phrase until Celia ended the lesson with a sullen, "I'm hungry."

There was a line forming in the yard for a new game of crack-the-whip, led by Cynthia and Jim. They were pairing off boy-girl, boy-girl, down to the curly-haired blond boy who sat next to Celia in class. Martha was rambling on again about her marriage plans, and Celia fidgeted in the damp swing seat, stealing secret glances across the road. Cynthia had gathered the players around her in a tight group, and Celia was wild with curiosity to know what they were saying, having no idea that she herself was the object of their heated discussion.

"I don't give a damn if she is a snooty stuck-up," Cynthia was whispering. "She's still family, and we can't have her playing around with old Martha Whiting." Since she was the newly elected class president, Cynthia's words carried considerable weight, but there was a long argument before she won her way and began outlining a plan of action. The line formed, but instead of swinging wildly across the open sandy grounds, it began a slow, graceful procession around the live oaks, across the sandy road, and over to the fence enclosing Martha's and Celia's swings. Celia hoped they hadn't seen how closely she had been following their progress.

"—and we'll have a big family," Martha was saying, her nimble fingers halving the pound cake. "All blonds, like him, and I'll do all the sewing for the children, and make his shirts, and—"

"Hey, Celia! Come here a minute."

They were smiling, and they had called to her. Heart pounding, Celia slid from the swing without the slightest hesitation and raced to Cynthia. The group closed around her. A hand patted her shoulder, voices crooned at her ears. "You don't want to play with her!" "No—she's not nice." "My dad's a deputy, and he says the Sheriff is just waiting to run them out of town." "Her mother's a tacky whore."

"Actually, I just feel sorry for her. She's certainly the dumbest girl I ever met." Celia's voice was louder than she intended, and she realized with an icy chill that Martha had clearly heard every word of her treachery.

"We voted you into our club." The blond boy took firm hold of her hand, and the line formed again. This time she was in its midst.

She belonged! Through some miracle not of her own doing, she belonged, and she laughed aloud in an ecstasy of relief, feeling close to fainting in her lightheartedness.

They began to run for the open grounds.

Celia tried not to see Martha sitting in the swing, motionless, holding two pieces of pound cake and watching her with the wild gaze of an injured animal. She was still sitting there when the bell rang. Celia took the proffered hand of one of her new companions and ran for the pink verandah without looking back toward the swings.

Martha did not come back to class.

That afternoon, Celia found the two pieces of pound cake in the white sifting sand under the swing, right next to her own smashed lunch box and thermos.

31

After a week, when Martha failed to appear at school, city authorities came and went from her little whitewashed house, and there were whispered rumors of "illness." "Some illness!" Jim snickered, pantomiming a heavy belly.

As the days passed, Celia's nagging guilt began to abate, and she was glad Martha was out of the way, unable to cast the slightest shadow over her growing popularity with her classmates. But she made a point of always walking home on the opposite side of the street from Martha's house, careful to conceal her furtive glances toward the front porch and its beer-drinking occupants. Through the rest of that month, Martha was occasionally seen sitting with her mother and varying male companions. One afternoon, she was in the porch swing, snuggled on the lap of the fat man with the scarred lip. He was laughing, hugging her hard, and running his hands across her slender hips and stomach, forcing her legs apart with a sharp upthrust of his knee. Martha showed no consciousness of his actions. She was immobile, staring hard at Celia walking by with Cynthia and Jim. Martha's eyes were still enormous, but hard and bitter, uneasy reminder to Celia of something she couldn't identify. Only once again did Celia ever see their gentle, lost expression.

At the end of the month, Celia's report card read straight A's and bore a note of praise from her teacher for "startling adjustment and excellent cooperation." The note added that Celia was now helping to coach the slower pupils in her class. Arms entwined with Cynthia's, Celia was giggling along toward home and a party when they noticed the commotion in front of Martha's house. Armed M.P.'s were escorting three partly dressed Marines to a government vehicle parked behind the Sheriff's car, while Harlan and his two deputies strode up and down along the sidewalk, holding back a group of angry townspeople. The shack door slammed open. Hair hanging stiffly awry, Martha's mother was dragged down the steps to the Sheriff's car, shrieking obscenities and gesturing lewdly to onlookers. She wore only a pink satin slip, and in the thin afternoon sunlight it clearly delineated the lines of her bare, sagging breasts and haunchy buttocks. She yanked one arm free to wipe a drunken spittle from her chin. "Gimme a coat for crissake you bastard it's cold out here."

"I'll bet it just is, after all your exercise." Harlan's mouth twisted in a prurient smirk, and he went back into the shack.

A hard shove thrust Celia to one side. She looked up to see the lip-scarred man. His breath came heavily, and his snicker became shrill as he wiped at his wet lips as though drinking beer. Celia shivered and brushed at the spot on her shoulder where he had touched her.

Across the street, Harlan returned to the porch, leading Martha by the arm. Her bare feet were thrust into oversized bedroom slippers and she, too, wore only a slip. It was dainty and blue, a full ruffled crinoline skirt with soft lace top that clung to the tiny buds of her breasts. The Sheriff unfolded several garments crumpled over his arm and draped the dark blue blazer around Martha's shoulders. Celia could see the gold embroidery on the pocket glinting in the sunshine as Martha hugged it to her, her delicate fingers playing nervously over the cloth. She stood listless and unprotesting, her face turned up to the sunlight, waiting while Harlan and a deputy nailed the door shut behind her. She might have been on the way to her own wedding, her gaze was so wide and wondering. And then she saw Brown beside Celia and the gape-mouthed gathering of children, and her eyes went fierce and cold again, as accusing and lifeless as those in the severed chicken head. Celia turned away from Martha's stare.

Harlan shoved Martha down the steps and into the back of the car beside her mother. Martha leaned across to the open window. "*Bon voyage, cheri!*" she caroled, her voice and inflection a perfect imitation of Celia's tone.

Red lights flashed, sirens blared, and the two cars pulled away.

Celia was clutching her report card and note so tightly that she had torn them almost in two. She unfolded the card and read the enclosed note of praise, oblivious of the chattered obscenities around her. She read it once more, then ripped the note into

33

shreds, folded the card, and rammed it into her pocket. She left Cynthia and walked home swiftly, knowing she had helped put Martha in that car, and already certain she could never ease the memory of a slender girl standing on the steps searching for who knows what in the sunlight, while her fingers traced the blazer's embroidery: Honor, Love, Beauty, Learning.

3

FOR SOME DAYS, Celia's guilt enmeshed her in preoccupied, troubled silence. One morning Cynthia asked her what was the matter. When Celia told her, Cynthia snorted laughter, insisting that Martha was "nothing but a tacky old whore." Celia burst into tears. "Aw, come on," Cynthia said kindly. "What do you care?" Celia wept harder. "Tell you what," Cynthia said in a burst of generosity. "Me and Jim have got a secret, private club—and we'll let you join." Celia was dubious. "Honest. It's so we don't have to play with those dumb cousins."

"But you go over there all the time."

"Sure. Mother doesn't bake cookies the way Aunt Annie does. And then sometimes Uncle Alan sneaks us two out on the boat. He knows about the club—he even lets us meet in the attic over his garage."

Celia was a swift convert. By the end of ten days of secret ceremonies and raucous picnics along the seawall, she was so enamored by the sense of total acceptance that she openly mimicked Cynthia's statement that Martha was, after all, "nothing but a tacky whore."

The one drastic change in her life that Celia detested was the upheaval of traditional family Sundays. When they lived abroad, Sunday had been a cherished day of leisurely brunches in bathrobes, then a picnic, or a concert, or some other special outing. Now, abruptly, Evelyn insisted that Celia attend church almost every Sunday. Evelyn had gone back to the Baptist church of her childhood, and every week she dragged the protesting Celia along with her and Sallie. "She needs it," Evelyn answered George's mild questioning. The first Sunday, George agreed to go with them. But he intensely disliked the sing-song, haranguing delivery of the minister. Then the leading soprano rose to deliver her weekly solo. George recognized Mrs. Beezely, a lifelong friend of Sallie's. He was surprised she was still singing. She was a thin little woman in her seventies. The delicate features of her face were gouged by a black, gap-toothed smile that made George think of Halloween pumpkins and hockey players. He averted his amused gaze to a hymnal and shook his head sternly at Celia's snickering. When Mrs. Beezely lifted her shoulders and attacked "Let a Little Sunshine In," her voice shrilling to the high notes in a cracked quaver, George muffled his laughter in an outburst of choked coughing. No one noticed him because of Evelyn's frantic attempts to stifle Celia's convulsive giggling. From then on, when George did not go fishing, he attended the Episcopal church. Celia contented herself by sitting in the back pew with Cynthia, and the two girls whiled away their tedium with convoluted notes and smothered giggles at Mrs. Beezely's singing.

Sunday afternoons there was a regular secret club meeting. George was becoming acutely aware of the amount of time Celia and the two cousins were spending with Alan, trailing him around the boat dock or down to the hardware store. It disturbed him, for no specific reason he could name.

Despite the deliberate efforts of George and Alan to be friendly toward each other, a growing antagonism sprang up between the two men. Neither would admit it. On George's side, there was sharp resentment of Alan's many disdainful prejudices. Alan distrusted journalists, refused to listen to radio news, bragged about never reading a book "all the way through." "We sure had a bunch of outlanders in the store today," Alan had said in an unguarded moment, and George had answered quickly, "I bet

36

they must have come from all of ten miles away." Alan in turn resented the easy confidence George's travels had given him, his casual way of saying, "When I was in Rome—" or "After we sailed from Trieste—" Alan had been out of the state only twice, once to a convention in Georgia, and once on a short trip to the mountains of Tennessee. The two men continued a pretense of friendliness for the sake of family ties, but George distrusted Alan, and he felt a growing concern for Celia's obvious adulation of the man. "I don't like it," he remarked one morning.

"Why, George, I think you're jealous!" Evelyn laughed. "Alan's a pixie! An overgrown pixie. All the kids adore him— and they dote on Annie, too. That's why they're over there so much of the time." She stopped his quick comment. "Oh, I know he joshes you a lot—and I can see why you'd feel antagonistic toward him. But he's always been a big tease. Always."

George said nothing more, but he began seeing to it that Celia did not go visiting so often when Alan was home.

One morning, George reluctantly accepted an invitation to go fishing in Alan's cruiser. He was disgruntled with himself for being pressured by Evelyn into accompanying Alan, but he couldn't think of a polite way to refuse. Should have told him to go to hell, he was thinking, when a great white fish surfaced just off the bow. In shocked astonishment, George dropped his new fishing rod overboard. Alan's snide laughter infuriated him.

"Good gawdamighty, George. That's only our white porpoise. See the small gray fellow with her? That's her son. Everybody knows about them."

A few minutes later, George's humiliation was complete when the magnificent porpoise surfaced again closer to the boat and he lost the handline Alan had rigged for him as a substitute. The story, he knew perfectly well, would be all over town by suppertime. When they got back to the family dock, George walked straight downtown to Gus the Greek's Marina and, chuckling at his own childish behavior, ordered the boat he had been considering. It would give him an excuse not to accept any more of

37

Alan's crudely jovial invitations to go fishing on his crusier. Better yet, it would make a good wedge to take Celia away from the long hours she spent bantering and teasing with Alan.

The Saturday morning George was to pick up his new boat dawned crisp and clear, with a soft wind drifting through bronzed and falling leaves. George lit the fire and flexed his back, feeling slow warmth touching a sore twinge in his chest. Too much raking, probably. No. That was a lie of old habit. There was no longer need to hide the pain that came on him with the first cold of winter and nestled beneath his ribs until summer heat momentarily absorbed it. He'd managed to conceal it through his last three medical examinations. No sense retiring for physical problems when he was so close to retiring on thirty years' service with a higher pension. But now, why not admit it was rheumatism, or arthritis, or some other damn thing? He took a deep breath and winced at the sharp slash through his chest. Worse than last winter. Best to have it checked. Yes. But sometime when Evelyn wouldn't suspect. He heard Celia tiptoeing downstairs toward the warmth of Sallie's wood stove and hurried to finish dressing. Gus the Greek had promised to have the boat ready early so George would have full advantage of the incoming tide for his first outing. Alan insisted on showing him where and how to tie-off at the family dock. Because of an average seven- to eight-foot rise and fall of water, use of the dock depended on the constant variance of the tide. Following the mysterious rhythm of the moon, it would be high at six this morning, low at noon, then reach its extremes approximately one hour later each day. Alan had remarked in his rough fashion that he didn't want George to smash up his cruiser through "outlander ignorance of the tide." George grimaced. Even acquiring a boat didn't seem to eliminate Alan's pervasive presence.

Midway down the steps, Celia had come to a slow halt, the hair on her neck tingling at a mysterious, unearthly sound. Holding one foot off the edge of the tread, she held her breath, listening. For long moments there was nothing but wind and creak-

38

ing house. She took the next step, hesitating with her other foot in midair when she heard it again: a deep guttural flow of incantation. It was coming from the downstairs kitchen, a torrent of rasped muttering. This time it terminated abruptly with "No, sir! I won't stand for that, and I don't mean maybe." Celia recognized Ethel's voice and let out her breath in a puff of relief. She eased through the long hall and into the serving pantry, ashamed to be spying, but overcome by curiosity.

Ethel was leaning hard against the sink, knees bent, shoulders hunched, eyes staring into something beyond vision. Her great weight was held upright only by the strength of her two hands clutching the sink's edge. She inhaled with a spasmic catch of breath, and the muttering began again, senseless sounds spewing from loose, wet lips. She seemed to be in the grip of some terrifying attack, and forgetting she was supposed to be spying, Celia ran to take her arm. "Ethel! Are—are you all right?"

The glaze in Ethel's eyes wavered, slowly absorbed by normal focus. With a hard shake of her head, she straightened up, releasing her grasp on the sink. "Morning, honey. You ready for some breakfast?" She smiled cheerfully, oblivious of the bleeding wound in her palm where the rough under edge of the sink had punctured her skin.

"Ethel—Wh-who were you talking to?"

"The Spirits." She rinsed her hands, totally calm.

"Wh-what spirits?"

"The Evil Spirits all around out there on that water."

"What?"

Ethel tied on an apron, struggling to choose her words. "Mind you behave yourself out there, every minute you're around that water, or those Spirits will mark you and pull you right down— deep down under—with them."

"Why?"

"Because when you're on the water, you'll be looking straight into the eyes of God, and you'll make the Evil Spirits jealous, because they not allowed to. But you getting a boat, you going to be doing it all the time." She shook up banked ashes in the

39

wood stove and added two pine logs, coaxing them to quick flames.

Celia leaned against her favorite spot at the thick, wooden-topped mixing table, savoring the heat and incense odor of resin. "How do you know they're jealous?"

"Because I just was talking to them."

"Do they answer you?"

"Sure do."

"Out loud?"

"No. But I hear them." She began mixing biscuit dough, measuring scoops of flour instinctively with her uninjured hand. "Nights, walking by the cemetery, I can hear the Good Spirits arguing with the Evil Spirits, fighting to keep from being taken."

"Taken where?"

"Down to Hell." Ethel shook her head mournfully. "The Evil Spirits are always out to catch the Good ones, and they fight something fierce."

"It must be awful noisy."

"Worse than a hundred cars loaded with skeletons, all smashing together." Ethel paused in her mixing to lift her head slowly, shutting her eyes as she recaptured remembrance. Her white maid's cap slipped over one ear, and wiry gray hair protruded to frame her face in ragged wisps.

Celia bit her lip. "Can I hear them . . . Ethel?"

She opened her eyes and smiled at Celia with deep compassion. "No, honey. You not marked. You not Good Spirit or Evil Spirit. Yet. But you mind what I say. Mind what I tell you."

"Oh, Ethel!" Celia made no attempt to stifle laughter. "You don't really believe all that rot!"

Ethel's gigantic hands shot from the flour to seize Celia's arms in a powdery vise. She shook Celia hard, knocking away the smirk. "There's more things on this earth than any one little huffy girl knows about." Celia began to tremble before the belief of a true visionary, and Ethel shook her again. "You remember what I say. You hear me?"

40

"A-all right."

To Celia's relief, there were quick footsteps in the hall. Ethel released the grip on her arms and went back to the table, humming over the biscuit dough. Sallie bustled into the kitchen, her eyes lighting with pleasure when she saw Ethel. "What are you doing here so early!"

"We can't send them off on that cold water with nothing between them and the chills."

"No!" Celia protested, stamping the floor. "We don't have time to eat—we'll be late."

Ethel wagged a stern finger at her. "Nobody stamps foots at me. You won't be late, I promise. But I'm not having you get so cold and wore out those old Evil Spirits can get a chance at you. No telling what'll happen out there."

"Now, Ethel." Sallie began squeezing orange juice. "Stop frightening the child. Only thing apt to happen is they'll come down with bad colds."

The phone rang.

"Drat." Sallie fumbled with the oranges. "It's Miss Effie's gossip ring. Do go answer it, child, before she wakes up your mother and the whole derned neighborhood."

Celia went to the phone. "Good morning, Miss Effie," she managed, only to be overwhelmed by a torrent of comments and questions.

"I happened just now to hear Jim calling your cousin Mary," Miss Effie began, "and I'm telling you, you're crazy fools to go out at this hour in this cold. Tide's swift and the wind's coming up, and—" Miss Effie's piercing voice droned on and on. Celia leaned against the wall and yawned heavily while Miss Effie recounted the history of innumerable boating accidents, all of which seemed to have occurred early on winter mornings with an incoming tide.

"'Scuse me, Miss Effie," Celia finally interrupted with a saccharine, demure tone. "Grandmother's calling me to breakfast, but I'll let you know what happens."

Miss Effie's cackle reminded Celia of a bad witch. "No need.

41

I'll be watching. Your dock is right down left from my window, and—"

Celia slammed down the receiver against another stream of comment. She folded her hand around the mouthpiece and whispered in perfectly accented imitation of Alan's habitual comment, "You goddamn nosy old bitch!" There was a creak on the steps above her head, and Celia looked up to see her father standing directly above her. She braced herself for a sharp reprimand.

His expression was immobile, inward. "Come on. Let's get some breakfast."

Ethel kept her promise to hurry, and before first light they had finished a meal of fried shrimp and hominy, with puffy biscuits hot from the oven. Celia was grateful for the warm glow in her belly when she felt the lash of damp salt air. George grunted and buttoned the neck of his old trench coat. Thin remnants of cloud scudded across unblinking stars and a sliver of new moon. Frost absorbed the dim light, giving it back in an eerie phosphorescent glow. Celia pressed close to George's arm. "Daddy, did you know Ethel talks to spirits?"

"Yes. Why?"

"I caught her at it this morning." With a glance over her shoulder to reassure herself no spirits were currently present, she began relating their conversation.

George's steps slowed. "And you laughed?"

Celia was taken off guard by his tone of disbelief. "Sure I did. Talking to spirits, and all that stuff—it—it's funny."

"You disappoint me. I knew you were deliberately making your speech 'southern provincial bastard,' but I fail to see the necessity for following suit with your thinking." He began filling his pipe, jabbing at the tobacco to underline his words. "Tell me, when we were in England, did you laugh at your little Buddhist friend?"

"No."

"Or the Catholic boy? Or the little Shintoist girl?"

"No, but—"

"But what? Why at Ethel?" He struck a match, his face stern in its flickering. "Answer me. Why."

"They—the others—that was a religion, but Ethel's talking like that, it's—uh— You—you don't believe her, do you?"

"Whether I believe is not the question. Point is, she believes it."

"But it's so dumb!"

"Is it? Any 'dumber' than lighting votive candles, or singing hymns, or burning incense?" Celia fidgeted away from him. "But you led her on with all sorts of questions about something deeply personal to her. And then you laughed."

"Well, Uncle Alan says she's crazy."

"Oh, Celia, Celia. Don't you see what you're doing? You're selling yourself out in every direction just to run with the crowd. You're looking down your nose and making fun of Ethel because everyone else does. And why? If she chooses to see her God in earthy creatures, or in the waters of the Sound, that makes just as much sense as some folks who only see theirs in a church altar, or in a bottle of holy water, and no place else. More sense, maybe. And don't you ever—ever—under any circumstances—let me hear you laughing at Ethel again. Understand?"

Celia nodded quickly, anxious to end the lecture. "I-I'm sorry."

"It's Ethel you should apologize to, not me. Who knows? She may even have the grace to forgive a selfish, stupid little girl. Now come on."

Cautiously waiting until her father had moved a few steps ahead, Celia stuck out her tongue at his back. "Old fool!" she hissed softly.

In silence, they walked the brief block to the foot of the bridge. But instead of crossing right along Main Street, George turned left and led Celia to the small general store on the opposite corner.

"You're going the wrong way." Celia snickered.

"No, I'm not. Come on."

43

Old fool really was senile. Celia stopped and waited for him to realize his error.

"I said, come on. You're going to meet Miss Effie."

"But we'll miss the tide!" Celia whined.

"No, we won't."

"Well, I don't want to meet her. She's nothing but a—a—"

"—goddamn nosy old bitch," George finished quietly. "You've picked up your Uncle Alan's attitudes very nicely, haven't you? However, I did not ask if you wanted to meet Miss Effie. I said you were going to."

Celia dragged along behind him. He'd gone crazy. Old fool really was an outlander, like Uncle Alan always said.

They went through a short, sandy driveway toward the gasoline pump behind the store, picking their way through a clutter of empty oil cans. Celia knew Mrs. Beezely owned and operated the general store, and frequently saw her servicing cars at the hand-cranked gasoline pump. But Celia's eyes flicked in astonishment to see Mrs. Beezely now. She was standing beside an oxcart, stroking the neck of the work-weary beast and conversing with the stocky, gray-haired Gullah Negro driver. They were laughing together when the ox caught sight of George and Celia. Its great head came up with a snap of leather, and Mrs. Beezely turned toward them. "Why, morning, Major! Good to see you!" She smiled her grotesque cavity of black and broken teeth.

"Morning, Mrs. Beezely." George shook her oil-stained fingers.

Her interest aroused, Celia forgot her antagonism toward her father and ran to stroke the nose of the ox. "What's his name?" she asked the driver.

"Yes'm. Sure is. Beautiful morning. Jus' beautiful."

The little woman laughed, an unaccountably girlish sound from the ugly mouth. "This here's Old Deaf Donald, child. He can't hear a word you're saying." She turned her face up to the old man. "Sure you got everything, Donald?"

"Yes'm. Ever-ting."

"And you be sure and feed Marigold those oats I gave you as soon as you get home. He looks all run down."

"Yes, ma'am. Soon as I get home Ol' Marigold gonna eat 'n eat."

"Marigold?" Celia snickered.

"Marigold," Mrs. Beezely confirmed.

Donald touched his shapeless felt hat and gave a gentle flick of greasy reins along Marigold's neck. The oxcart moved down the driveway with Donald slumped on the seat in dejected resemblance of his ancient beast.

"How come he hears you?" Celia was careful not to look at Mrs. Beezely's face.

"He doesn't. But we grew up together on Papa's farm, and I guess Donald sort of reads my lips. At any rate, I'm the only one around he can—you know—converse with—so he really enjoys his weekly stocking-up trips." The tiny lady peered at Celia over grease-clouded glasses. "This here must be Celia."

"That's right." George put his hand on Celia's shoulder.

"I've seen you in church, Celia. But you always skedaddle before I can say hello."

"Mrs. Beezely is Miss Effie's sister," George explained to Celia.

Oh, lord, Celia thought. Wouldn't you just know it?

"You two come on in. Come in—come in. Me and Effie have been wondering how come you never stopped off to say hello, Celia." She threw open a sagging screen door adorned with a bright red Coca-Cola shield. It swung wide with a bawdy shriek of metal hinges. George and Celia stepped over a worn stoop onto a sloping wooden floor. They were in Mrs. Beezely's "living quarters" at the back of the store. The small room was a clutter of old mismatched furniture and faded photographs. Most of the pictures showed a wide-eyed, grinning boy, from all stages of infancy to gangling youth, his vibrancy grayed by a faded patina that seemed to flow from the pictures to lie across everything in the room. Celia edged past a four-poster covered by patchwork quilts. On it was a tattered packet of letters and

45

an apparently new leather Bible, still in its tissue-lined cardboard box that smelled faintly of mothballs. A hand magnifying glass lay across the cover, enlarging ornate gold lettering: "Mrs. Emma Ellen Beezely."

Mrs. Beezely caressed the cardboard box, careful to keep her dirty fingers away from the leather binding. "From my son, Eben," she explained shyly. "He sent it to me from France, just before he was killed." She pointed to the ancient letters. "He was a good boy—always thinking about me."

Embarrassed by the tears suddenly coursing down Mrs. Beezely's face, Celia ran to the red drape that served as an interior door.

The store was even duskier than Mrs. Beezely's room. Rows of clutter surrounded Celia on every side, made dimmer by the contrasting glare of the rising sun at the front of the building. She was engulfed by high shelves of snuff and tobacco adjacent to cookies, fishing gear, chick feed, canned goods, and rubber boots. Celia breathed deep, absorbing a tantalizing blend of smells. Her eyes adjusted to the dim light, and she was able to see the far end of the store. In sharp contrast to the back part, the front was immaculate. Sunlight poured through picture windows across lush potted plants. A wooden rail separated the building halfway, and beyond the rail a second wispy, gray-haired lady was busily mopping an already shining floor. Except for her gleaming false teeth, she was a replica of Mrs. Beezely: wiry, thin to emaciation. But she worked from a wheel chair, her arms flailing to catapult her chair-prison across the floor. At one side of the room was a single maple frame bed with matching dresser. Behind her, against the only other unwindowed area of her portion of the store, a high oak switchboard buzzed and glowed with Medusan tangles of knotted wires. The switchboard stood beside an aerie of glass. At a glance, Celia saw that Miss Effie commanded an unobstructed view of the bridge in front of her and of the homes to the left along the waterfront to Alan's house and the family dock. To her right was Main Street with the post office, the police station, and Villiers hardware store, funeral home, and ambulance service. Very few activities could escape Miss Effie's vigilant scrutiny and pointed comment. A sudden insistent buzz sent Miss Effie rolling to the switchboard. With a quick flip, she disconnected the call and wheeled her chair to George. "Well? Have you gotten your boat?"

"You old fake." He leaned across the rail and tapped the small binoculars sitting on the switchboard. "You know damn well I haven't."

"Oh, those." Miss Effie pursed her lips. "I was merely watching the new bridge construction." Her innocent expression melted under George's knowing grin. "O.K., Major. Truth is —I don't want none of you falling overboard or anything. I mean, without some help at hand."

"Well—keep a sharp eye on us. We're off to get the boat right now. We just dropped by on our way to say hello." He took Celia's hand.

"Wait!" Mrs. Beezely darted to a pungent barrel, its liquid contents coated with a creamy foam. "Here." Picking up a small square of oil paper, she yanked up her sweater sleeve and thrust her arm into the brine to present Celia with an oversized dill pickle. Celia thanked her dubiously. "Go on—go on—taste it."

Celia shut her eyes and tentatively bit into the nubby treat, then took a larger bite and smiled at Mrs. Beezely and Miss Effie. "Oh! Thanks ever so much!"

George grinned at Celia's inadvertent lapse into her English accent.

"Come back," Miss Effie said. "If you come again, I'll show you how the switchboard works. And Sis always has plenty of pickles."

Walking along Main Street, George was silent, waiting. They were halfway to the Marina before Celia tugged at his sleeve. "Yes, Celia?"

"Do you like Mrs. Beezely's singing?"

It was the one question he had not expected, and he coughed, choking back his laughter. "Her—singing?"

"In church, I mean."

"I know what you mean."

"Do you?"

"Uh—I—" George stopped and briskly knocked out pipe ashes. "Did you like Mrs. Beezely?"

"That's not fair," Celia protested. "I asked you first."

"Celia, I—uh—I don't believe that a person's talent is commensurate to the friendship you might feel for them. That is to say, lots of times you have to put up with more so-called talent from your friends than from—"

"You don't like it." Celia licked juice from her fingers.

"I—uh—in a word—no."

"Neither do I. She's terrible."

"But I like Mrs. Beezely," George added hastily.

"So do I. Long as she's not singing in church." She kicked pebbles off the sidewalk, and George waited, silent again. "How come you didn't ever tell me Miss Effie is a—a—"

"Cripple?" George finished harshly. "If you could be so quick to call her a 'goddamn nosy old bitch,' why do you hesitate at 'cripple'?"

"I-I don't know. It—it gets different if—I mean—

"You mean you were perfectly willing to accept your Uncle Alan's comments about Miss Effie without knowing anything about her, the same way you behaved about Ethel." Celia glowered resentment. George looked at her a long moment, then said in a mild tone, "Come on. Let's get the boat and I'll help you steer it to the dock."

Main Street was still deserted as they crossed to the alley running beside Villiers hardware store. A vacant lot lay between Magnum's Clothing and the narrow alley and emphasized the demarcation line of heavy piers supporting the stores on the water's edge. The front of the weed-choked plot was fenced at the sidewalk by three tiers of sturdy wooden rails running the width of the lot and topped by a backless board bench. "Buzzard's Roost—White Only" was neatly printed on the bench-perch in faded blue letters. Three men were huddled against the salt air, drinking coffee from soggy paper cups. Gus the Greek saw George and Celia crossing the street and waved to them, holding up the boat engine crank. A swarthy man with an unpronounceable last name, he ran Main Street's only restaurant in conjunction with the Marina shop. Alan lounged on one side of Gus, talking to Len Finch, the town printer, who was seated primly on his other side. Len blinked at them, his pale eyes watery, unaccustomed to daylight.

A heavyset man strode unevenly from the shadow of the hardware store and shuffled toward Buzzard's Roost. Celia recognized his form, the wheeze of his liquored breathing. Mr. Brown from Martha's porch. She edged toward her father, grateful for his automatic protective arm around her shoulder.

The heavy man stopped at the edge of the sidewalk opposite Alan. Celia was fascinated and repelled by her recollection of the way he had handled Martha. Brown shifted from one foot to the other.

"What you want?" Alan rinsed his mouth with coffee and spat the dregs toward Brown's feet.

"Out at the bridge—we need some things. Fast."

"Fast, hunh?"

"Yeah. Mr. Thatcher said to tell you."

"Store's not open 'til nine."

"I know. But seeing as how you're here, and the store's just there—" He lifted one elbow as a pointer. "I thought—"

"You thought wrong." Alan spat again.

"But at the meeting the other night, you said—"

"I'm busy!" Alan cut in abruptly. "Too busy for outlanders, that is. I'll talk to you at nine o'clock. Not before."

Brown's face went scarlet, and he shuffled away from the staring men.

"Meeting?" Gus asked curiously. "With that bunch?"

"Uh—yeh. Sort of. Out—out at the bridge site. Yeah, you know. Trying to figure some organized way they'd order from me. Instead of sending that bastard. He comes wandering in all the time, any old time."

49

Gus chuckled. "Never thought I'd see you meeting with outlanders."

Alan clenched his teeth until his jaw bulged white streaks. "You know how it is. Business. Business—uh—makes strange bedfellows." He laughed quickly. "But, hell, Gus—I even talk to this outlander brother-in-law of mine."

Celia's thinking was lost in a muddle of feelings. "Outlander," Uncle Alan had called him. Outlander. Right to his face. At least he'd never said that to her, so now she must really belong. She looked quickly at her father. Way he acted, maybe he really was an outlander. "Old fool," she muttered again, and started squirming along the alley toward the Marina ramp. "Grown-ups," she breathed through tight lips. Damn fools. All of them. Ethel talking to spirits, and her father taking up for her. Bunch of damn fools.

George nodded to the men. "What are you doing here, Alan? Thought you were going to meet us at the dock."

"Oh, I'll be there ahead of you. Don't worry."

"Uh—O.K." George sensed he was being baited.

"Say, George . . ." Alan spoke slowly, derisively. "That's some granny boat you let Gus unload on you. In fact, it's not a boat at all. Just—a thing."

"It won't turn over with the kids in it, which is the reason I chose it."

Celia stopped, staring down the sharp slope of alleyway in shocked disbelief. There was a small-engined, flat-bottomed craft bobbing in the water, the only boat beneath the dock. She had envisioned a sleek, fast motorboat for racing. "Is that it, Daddy?"

"That's it." George's smile faded at her disdainful tone.

Alan slid down from Buzzard's Roost, crumpled his cup, and flung it in the general direction of the trash basket. "I'll go home and wait for you at the dock, if you think that put-put will make it before nightfall."

"We can always row," George said, more sharply than necessary.

50

"Might be faster, at that." Alan hitched up his trousers with an impudent grin.

"Daddy . . . I-I'll walk over with Uncle Alan." Celia ran to catch his hand, and Alan seized her wrist, swinging her in a wild circling arc.

"Goddammit all to hell," George said, watching Alan's swaggering gait and Celia's dogtrot beside him.

Gus jumped down to the sidewalk with a friendly clasp on George's arm. "Sometimes Alan can be a real bastard, you know that? Don't worry, Major. That kid'll be crazy about the boat once you start letting her handle it."

George took little pleasure in the boat's easy maneuvering, but steered mechanically under the bridge. Brown's truck roared by overhead, and George started at the sharp clatter of loose planking, the creak of antiquated pilings. The structure looked worse from the water than it did driving over it. The new bridge was long overdue, George thought, glancing at the construction site on the opposite shore. He could see workers already assembling, moving slowly around the first spindly pilings. It was curious how long they seemed to be taking. When he picked up Celia, he'd ride over and take a look. It would be easy for her to start learning to manage the boat on the broad expanse of the Sound. Suddenly whistling cheerfully, George turned his attention to the marsh grass at his left, edging the prow into a narrow creek leading to the family dock that would be inaccessible on the low tide.

Celia was the first to spot his approach and pointed him out reluctantly to Cynthia and Mary. Alan gestured George to the sheltered far side of the dock, beyond his powerful cabin cruiser. "Did you buy a tie-line?" He laughed at George's dismay. "You outlanders. Figured you'd forget." He threw a new rope down to George and lowered himself into the boat to help tie it off.

There was an anguished squealing from Mary. Alarmed, George stood up to see Jim, Cynthia, and Celia shove Mary from the seawall to the narrow strip of dry beach below it. Her skinny arms clung briefly to Jim's legs, but Cynthia threw her bulky

51

weight against Mary's narrow shoulders. Mary's grasp loosened, and she slid down the rough surface of oyster tabby wall. "You stop that!" Mary tried to pull herself up on top of the seawall only to have the three cousins thrust her down again, stamping their feet at her grasping fingers. Their eyes flared with excitement at Mary's distress as she slipped under Celia's hard push and fell to her back on the cold sand. "Daddy!" she called to Alan, beginning to cry.

Alan glanced over his shoulder, his hands working at the stiff new rope. "Don't be such a goddamn cry-baby, Mary."

"Cry-baby! Goddamn cry-baby!" Celia instantly echoed.

George climbed the ladder to the top of the dock and ran to the seawall. Yanking Celia aside, he jumped down to lift Mary to her feet and brush sand from her hair and her spindly legs. Jim and Cynthia stepped back from his anger, and George lifted Mary to the top of the wall. Sobbing piteously, she ran across the lawn and into the house to Annie. George vaulted to the top of the wall and confronted Celia. "What the hell's gotten into you?"

Her lips trembled, her hands clenched and unclenched at her slacks. "We—we were just playing."

"You call that playing?"

Celia's head came up defiantly. "We three—we've got a club, and nobody else can belong, and Mary's always trying to horn in."

"You don't miss a chance at running with the crowd, do you?"

"Ah, hell, George. Leave 'em be." Alan came shuffling along the dock. "Kids will be kids. And Mary's a dull one, that's for sure."

"Now, look, Alan—"

"Kids will be kids, I tell you. There's nothing wrong with clubs. Most natural thing in the world."

"Goddammit, Alan. Keep out of this."

"Why—why, sure, George."

Jim and Cynthia ran to the end of the dock and jumped into the new boat. "Hey, Uncle George, this is great! You could even dive off it without turning over." Their voices rose in excited comment, and George saw Celia's pout beginning to soften at the cousins' boisterous praise. "After Celia, can I steer, Uncle George?"

"Not this morning, Jim. Celia gets the first trip."

"Aw, Uncle George."

Alan smirked at George. "Come on, Jim. I'll give you and Cynthia a ride in a real boat. No sense wasting this good tide."

Shrieking laughter, Jim and Cynthia scrambled to the dock and leapt onto the cruiser. Celia started to follow, but George caught her arm, holding her beside him.

"Maybe you and Celia want to come, George?" Alan called.

"No, thanks. We'll take our own boat."

Celia stamped her foot in fury. "I want to go with Uncle Alan."

"Not today, I said." George was bitterly regretting his refusal of Jim's request, but he held tight to Celia's arm as they watched the big boat gun away from the dock. "Look at that wake!" George remarked. "That's one boat you couldn't steer just yet. I think ours will be more fun. Come on. I'll show you how to crank the engine, and—"

"I wanted to go with Uncle Alan—not in that—that old granny boat." Celia spitefully turned away from him.

"There you go again, Missie, copying Uncle Alan." George shook his head sadly. "All right, Celia. When you're ready to learn how to handle the boat, you let me know." George walked slowly away toward the end of the dock.

"Old fool!" Celia murmured, and skipped away for home.

4

AS THE DAYS PASSED, Celia stubbornly refused to ask permission to join George in his daily boat rides. George said nothing more about going with him. But all that week he rose early to catch the incoming tide, varying his meal hours to take advantage of the high water. Celia maintained her silence about the boat for another week. The following Saturday, when the tide had shifted back to an early morning schedule, George found Jim and Cynthia waiting for him on the dock. At their eager request, he took them along, grinning to see Celia hiding behind the bushes and watching enviously.

That morning, the white porpoise surfaced twice behind the stern of the boat, sending Jim and Cynthia into squeals of excitement. "We've heard about her," Jim explained, "but we've never seen her before."

When Jim and Cynthia told Celia about the white porpoise, its description was so outlandish she was convinced that the cousins were teasing her again, "joshing," as they called it. "But I fixed them!" she bragged the next morning over breakfast.

Sunlight streamed into the glassed-in porch, pouring across the table with a dancing shadow play of dried and falling leaves. George squinted his eyes, shutting his mind to the child's prattle. Why was it she talked so much these days? Was it, as Evelyn said, "just a phase"? He blinked, glancing at Celia. Her mouth was moving rapidly, without pause for the spoonfuls of steaming oatmeal she was swallowing down. He said—she said—

teacher said—they said—I said, and who gives a damn? George decided he really liked the child better when she was "maladjusted." And silent.

Celia was giggling through her last mouthful of cereal, oblivious to a large glob of it on her cheek. "—so I told them I couldn't get up at dawn to see any old white porpoise because I had to be up at three A.M. to see the purple comet." She choked with a hysterical outburst of mirth and coughed into her napkin. "And they believed me! They're coming over tomorrow at three A.M. to watch through our telescope! Isn't that just a riot?"

George scowled at the spilled mess of sugar and cream around her plate and down the front of her dark green jumper. "Hm? What telescope?"

She pushed her cereal bowl away with an aggravated thrust. "That's the whole point, Daddy. We don't have one, but those stupes are getting up at three A.M. tomorrow to come over and look at something that doesn't exist. That's the joke."

"Oh, very funny." Evelyn set down a steaming platter of scrambled eggs and shad roe. "And you know who they'll wake up at that hour of the morning—me, your father, and your grandmother—while you sleep through the doorbell. You phone them right back and tell them you were kidding them, the same way they were kidding you about a white porpoise."

George's attention came back to the table. "What are you two talking about?"

Celia sighed. Lately, it seemed she had to repeat everything to her father to get him to understand. She watched him mixing butter into a large portion of hominy grits. Probably he was getting deaf, or—or senile. That must be it. Senile. He was, after all, an old man in his fifties. But however decrepit he might be, he was still quick to discipline impudence, and Celia spoke cautiously. "I just told you."

"Sorry. I was—uh—thinking about something. What did you say?"

Celia toyed with her fork. "Daddy, you get mad when I don't listen to you."

"True. On the other hand, I don't talk all the time."

Evelyn hurried in from the kitchen with a pot of coffee, hoping to avert the explosion. She filled George's cup, amused by their similar profiles, the stubborn thrust of squared chin lines. Celia's hair hung stringy and ragged around her face because of her insistence on letting it grow, but the set of angry blue eyes beneath arching brows was precisely that of her father's. Evelyn spoke lightly. "Those cousins! They've been making up wild stories again. This time they've been trying to persuade Celia to get up at dawn to go look for a big white porpoise. Can you imagine? As if Celia were stupid enough to believe such a fib."

To her surprise, George threw back his head with a hearty roar of laughter, his eyes sparking from irritability to mirth. "But there is such a fish."

Celia was profoundly indignant, and George held back his laughter. "Honey—I can understand why you'd be suspicious, but—" He took several sips of coffee, hiding his smile at the recollection of Celia's city-bred gullibility, even more naive than his own. She'd spent one day stumbling through burr-choked pine woods on a traditional snipe hunt, and an entire sweltering afternoon floating in a boat over a mud bank, trying to catch an oyster on a hand line baited with a red marble. "You just drop it in an open shell," Jim had told her, "and that old oyster thinks it's a pearl, and—wham—he snaps shut and you got him." George wiped his mouth and managed to look Celia straight in the face. "Those cousins of yours don't have any manners worth a damn, but their imaginations are superb. However, there is a full-grown white porpoise in the Sound, traveling with her son." He described what they had seen from the boat, what he had learned from Gus the Greek.

"That's exactly what Jim said." Celia's eyes were wide.

"Oh, come now, George." Evelyn reached for the sugar bowl. "Eat your breakfast—both of you. White porpoise, indeed. You're worse of a tease than those children."

"I'm not kidding."

56

Evelyn chewed thoughtfully. "Let's use a little logic. How come this fish only shows up at dawn?"

"Gus the Greek says the bridge crew have been taking shots at her. Ever since they've been in town, she doesn't go near the bridge site. And she's never seen any more by daylight."

"Why would anybody shoot at her, Daddy?"

"Lord, honey, who knows? Sport, I suppose." Not wishing to alarm Evelyn, George was careful to disguise his distaste for the bridge crew, his dismay at their brutal, crude behavior. But he had observed their deliberate jostling of women on the sidewalks, their drunken invasion of Gus the Greek's restaurant, their foul obscenities to slow-moving elders, their deliberate fights with Marine Corps privates on afternoon leave in town. Given a chance, God knows what they'd do to Celia or Cynthia. It was ironic to accept Beldon's educational limitations for the sake of Celia's physical freedom, only to have the town become increasingly dangerous for a little girl to wander in alone. Without comment, George had begun keeping careful check on the children's activities. Some of the bridge crew had criminal records. At best, they were cynical, rootless men—outlanders, indeed. He grimaced at finding himself using that term. George realized Celia had asked him another question. "What, honey?" He frowned at her obvious exasperation, her overly precise enunciation to him.

"I said—how could a porpoise be white?"

"Is it a lighter gray, maybe?" Evelyn suggested.

"No. White."

"Completely, positively, absolutely white?"

"Well—off-white."

"Aha." Evelyn grinned. "Which would be gray."

"No, dammit, *white*. Or at least what I call white. You women would probably call it Mushroom Mauve or Titillated Teak or some other fool thing. But it *is* white."

"Honestly, Daddy?"

"Oh, my god." He slammed down his coffee cup, spilling a

slosh across the tablecloth. "Do we have to spend the whole damn breakfast hour arguing about a simple statement of fact? That damn porpoise is white and I don't want to hear another word about it."

The wind dropped off, and a heavy shadow of leaves settled across the soiled table top. Head throbbing, George picked at his food without appetite, wondering why he'd lost his temper. There was the sharp rattle of a pecan falling on the tin roof and rolling into the gutter, a heavier thunk, and the steely scratching of claws. George started and dropped his fork.

"It's only a squirrel." Evelyn's tone was the soothing one she usually reserved for Celia, and it increased his irritability.

"I know it's only a squirrel. I don't see why the hell they can't collect nuts down on the ground like everybody else."

Evelyn began eating, and for a time the only sound was the clink of her fork touching the plate. George looked at Celia, who was staring out the window toward the Sound, her face vibrant with aroused curiosity. "Mother, if it really is out there, can I go with the cousins to look for it?"

"No, ma'am!"

"Please."

"No! It's not safe to have you wandering around by yourselves in the dark. I won't have it, and that's that."

"Uh . . ." George touched his napkin to his lips. "Tell you what. Tide's not high till around ten tomorrow morning. But there'll be enough water in the creek to get out by five-thirty or six. If you want to get up that early, I'll take you on a quick run to look for her before you go to school."

"Oh, Daddy!" Celia bolted from her chair to fling her arms around his neck. "Would you?"

"Sure. That is, if you don't mind riding in the granny boat."

"Oh, Daddy—it's not a granny boat. It's really sort of—sort of cute." Contritely, she hugged him again harder.

He gritted his teeth as her clutch wrenched his sore chest, but Evelyn's secret smile to him made the ache unimportant, and he even impetuously agreed to take all the cousins along.

Evelyn flatly refused to get up before dawn to "look at any fish, white, purple, or otherwise," and that first morning, George admired her wisdom. There was a light frost on the ground, and the old house was creaking and groaning with icy drafts. But when George and Celia got downstairs, Ethel was waiting for them with waffles and sausage and muttered comments about the Evil Spirits. She sent them on their way with thermos jugs of coffee and hot chocolate, and a shoe box of sandwiches for the cousins. "I know Miss Annie and Miss Agnes ain' going to be up at this hour." George thanked her and led Celia down the back steps. Ethel watched them from the window, her muttered incantations blending with a sharp north wind. Celia shuddered. In the dim starlight it was easy to imagine Evil Spirits in every shadow, and she was glad her mother had not let her go out alone.

At the dock, uneven whitecaps shook the pilings. Following George's sure stride, Celia made her way gingerly across the twenty-foot length of planking, shivering at the thought of icy water and mud beneath them.

"Hey!" Jim called out as he heard the hollow echo of their footsteps. "Where you been?"

Celia was holding her breath and waited to answer until they had reached the security of the broad surface of the dock. "Ethel made us eat." She sank down beside him, swinging her feet over the edge.

"Your're lucky." He licked his lips, eyeing the pungent shoe box. "Mama wouldn't get up with us."

"No." Cynthia and the others crowded around and Celia surrendered the box. The hot chocolate was gone before George could uncork his thermos, and he was selfishly delighted none of the children drank coffee. He shifted his steaming cup from one hand to the other, snugged his coat close, and paced the dock for warmth, grimacing to himself at the two hours ahead. The children had begun a lively squabble that made no sense whatever to George. But he envied their lithe young bodies, impervious to the cold wind in their sweaters. Celia was crouched in their midst, and as he turned in his pacing, he realized with a start that he could scarcely distinguish her appearance from that of the others. She was even beginning to sound like them, with her deliberate imitation of their thick, syrupy drawl. He sighed and leaned against the farthest palmetto pile. It was scaly beneath his hand, pungent with creosote. It was one of a pair of piles that rose eight feet above the dock's surface. They supported heavy boat slings intended to lift Alan's cruiser for cleaning or repair. The cross beams at the top were retracted, and their heavy canvas loops dangled before him, two shadowy hangman's nooses for giants. George lost himself in study of the double pulleys, concentrating to recall the mathematical formula for weight reduction per pully, and was finally able to shut out the children's shrill, senseless bickering. First light began to brighten the east, bringing color and third dimension to the seascape. Emerald green marsh stretched away along the winding creek, rippling in the wind and bobbling with packed gray mats of dead growth floating at its base. The tide was rising fast, whipped by the sea behind it. Water covered the hard white sandbar at the creek mouth, and waves were slapping at the ladder leading up from the ragged water just below him. George raised his binoculars with a fervent aside to Ethel's spirits to let the porpoise appear immediately and put an end to their chilly watch. He scanned the shoreline from the drawbridge along the sweep of causeway to the new bridge site, to be rewarded by nothing but a close view of more gray waves with frothing white caps. He knew with certainty that if the white porpoise did surface anywhere in the area, they would be unable to see her in the foaming white caps, but he was determined to keep his promise to Celia.

When the children finished eating, George began the first of six runs in the boat. Celia made each trip, sitting on the back seat beside him. Despite insistent pleas, George refused to load all the children at once and alternated Jim, Cynthia, and Mary with Little Sally, Charles Two, and Louisa. George dreaded

60

the runs with the smaller children. Rowdy and undisciplined, they required his full attention to keep them from falling overboard. With the older cousins, George could concentrate on teaching Celia to maneuver the boat, and he was delighted by her instinctive feel for the little craft. Only once did he have to caution her about being sure to head into the waves to avoid being swamped. But the cold air had begun to slice through his sore chest, and after the sixth run, George insisted that they go in.

Celia confronted him with hostile suspicion. "Is there really a white porpoise, or were you kidding me?"

"I told you once before, didn't I?" His voice had a sharp edge.

"Then can we come back tomorrow?"

"Oh, lord. I guess so. If it doesn't rain."

"Old fool," she murmured to Jim, behind George's back.

George sighed and pulled his coat closer, feeling at the moment very old, and certainly some kind of fool.

The next morning Charles Two developed asthma, and Annie kept him at home in spite of Alan's sarcastic comments to his son. Little Sally and Louisa announced that they could see the Sound from their bedroom, and asked to be awakened by shouts if the porpoise showed up.

Alan swore profusely. "No spunk. My own children, and they haven't got an ounce of spunk. Get up!" He prodded the girls roughly.

"Alan, leave them alone." Annie tucked the bedclothes around the two little girls. "I don't see you out there these cold mornings."

"Do we have to go, Mama?"

"No, Louisa, 'course not. Later on you two can help me bake a cake."

"Bake a cake!" Alan repeated sarcastically. "Goddamn. Some kids I've got."

This left only Celia, Jim, Cynthia, and Mary. Mary would have preferred sleeping in with her two little sisters, but she was grimly determined to win her father's approval and marched down to the dock, her lips blue and trembling in her pale, thin face.

George continued to bring the box of sandwiches, returning it invariably empty an hour or so later. The weather went into an unexpected warm spell, and with the younger cousins out of the way, they could all go out in the boat at one time. George discovered with pleasure and surprise that the older three had interests other than inane games and squabbling. They questioned him about his travels and military service. Jim was an avid history reader with expert knowledge of battles George had been in, including the torpedoing of his troop transport. And once George had penetrated Cynthia's doltlike shyness, she showed a keen grasp of varying art styles and crafts around the globe, sending him straight to the encyclopedia morning after morning when he got home. Mary's quiet talent was for music, and she was a good listener. But privately, grudgingly, he came to understand Celia's preference for the company of Jim and Cynthia and to sympathize with their club. Mary was, as Alan said, a dull one, silent except for occasional comments about the fudge she planned to make, or the dress she was sewing. Talk among the other three was incessant and wide-ranging. George joined in, quiet and companionable, and when he saw the occasional glints of admiration in Celia's eyes, he felt a deep fondness beginning for her cousins.

Always around them was the vast, ever-varying seascape. On calm days, the dome of sky reflected its mirror image on the glassy Sound, and the little boat projected them into a heady, swirling globe of clouds with earth delineated only by a thin green perimeter of distant shoreline and marsh. Those mornings Jim would lie on his stomach, his chin on the edge of the prow, and outline his determination to become a flyer. On windy days, the water churned beneath them, dirty gray one morning, turquoise blue the next, and Jim talked of running away to sea. With the warm spell, George no longer needed his coat. He began taking his new Leica along, making color shots of the endless kaleidoscopic drama of dawn. To his amazement, he found himself actually anticipating the mornings with boyish eagerness.

In spite of Evelyn's comments that they were all insane to get up at that hour, the unsuccessful watch continued for several weeks. When the hourly shift of the high-tide schedule left the creek a mucky slit of outgoing water and they could not use the boat, George borrowed additional binoculars and they kept their vigil from the mud-locked dock.

Monday morning, a full moon hung low over the horizon, and Ethel muttered dire prophecies with gloomy shakes of her head that kept her white cap constantly askew. "You mind, Major! You take special mind . . . those Spirits fight something fierce on the full moon."

"Don't worry, Ethel. We can't even go out in the boat today," George reassured her.

"Even so . . ." Wiping her eyes, Ethel stepped into the pantry, and her gutteral incantations began before George and Celia could finish eating.

Celia stifled a giggle and bolted down her pancakes. But once outside, her mirth subsided into awe. The moon lit the back yard with unearthly opalescence, painting live oaks and tin shed alike in pale pewter hues. George and Celia made their way slowly across the sand, filled with wonder at the supernatural appearance of familiar shrubs and barren pecan limbs.

At first, the dock appeared empty. George peered anxiously around the front lawn and the strip of beach the outgoing tide had left by the seawall. "Don't tell me they've all dropped out on us."

"Look." Celia pointed to the dock.

By squinting, George was able to make out a slim form sprawled face down beneath the boat sling, and he sprinted across the walkway without regard for the uneven planking. "Who is it? Is something wrong?"

Mary lifted her prim little face. "Uncle George, there—there's something down there."

He sat down beside her and wiped his clammy forehead with his sleeve. "Like what? Water, maybe? Or mud?"

"No. Some k-kind of swimming thing."

"I should hope so." He stretched on his stomach beside her, peering into the carbon silky water. Celia joined them, moving cautiously to the dock's edge. The tide was half low, racing out from the creek with viscous suckings as it slipped away from mud and marsh banks. On the piles directly below them, barnacles crackled, and an oyster made a loud pop from the bed across the creek. Wide ripplings began at the shallow end of the creek, flowing soundlessly toward the dock. Forming a V-shaped wave, a dark form broke the oily surface of the water beneath them, sped ten feet to the mouth of the creek, flung itself against the white dam of sandbar, and flopped back under water with heavy splashing.

"Wh-what is it?" Celia asked.

George shook his head in puzzlement. "I don't know. Where're Jim and Cynthia?"

"Gone for a flashlight." Mary pointed. "Here it comes again."

The rippling wave began in the shallows, shooting by at greater speed to hit the sandbar with a hard thud. The dark form was higher out of the water, and George could dimly see the head and fins of a young gray porpoise as it floundered desperately in the shallows. "Oh, my god. Poor thing's trapped in the creek, and the tide's going out."

Jim and Cynthia came pounding along the planks, carrying two large flashlights. "Did you see it, Uncle George?" "Did you?"

"Yes." Jim flashed the sharp beam of light at a beginning ripple, and George snatched it from his hands. "Don't. You'll blind him. Wait until he gets to the sandbar." When they heard the thud, George swung the light along the sand. On the creek side of the twelve-foot-wide sandbar, outgoing water had cut a concave wall, and they watched the gray porpoise in its frenetic thrashing as it struggled to make its way up and over the steep three-foot crescent that was rising sharper by the moment as the

64

tide drained away. Once again the porpoise failed and floundered back into the water. Jim and Cynthia moaned in disappointment, and George cut off the light.

"Daddy, what happens if he can't get over?"

"He'll die. He can't live six hours out of water until the tide comes back in."

"Oh, no." Celia groaned as the thrashing began again, ending in another heavy splash. "What'll we do?"

"Hope he makes it in the next few minutes."

"We could build a dam, couldn't we?"

"Naw." Jim thrust his hands into his jeans pockets. "That water goes out through a billion rivulets in the oyster banks."

They sat along the dock edge in gloomy silence, watching the porpoise wage its relentless struggle. The horizon became banked with heavy clouds, muffling the sun's first rays, and dawn came with a sad, nacreous light. Sky and water flooded gradually with cold tints of gray and pink, and the Sound heaved with long, crestless swells. Abruptly, beyond the sandbar, the water was rent into foam by a long, gliding wave running against the tide, and with an anguished squealing, the enormous white porpoise surfaced. Her appearance brought George and the children scrambling to their feet, struck dumb by her sheer strength and beauty. She was twice the size of the porpoise trapped in the creek, and her sleek bulk was an iridescent, satiny white with soft peach undertones. As they watched, she surfaced again, her head cutting the surface to lead the long gliding arc of her body until, with a flick of her tail, she disappeared. They kept looking at the bubbling water where she had been, blinking after a ghostly apparition that seemed at the instant to be a creature of their imaginations, a fusion of dawn hues created by the strength of their desire for her existence. A curving fin of white disrupted their hypnotic trance, and she surfaced again, swimming directly toward them. Again her shrill squealing broke the silence. She was close enough for them to see the humanoid face, and Celia unconsciously turned her head to avoid the pained, grieving eyes of the porpoise. She

65

surfaced again, even closer to the sandbar. Mesmerized, Celia turned and stared directly into the face of the magnificent creature. The eyes drew her, held her. Staring, unable to break the contact, Celia shivered with recognition. The eyes were just like Martha's. Martha when she left her in the swing; Martha standing on her porch; Martha in the sheriff's car. And accusing, like the eyes of the severed chicken head on her first day home. Celia bit her knuckles, fighting to hold back a trembling nausea.

"What's the matter?" Cynthia asked.

"Nothing." Celia shook her head. It was something, but nothing she could explain, not even to herself.

The white porpoise dove underwater only to reappear instantly, swimming back and forth before the sandbar with a wild, pathetic shrieking, answered at last by a diminishing squeak from the trapped porpoise. George sat down heavily, overcome by infinite sadness. "I'm afraid it's her son in the creek," he said.

In the flooding daylight, they could see the smaller porpoise through the entire length of its desperate swim, clearly visible in the shallow creek water. He was perceptibly weaker, scarcely able to make an assault against the growing scoop of sandbar.

Jim pointed across the Sound to the bridge site, where an assortment of workmen were assembling. "If she don't get away from that sandbar, somebody's apt to shoot her, Uncle George. She's right on target from the bridge site." His voice broke as the white porpoise swept past them again.

George rose and paced the dock, studying the boat slings. Opened wide, the one on his right would hang just above the crescent edge of the sandbar. "How much more time before the creek's dry?"

Jim eyed the familiar landmarks of oyster beds, dock ladder, and sandbar. "About an hour."

George strode to the boat sling, unknotted the ropes that secured the swinging beam, and struggled to push it open. "Jim. Give me a hand. Quick." Salt-rusted hinges squeaked and moaned as they swung the heavy beam out into place with the canvas loop dangling directly over the sandbar.

"What you going to do, Daddy?"

"Try and haul him over." He lowered the canvas to lie loosely on the sandbar, and handed the line to Jim. "Think you can handle it?"

"Yes, sir! I help Uncle Alan all the time cleaning his boat."

"All right. But don't pull until I tell you to. Come on, girls, let's go bogging. Take off your sweaters. No—leave your shoes on, Celia, or you'll slice hell out of your feet on the oyster shells." George climbed down the ladder and lowered himself into the icy water. It was barely over his knees but rose to his hips as he sank into the thick, muddy bottom. Cynthia and Mary were quick to scramble after him, but Celia was horrified at the thought of the rancid muck and hung back at the top of the ladder. George steadied himself with one hand resting gingerly between razor-edged barnacles covering the piling. "Celia, I need all three of you." He squinted up at her.

"...I-I...c-can't..."

"Scaredy-cat!" Jim gave her a hard shove. "Go on!"

"Jim, no. Don't touch her." George held out his hand to Celia, speaking softly. "Come on, honey. We're all scared. Come on, take the first step—that's the hardest one. After that, it's easy."

She licked her lips, edging her foot to the top rung of the ladder.

"That's the way! Now the second step. Come on—one step at a time."

Following his coaxing instructions, Celia turned and climbed down the ladder, blubbering with terror as a frigid ooze of slime clamped around her legs and sucked her waist deep down into the shallow water.

"S-summertime, this'd be fun." Cynthia's teeth were chattering, but she managed a cheerful smile.

They began making their way along the boggy oyster bed toward the sandbar. George led the line, fighting to maintain his

67

balance while he lifted one foot above the oil-stained slush to take a short, groping step. His foot was sucked back down into the mud bank, until his heel found purchase against a clump of oysters. He turned and held out his hand to steady Mary on her step, then Cynthia, and finally, Celia. It took them fifteen minutes to flounder their way across the ten feet separating them from the safety of packed white sand. George scrambled up the four-foot crest now showing above the tide and lifted the girls out of the shallow mud. The white porpoise swam closer, trumpeting shrieks of angered warning to her trapped son. George clenched his arms across his throbbing chest and knelt down to observe the young gray porpoise. He had stopped struggling and was floating against the sandbar in the remaining creek water, a pool eight feet across and approximately three feet deep. The water was disappearing rapidly, shrinking away from its cup of mud and oyster clumps.

"Another few minutes," George muttered. "And stop that sniffling, Celia. We're all just as cold and wet as you are."

When the dorsal fin of the porpoise began to show above the water, George took hold of the canvas loop, spread the cloth to its full four-foot width, and slid down into the pool beside the creature. It wriggled feebly, imprisoned on all sides now by mud and sand. George worked his way to the tail of the porpoise. "Girls, when I get the sling under him, grab the front edge, Celia and Cynthia—and Mary, you grab the back edge. Hold it as tight around him as you can—and pull. Understand?

They nodded, and Celia gave one final sniffle. "Will he—will he bite?"

Mary and Cynthia giggled, but George gave a snort of exasperation. "Think I'd put you girls on the front end if he did? Ready, Jim?" He looked to Jim, who was braced to haul the dead weight of the porpoise to the rim of the sandbar.

"Ready."

"Here goes." Holding the canvas loop open, George eased it around the tail fin of the porpoise. At his touch, the animal lashed in panic, knocking George to his back in the mud.

68

"Gee." Cynthia gave a low whistle of respect. "He kicks worse than a derned old mule."

"Jim! Hold on tight to that line."

"Yessireeee!"

George pulled himself upright with the aid of the sling and struggled back to the sandbar. Edging past the tail flukes, he laid the weight of his body along the lower section of the porpoise and wrestled the sling over its slithery tail, working it along under the heavy body.

"You got him, Uncle George! You got him!" In a thrill of excitement, Jim threw his full weight against the pulley line. The porpoise shot clear of the water, twisting wildly, only to slip nose first from the sling back into the muddied puddle.

George barely scrambled clear as the porpoise fell. "Dammit, Jim! I told you to wait."

"I-I'm sorry."

"Once again. And this time, wait until I tell you." It was harder to get the sling under the porpoise as his weight began to rest on the treacherous creek bottom. George thrust his hands into the mud, forcing the sling up under the tail to the creature's belly. He winced as oyster shells slashed his arm, but held fast, spreading the canvas loop forward from the belly of the porpoise to its heaving throat. "Now, girls—when he comes out of the water—be ready to grab the sling. But all of you, whatever you do, don't jerk him. I'm afraid this is our last chance." George rested a moment, breathing hard. "Ready, Jim?"

"Yes."

"Gently, remember." He threw his arms around the tail, bracing himself to hold the lashing body of the porpoise. "O.K., Jim. Pull."

Jim planted one foot against the dock edge and hauled at the line with slow, steady pressure. The porpoise rose three inches, then six. George swung him sideways against the sandbar, where the girls could reach the sling, and they grabbed for it, holding the porpoise firmly in a soft clutch of canvas. George found secure footing in sand and steadied the tail as they raised the animal within a foot of the top. He could reach no higher with any strength and called back to Jim, "Hold it, right there. Now hang on tight, all of you." George let go, and the porpoise dangled loosely, immediately beginning to lash again. George leaped for the top of the sandbar, throwing himself flat on his stomach and seizing the tail fin before the porpoise could wriggle free from the sling. "Pull!" he shouted to Jim. "Pull hard this time!" With a final tug, the porpoise slid up and over the top through the crescent of sand and dropped onto the flat sloping surface of sandbar. Heaving and grunting, George and the girls dragged him across the smooth sand toward the safety of the Sound. Four feet from the water's edge, George slid the sling free. In a desperate surge of strength, the porpoise began a wild thrashing, flopping his way swiftly into the slapping waves and safe deep water. Instantly, he sank from sight while George and the children cheered wildly. For a moment, the water billowed empty before them, until both porpoises appeared off to their left. They surfaced and swam past the sandbar with their graceful, effortless arcs, swung back and returned, made a final sweep before them, and disappeared into the depths of the Sound.

"They were saying thank you!" Cynthia clenched her hands in awe. "I know they were! They were saying thanks!"

"Yes! Did you see her face? She was smiling! I swear to goodness! Did you see her, Daddy?" Celia swung around to find George sitting on the sand, slumped in a clumsy heap and clutching his chest. Too late she remembered Ethel's stern warning and cried out in shocked apprehension.

"It—it's all right." He pushed away their fumbling hands. "It's all right. Just let me—sit a moment." His breathing was a painful rasp as sharp pains sliced back and forth through his chest, but he smiled up at Celia. "The 'old fool' just pulled a muscle, that's all."

"Oh, Daddy—I-I never meant—"

"I—know. Used to—feel the same way—'bout my own father."

Jim hovered anxiously at the dock edge. "Should I go get Uncle Alan?"

"No! God, no . . ." Taking shallow breaths, George forced himself to stand up and face the torturous effort of slogging back to the ladder. This time it was Celia and Cynthia who helped him, pausing after each step while he gasped for air. The last trickle of water was gone from the creek when they reached the base of the dock. Jim held an oar down to him, and George floundered quickly to the foot of the ladder. Safe on the dock, he sank down to rest, and the children clustered anxiously around. "Go—on." George waved them away. "Go on. You'll be late to school . . ."

Cynthia and Mary moved obediently toward the walkway, but Celia clung stubbornly to George's arm. "I'll wait for you."

He nodded his head, unable for the moment to speak, and Celia sat down beside him. Jim saw the terror in her face, and came back to wait with her. They were silent until George caught his breath, then helped him struggle to his feet. Together, they walked George slowly home with his arms resting heavily across their shoulders.

At the back steps, he stumbled and fell against the banister, and Ethel immediately appeared in the window of the kitchen. She gasped, seeing them caked with stenching mud, their faces wan with exhaustion. With a low, hopeless keening, Ethel dropped the pan of beans she was shelling and bolted down the steps to George's side. "Oh, Lord, I said something bad would happen. I knowed it!" Ethel brushed Jim and Celia aside, took George's arm across her own massive shoulders, and half-carried him up the back steps. "Miss Evelyn! Miss Sallie—come quick!"

Celia ran to open the door, and Evelyn darted past her to George's side. "George! What is it? What happened?"

In a spasm of pain, he couldn't answer. "He sort of—sort of fell," Celia stuttered, following Evelyn and Ethel as they helped George up to the bedroom.

"He's all right," Evelyn said. "Run on to school, honey."

"No!"

"All right—but stay quiet." Evelyn kissed her on the forehead, then shut the door firmly in her face.

Celia drifted back down the hall steps in a house made strange and alien by tension. Sallie was cranking the phone angrily. "Miss Effie . . . this is an emergency. Find Dr. Phelps and— Oh? You did? Well, I'm glad you happened to see all of it. Thank you." She hung up the receiver and wiped her eyes. Hurrying upstairs, she shut the door behind her.

Celia sat down on the stairwell steps, pressing her forehead against the cold plaster wall. In a few moments, breathless and red-cheeked at the fast walk from his office three blocks away, Dr. Phelps burst through the front door without knocking. A small, gray-haired man, he nodded brusquely to Celia, having no idea which child she was. "Where's your Uncle George?"

"He's not my uncle, he's—"

"Never mind your genealogy, girl. Where is he?"

She pointed to the door at the head of the stairs, and he dashed past her, wafting a strong, clean odor of antiseptic.

Ethel came slowly out of the bedroom, closing the door behind Dr. Phelps. She stepped over Celia without comment and headed straight for the kitchen. Her gutteral, earthy muttering began at once. Trembling sickly, Celia huddled in the shadows waiting through the eternity of minutes it took for Dr. Phelps to examine her father. When he emerged from the bedroom, he turned in the doorway. "That's exactly right. Angina," he announced indignantly. "Serves him right, the derned fool. Grown man out bogging in the dead of winter like a twelve-year-old kid. Lucky for him it's not a stroke. I'll check you over tomorrow, George." He slammed past Celia, grumbling to himself about animals in general and two-legged animals in particular.

"Angina," Celia repeated, additionally frightened by the unfamiliar and ominous word. In the stilled household, the only sound was the breathy incantation flowing from the kitchen. Celia raised her head, hoping for consolation from Ethel's words of intervention. She listened intently, her arms locked around her knees, rocking on the steps in her misery. The muttering remained indecipherable. Celia stood up and went down the hall into the kitchen. Ethel was kneeling before the window, fists

72

clenched, arms stiff along her sides. Her eyes were squeezed shut, and her entire body vibrated rigidly, sending rolls of sweat cascading from her forehead. Celia knocked timidly at the door frame. "Ethel?"

The stiffness relaxed; Ethel's breathing slowed; her flashing black eyes opened. She wiped a foam of saliva from her lips. "What you want, girl?"

Goose pimples covered Celia's body at the harshness in Ethel's face, the defensive antagonism. Celia forced back her pride and spoke softly. "I—I came to apologize. For before—when I laughed . . . I didn't mean to hurt your feelings. Honest."

"I know."

"And—and when you talk to them—the spirits—would you ask them to look after Daddy and to please—forgive me—f-for being so dumb—a-and so rude . . ." Her voice quavered into tears.

"You didn't have to ask, honey. I done that the first morning you come here, and every day since." Ethel held out her arms, and sobbing openly, Celia ran to bury herself in Ethel's awkard embrace.

"I'm scared, Ethel—I'm real scared for Daddy—and everybody's too busy to talk to me—and—and I'm so scared . . ."

"That's 'cause you're marked, honey. They after you now. You done been marked by them Evil Spirits. And once you marked, you stay marked."

"Ethel . . ."

Ethel touched her hair, looked at her with deep compassion. "Marked," she muttered, and turned toward a bowl of eggs.

5

CELIA SPENT a sleepless night. Marked, she kept thinking, shuddering and pulling the covers over her head. Marked by Evil Spirits. Of course, she didn't really believe it. Nevertheless, around midnight, she eased her door shut, turned on the reading lamp, and stripped herself naked in front of the full-length mirror. Shivering in the icy room, she examined her image critically. Except for the regular strawberry birthmark on her rump, there wasn't a mark on her body. She noted with considerable satisfaction that she was beginning to show a bosom. Or was it fat? She turned, admiring her profile, thrusting her unformed breasts up with the palms of her hands, eager for the day when she could justifiably demand a brassiere. Then she remembered what she was looking for. Or maybe that was how Evil Spirits marked you—with tits. Only that couldn't be so, because then every woman in the world was "marked." Head reeling, she made another hasty check of her body, pulled on her flannel pajamas, and jumped back to the warm security of bed and body-warmed sheets. Marked. What the hell did Ethel mean? She couldn't ask Uncle Alan. "Everyone in town knows that goddamn old nigger's crazy as a coot," was his usual comment about Ethel. She couldn't ask her father, sick as he was. And anyway, he would probably lecture her again about Ethel. And her mother . . . she'd only tell her to go out and play. Or even worse, give her a laxative. No. No sense trying to talk to her. Celia tossed and turned, unable to sink into sleep.

Even the old house was restless. Gusty winds came curling

74

across the Sound, rattling windows, buffeting curtains, creaking through the attic. Celia dozed but was awakened throughout the night by Evelyn moving up and down the steps with warm milk for George, a hot water bottle for his pain-racked chest. Marked. She'd ask Cynthia about it in the morning.

The next day, it was a relief to escape from a household geared down to illness. Celia bolted a skimpy breakfast under Ethel's muttered disapproval, then ran outside to meet Cynthia in the back yard. Hand in hand, they walked toward school, conversing earnestly about Celia's problem.

"But, Celia, if you didn't find any marks, then how do you know you are?"

"Because Daddy got sick, stupid. He was O.K. when we started—so it had to be my fault—you know, because of the Evil Spirits."

"That's true." Cynthia was silent a moment, contemplating this irrefutable piece of logic. "But Ethel's just a dumb old nigger. You're crazy to listen to her."

"I guess so."

"Oh, come on. There's the bell . . . hurry up, Celia—we'll be late . . ."

Celia ran after Cynthia. The sun was well up, and the blazing light made her feel better. Cynthia was right. Ethel was just old and dumb, and nothing but a—a—Well—she was.

The first morning George felt well enough to leave his bedroom was Saturday, and he toyed with the idea of taking the boat out. Rising shakily, he changed his mind but forced himself to join Evelyn and Sallie in the downstairs living room. Agnes was with them, sitting stiffly erect on the edge of Sallie's beige recliner. She held a scoop of worn black fur cape in her lap and was running her hand back and forth against the pelt. Her mouth was clamped in its usual pinched expression of disapproval as she watched Sallie working with a bolt of heavy red wool on a card table pulled close to the fire.

"George!" Sallie dropped the red material. "Welcome home, welcome home. I do declare, it does seem you've been away on a trip." She poured him a cup of coffee while Evelyn settled him in the leather chair and tucked a wool afghan around his legs. "Warm enough?"

"That's fine, thanks." He snugged down between the wing backs.

"Well!" Agnes gave a sniff and delicately wiped the tip of her nose. "So you finally decided to quit playing invalid, eh?" Her laugh was nervous, mirthless.

" 'Playing invalid'?" George repeated dully.

"Agnes!" Evelyn whirled to face her, and Sallie stopped cutting cloth.

Agnes tried to laugh again, a self-conscious snort. "Just making conversation, that's all. If a person can't take a little joshing . . . but then, of course most outlanders can't."

Sallie went back to the cloth. "Agnes, sometimes you're just a derned old fool."

"Jesus," George thought, bitterly regretting his decision to come downstairs. He sank down behind the town newspaper, the *Weekly Bugler*.

The fire flared with a sizzling roar, chewing turquoise and red flames from driftwood banked over pine kindling. Sallie's scissors snipped and burred, following the lines of a rough pattern she had fashioned from newspaper.

Tension bore down through the gentle, homey sounds.

"Agnes," Evelyn said suddenly. "Did I tell you I finally decided what to do with the living room and hall? White! Both areas, all white."

"Oh? White," Agnes repeated inanely. "Just like a derned old hospital. For your invalid, I suppose."

George snapped the paper and Evelyn spoke swiftly. "It'll brighten the hall. And think how our Chinese furniture will show up."

"No, no, no! No, I think you should use a formal wallpaper pattern—something striking—like roses on a trellis, or a street scene."

"With Chinese furniture? You're crazy."

"After all, I did have two classes in college on design and decor, and—"

76

She had pronounced it "deecor," and Evelyn corrected her absent-mindedly. "Daycor."

"Really, Evelyn—I'm the one who took the course, and I guess I know how to pronounce it."

"Have any of you read this issue of the *Bugler*?" George interrupted loudly. "Johnson Miles has a fine editorial on drunken vandalism caused by the bridge crew."

"Yes!" Sallie said quickly. "Johnson's a fine writer. Just fine. One of the best we've ever had—just fine."

"That bridge crew." Agnes sniffed again. "Outlanders—every last one of them."

George ground his teeth. "It says here, 'A *local* member of the construction crew, later arrested as drunk and disorderly, was observed using one corner of the post office lobby as a urinal, and—'"

"Really, George!" Agnes fanned herself uneasily with the tatty fur.

"Want me to read you some more?"

"No! I certainly do not. I think it's perfectly dreadful such—such—trash—should be permitted in a town paper. Johnson must be crazy. What if the children should read it?"

"Why, hell, Agnes. They've probably seen that and worse anywhere in town. That crew parties all over the place. According to this, they had a picnic at State Park Beach last week that 'evolved into a drunken orgy of nude swimming and public love-making, clearly in view of vacationing families and Boy Scout campers.'"

Agnes choked, sending a spew of coffee down the front of her dress. She began fanning herself again, glancing nervously around the room. Wrinkling her nose with a series of quick sniffs, she scowled at the furniture. "Really, Mother—as long as Evelyn's decorating, why don't you?"

Smiling broadly, George folded the paper open to page two. "It also says—"

Agnes's voice rose shrilly, drowning him out. "It's time you get rid of this junk and let me help you arrange some semblance of dee—uh—*day*cor."

77

"Why? It's got perfectly good decor right now."

"Oh?" Agnes's eyes were riveted on George as she rattled on hastily. "Papa's old chair and his handmade cherry table with a walnut feather-down couch? I mean, really, Mother! Just—just what dee—uh—style would you call it?"

Looking Agnes straight in the eye, Sallie said firmly, "Early American Mixed-up Leftovers. And I like it exactly the way it is."

"But, Mother! All this clutter! If you think about my house, and—"

George sat forward in his chair. "Your house! Exactly, Agnes. Your house and nobody else's. Without a single goddamn chair fit for man, child, or beast."

"Why—why, George!"

"You've been carrying on this stupid, bitchy conversation about furniture from the first day we set foot in this house, and I am sick and tired of this kind of crap. The town is in turmoil, the world is falling down around our ears, and you sit in your private, backwater, isolated swamp of mentality arguing about some goddamn paint and wallpaper."

"George, please—"

"Does it matter, Evelyn? Does it really matter what you paint something, or paper it, or if? Does anything matter? Anything at all?" He slashed the paper to the floor and struggled to free himself from the cocoon of afghan.

Agnes raised a protective hand. "Now, George, you know perfectly well that my intentions are for Mother's own good. She—"

"The hell they are! You—"

"George is right!" Sallie interrupted.

Their voices rose in a babble of inane bickering. "—and the stupid waste, the—" "Now, George, I—" "Oh, be quiet Agnes!" "Don't tell me to be quiet, Mother, he—" "—all the time and money down the goddamn toilet, while—"

"Hi, everybody!" Celia's cheerful greeting cut through their overlapping squabble. "Whatcha doing?"

There was profound and instant silence. Finally, Sallie

coughed. "Just—uh—talking," she said, and returned hastily to her pattern.

Evelyn froze by the leather chair, and George sank back against the cushions. "Morning, honey."

"Brrrr!" Celia ran to the fireplace and lifted her skirt, proffering a lace-pantied backside to the flames in imitation of her grandmother and her mother. "Uncle Alan said we can come down to the store and play today."

"Oh, did he now," George muttered dryly.

"Well? Can we?"

"Well . . ." Evelyn echoed, and looked to George, who said nothing but lowered his head into his coffee cup. "If you'll promise not to—"

"Oh, Mother! You're always saying that. We'll stay out of the derned old funeral home." Celia spun to the service tray and snatched up a biscuit. "What you making, Grandmother?" she asked, resorting to diversionary tactics.

"This? Oh, this here's a coat for Ethel."

"For Ethel?" Celia's voice rose in astonishment. "Red?"

"Yes. And it's going to have a black fur collar and cuffs."

"But—but why?"

"You know how big she is. All her life she's had to buy men's coats. Military surplus, mostly—like that old Army thing she's wearing now. But the other day, she saw my new red sweater and she had a conniption fit. Told me she'd always wanted a 'red lady coat.' So I'm making her one for her birthday."

"Really?" Celia giggled around her biscuit. "All that trouble for a crazy old nigger?"

George leaned forward and dealt Celia a heavy, sharp blow across her fire-exposed posterior. With a yelp, Celia dropped her biscuit and turned to face him. He was breathing heavily. "Don't you ever—ever again—let me hear you call anyone by that word."

"But—but, I only meant—"

"I don't give a damn what you 'only meant.' I will not have that word used in my home."

79

"It's my home, too. Supposed to be. But you'd never know it. You're always telling me what to say, what to do, what to wear, until I'm sick to death of living here." Terrified at what she'd let slip, Celia ran from the room and slammed out the front door before she could be called back and punished.

"Celia!" Evelyn rose angrily to follow her.

"Oh, let her go," George said wearily. "For god's sake, let her go. At the moment I'm 'sick to death' at the sight of her." He shook his head despondently. "Sometimes the girl drives me out of my mind. Selfish, self-centered—doing anything and everything to be part of the mob."

Sallie dropped her sewing into her lap. "Oh, George—do be patient with her. It's a terrible time for a girl, being in her twilight years."

"What?"

"No longer a child, not yet a woman. Not a human being, really."

Deep fatigue settled into his face and drained down across his shoulders. "Then perhaps you should say this whole damn town is in its twilight years." He rose with a grunt of pain and walked slowly, heavily up the steps.

Agnes gave a louder than usual sniff. "I think George was too hard on her. The child is absolutely right. All these hours you've been making a pattern, sewing, and now you want her to have a fur collar to boot. All for one crazy old—uh—" She faltered, catching Evelyn's expression. "—old darkie."

Sallie stopped trying to fight a new thread into her needle. "Agnes, you've had that derned moth-eaten cape in your attic for twenty-some-odd years. But if you don't want to let me have it for Ethel's coat collar, then you just take it right back home again."

"No, no, no. It's bad enough to see you waiting on your cook hand and foot. No need to spend any more money on that old —woman." She rose clumsily, her knees spraddling in the effort, exposing thick garters along lard-fat thighs. Dropping the worn pelt on the card table, Agnes waddled toward the door. "I'm going home where things make some sense." The door slammed behind her self-righteous departure.

"What's gotten into her this morning?" Evelyn asked crossly.

"Oh—Alan's been running off every night again—fishing, hunting, whatever. Fred's working himself to death, plus standing ambulance duty, and Agnes doesn't know what to do about it."

"I don't see there's anything she can do."

"There's not. And that's 'what's gotten into her.' This morning, and every morning." Sallie picked up the limp fur and ripped away its faded satin lining. "I reckon I can get enough good out this thing for collar and cuffs for Ethel." Her attention appeared riveted to the pelt stitching she was ripping. "Evelyn—do you think George is ever going to be happy in Beldon?"

"Why, of course. What a thing to say. He's always in a bad temper when he's sick. But he told me just the other night how much he was enjoying his retirement."

"Maybe so. But what folks say and folks are really thinking doesn't always jibe."

"Now what on earth do you mean by that?"

Sallie retreated before the edge in Evelyn's tone. "I'd best go fit this to Ethel again before I stitch it." She rose and walked stiffly toward the kitchen. Out in the hall, Sallie murmured to herself, "Stay out of it, Sallie. Stay out of it. You're a meddling old fool . . . hunh . . . getting bad as Ethel, talking out loud to myself . . . they'll be saying I'm crazy next thing you know . . ."

Once out of the house, Celia had met Cynthia next door and they had sprinted along the back way to the store. Alan and Thomas were crouched by the open sliding door of the funeral home, playing mumble-de-peg in sifted white sand. Jim was loading small cartons onto the pickup truck, his mouth-clamped expression a dirty replica of his immaculate father's.

Celia felt a heavy, involuntary shiver sweep through her body.

"What's the matter? You act like some old Evil Spirit just walked over your grave." Celia's fingernails left blood on Cynthia's arm. "Owww ... what the hell you think you ..."

Celia put a hand over Cynthia's mouth and gestured to the loading dock. Brown was leaning against the tailgate of the truck, making no move to help Jim stack the assortment of cartons. He held a pint bottle of wine in one fist and took long gulping swallows as he watched Jim's labors. He was pink-faced, smiley. And he smelled—partly from wine, partly from stale sweat. Celia wrinkled her nose and yanked Cynthia back into the shadow of the shed.

Fred came out on the platform with two more cartons. Brown squinted, swallowed hard. "If that nigger boy over there would get off his lazy ass, you'd get through a lot quicker."

Fred scowled down at him. "I told you twice—he's on a rest break."

"Since when do niggers get—get res' breaks?"

"Since they've been working overtime loading and delivering heavy supplies to your crew. Where you parked?"

"... Up f-front ..."

"You going to be sober enough to drive yourself back?"

"Shit yeah." Brown pulled himself erect and lurched up the alley toward the sidewalk. "Gotta pick up some wine. See you out at the bridge." He passed the two cringing girls without seeing them.

Fred shook his head and handed up a final carton to Jim. He paused to mop his forehead, and Alan whistled derisively. "Aw, is Fred getting dirty?" And when Fred ignored his first sally, Alan said for the benefit of the children, "Whatever happens, Fred, don't you get no dirt on you."

"Don't worry," Fred returned quietly. "God forbid I be mistaken for my brother-in-law." He eased into the driver's seat, and the store truck rattled away up the driveway with Jim happily jouncing around in the truckbed.

Thomas gave a final fling of his pocketknife with a hoot of glee. "Mr. Fred got you that time, Mr. Alan."

"That he did," Alan admitted sourly. "Goddamn old maid that he is."

Cynthia bit her lip but said nothing in defense of her father. Thomas rose and came to her side. "You know well as me that Mr. Alan's only teasing, so stop wrinkling up your forehead. This cold weather you're liable to freeze that way." Thomas sat down on the edge of the sunny dock, and the two girls quickly sat down beside him.

Celia rolled to her side, poking at the heavy key ring clamped to Thomas's belt. "Golly, Thomas. You got more than Grandmother. How many?"

He laughed, an easy chuckle. "Forty-one."

"Do they all work?"

"You bet."

"Grandmother's don't."

"I know. But these do." He pried the keys apart. "This here was number one, when I was eleven and first came to work." It was a fragile, smooth slip of a key, and even Celia realized that a cleverly wielded bobby-pin could act as substitute. "Mr. Alan gave me that the day he hired me—it's for the supply cabinet—you know, cleansers and toilet paper." His finger separated the next key. "This was number two . . ." One by one he reeled them off, a story of his progression with the store. Storage bins; warehouse; housing supplies; hardware; lumber; Alan's house keys and boat keys; funeral home; and finally, all the vehicle keys connected with the store. ". . . and every time Mr. Alan gave me another key, he gave me a raise."

"You must be a millionaire."

"Not just yet." Thomas laughed. He saw the store truck driving back across the bridge and arose with a swift flex of one knee, hurrying to meet Fred at the warehouse.

A deep quietude drifted across Celia and Cynthia. They were aware of gulls crying, of water lapping and rocking the pier. Celia stirred. "Now what'll we do?"

"Dunno. Go home, I guess."

"Might as well."

Toe-raking, heel-dragging, they sauntered silently along the alley. Cynthia caught her breath. "Celia. Look."

"Hunh?" It took several nudgings before Celia was aware that the sliding doors into the back of the funeral home stood wide open, totally unattended. Wordlessly, they crept to the open doorway. Referred to euphemistically as "the showcase," it was a large, stark tin shed. A profusion of mute-toned caskets loomed in the dim interior. Visible reminders of mortality, lids clamped tight, they emanated an aura of unrelenting watchfulness that sent shudders through Cynthia and Celia. Garish artificial flowers on fold-out wire stands marked an attempt to soften the brutal reality of the coffins. Raw-wired record amplifiers were bolted to the ceiling beams and garlanded with plastic ivy in an attempt to ease the pain of cheaply recorded organ music that would be dumped over the heads of the next family forced to make the brutal choice of color and cost to bury their lost one. "Cross your fingers." Cynthia's whisper was a hiss of command.

"Why?"

"Because you're s'posed to when you see a coffin." Celia dutifully crossed two fingers; then, taking note of the number of empty caskets, she crossed every finger on both hands. They eased to the edge of the ramp that gave loading and unloading access to the ambulance-hearse. "Look." Cynthia gestured to wide back doors at the rear of the warehouse. They opened into a glaringly white room. "Celia! Let's—" Cynthia took a tentative step up the ramp.

"No!" Celia yanked her back.

Cynthia tugged at her sleeve. "C'mon."

"I-I promised not to go in. I promised."

"So did I. But it's not exactly 'going in' with the doors wide open. We'll just peek. C'mon."

They moved forward slowly, each one's uneasy curiosity feeding the other's false bravado. The storage shed had an oddly crisp and lingering odor. New metal, satin linings, and sympathy cards for "families of the deceased" washed the air to a sick mockery of breathing. As they approached the inner door,

84

the cloistered odor became rancid, sterilized beyond human concept. "Phew," Celia murmured.

"Shut up!" Cynthia pinched her to silence.

Arm against pudgy arm, they crept into a blaring spill of light falling across the whitewashed doorjamb. Surgical tools; an oversized sink; white metal stool; cabinets with mysterious containers and tubing. They were brought up short by the permanent operating-type table under a floodlight in the midst of the room. Celia's immediate reaction was to a stainless steel pedestal with a foot control. Like the dentist. Or the veterinarian. Or their own Dr. Phelps. Or— Cynthia seized her arm in a bruising grip, her breathing quick, uneven gasps, unable to voice a comment. Following the line of heavy steel up to the operating table at its top, Celia returned Cynthia's grasp. An unmoving form lay stiffly along the table top. Draped in heavy sheeting pulled across its head and well down over its feet, it was distinctly human in shape and contour. The head, chest, arms, and legs were sharply delineated by crisp white linen, and Celia had a crazy concept of heavy work boots on the invisible, immobile pair of feet. "L-le's go home!"

As they began backing toward the doorway, a low, unearthly moan came from the table. Momentarily paralyzed, they watched the ghoulish figure. With another low, long moan, one arm bent sharply at the elbow, raising the sheet on the far side in a grotesque pyramid of linen. With further eerie sounds, the figure slowly sat up on the table, twisting to face them, arms extending jaggedly, imploringly. Shrieking terror, Cynthia and Celia almost knocked each other down running back through the open doorway, sprinting along the wide corridor between the waiting caskets. At the sliding door to the shed, they spurned the convenient ramp, flinging themselves headlong to the soft sandy driveway and bolting up the alley.

Thomas was standing on the sidewalk along Main Street. "Hey," he called. "What's the matter?"

Ashen-faced, they started toward his protective arms, just as Mr. Brown appeared behind him, carrying a clanking bag of wine bottles. At the noise, reminiscent of Ethel's description of Evil Spirits, Celia began screaming hysterically. Slapping away Thomas's hands, she ran for home with Cynthia close behind her.

"Nigger—you getting fresh with them white girls? You—nigger, there—I'm talking to you . . . ."

Preoccupied and troubled, Thomas paid no attention to Brown's slurred, drunken speech. He was looking down the alley, watching Alan lean against the side door of the shed. Alan was clutching a white sheet, his figure limp against the white-washed boards as he wheezed and coughed his amusement. Thomas walked slowly along the sloping alleyway. "Mr. Alan? You didn't—didn't pull that old trick . . . not on those two little girls?"

Alan's laughter died in a mean look of contempt that continued as he lit a cigarette and licked its end to the limp twist of tobacco he liked. Thomas felt Alan's look burning brighter than the tobacco ash. "You're just goddamn right I did," Alan said finally. "They've been told to stay out of there, and I don't like people snooping where they're not wanted. *Nobody*." Alan flung the sheet at Thomas's feet and swaggered stiffly toward the back of the store. Alone in a sudden chill of shadow and wind, Thomas knelt and scooped up the sheet, balling it to a hard twist between his strong dark hands, examining the spotless white linen as though he had never seen a sheet before.

The two girls ran for home without stopping. Evelyn and Sallie were still in the living room when they careened through the hallway and up the steps, taking them two and three at a time. Sallie dropped her scissors. "What on earth?"

Evelyn rose immediately to follow them upstairs to Celia's room. In the snug harbor afforded by Celia's double bed, Evelyn found the two girls twisted across the cover. "Mother!" "Aunt Evelyn" they gasped in confused unison. "Uncle Alan . . ." ". . . Uncle Alan didn't really do anything but he laughed . . ." ". . . and there was this Evil Spirit . . ." ". . . really evil . . ." ". . . and

86

all in white . . ." ". . . and he rose up and started after us . . ." ". . . trying to grab us, you know? . . ." ". . . and he was there . . . that awful man, and . . ." Evelyn finally soothed them to sleep with hot chocolate.

Half an hour later, back downstairs in front of the fire, Evelyn tried to repeat their incoherent dialogue. Sallie looked up from her oversized basting stitches. "I think I know what happened. Yes, I do know. And Alan should have his backside whipped, but good."

Celia was the first to awaken. She lay still, silent. Marked, she thought again. Ethel might be just a crazy old nigger like Cynthia said, but who else except someone who was marked could have caused an Evil Spirit to start moving around in a funeral home? Maybe Mr. Brown was the Evil Spirit marking her. Marked. She rolled from one side to the other, back again. Marked.

Cynthia awoke shortly afterwards, a victim of Celia's nervous, quick tossings.

"I'm marked," Celia whispered. "Really marked!"

"Yeah. And me, too."

"How you figure that?"

"Because you'd have been the only one to see it move—but I saw it, too."

"Yeah, but . . ."

They were silent, hearing Evelyn's footsteps in the hall. When she moved away from the door, they discussed their "problem" in earnest. After coursing their limited knowledge of hexings, folklore, and profanity, Cynthia suddenly sat upright on the bed. "I know the answer. I know!"

Celia was immediately upright beside her. "What?!"

"Celia"—Cynthia's fat hand came up in silent benediction—"we have got to go and join the church."

"The . . . what?"

"The *church*, stupid. Don't you see?"

"Uh—no—not exactly."

"You're 'marked.' Right?"

87

"Yes."

"You and yours Ethel said. Right?"

"Yes."

"Well, I'm your cousin, so that means me, too. Right?"

"Uh . . . yeah . . . I guess so . . ." Celia was reluctant to relinquish her martyrdom.

"So if I'm marked, and you're marked, all we can do is join the church."

"Hunh?"

"Stupe! If we join, and we're real members, those Evil Spirits can't touch us! Right?"

"Right . . . I guess . . ." Celia's hesitation was born from inbred reluctance for the tribal rites that surrounded induction to Baptist church membership. "But, Cynthia—all that pushing people under water . . . you know, you do your hair and all to look real nice, and then you get half-drowned . . . I mean . . . well, why couldn't we just go with Daddy and join the Episcopal church? They only sprinkle you over there."

"No." Cynthia glared at her. "Mama says you're only blessed where the water touches. We're in *real* trouble, and we'd best get blessed all over. 'Washed clean by the blood of the lamb,'" she recited, her eyes closing ecstatically. "And if we get washed —all over—then those old Evil Spirits won't be able to see us. Right?"

"Right. I guess." Cynthia's newly acquired zeal left Celia baffled, but she was determined not to reveal her ignorance to anyone a full year older than she was. "Washed clean . . . I guess."

To Celia's dismay, Sunday arrived as usual the very next morning. The girls took their customary places at the rear of the Baptist church. They were overgroomed, immaculate to a point of profanity on George's part, when the hot water ran out before he could shave. Evelyn was also distinctly aware of Celia's grooming, having run out of hot water midway through the breakfast dishes. A phase, she had decided. Another damn phase.

88

But four tubfuls of hot water for one little girl? She was relieved to hear Agnes and Fred make similar complaint about Cynthia.

The morning sermon droned along, endless as ever to Celia's anxious ears. She had hoped—prayed, indeed—for something related to Evil Spirits. Instead, the text dealt with Sodom and Gomorrah—whoever they were—with roundabout slaps at Beldon's city hall and the "founding fathers." Awake all the preceding night in a sweat of nervous apprehension, Celia let her head drop to her chest in an exhausted doze. She was awakened by Cynthia's sharp pinch. "C'mon."

"Hunh?"

"He just asked for all sinners to come forward and declare theirselves."

". . . Themselves . . ." Yawning, stumbling, Celia followed Cynthia down the aisle toward the indistinct, waiting figure of Reverend Dowde.

Of all the members in the church that morning, no one was more astounded than Reverend Dowde when the two girls presented themselves for baptism. His only acquaintance with them had been a paternal glowering toward the snickers constantly originating from the back of his church during what he fondly regarded as his eruditely conceived sermons. It had never occurred to him that he might have found a mark in two such young and mischievous girls. He folded his hands in reverential awe as he welcomed the two children into the "blessed fold of the church." "Suffer little children to come unto me," he intoned monotonously. "Why 'suffer'?" Celia whispered, silenced again by another fierce Cynthia pinch. Reverend Dowde wished fervently that the smaller girl was not yawning so audibly, that her sleepy visage might come closer to the burning eyes of her older sister . . . sister? . . . cousin? . . . friend? Reverend Dowde was never quite sure about the Villiers clan and, stuttering his confusion, gladly relinquished the girls to the attentions of an elderly deacon who obviously did know who they were. He jotted down their names and ages with broad winks toward the watchful congregation and toward an astonished Evelyn in particular.

At home, over their expansive Sunday noon meal with Sallie, George exploded at the unexpected news, striking the table with harsh, clenched fist. "What do you mean, 'Celia joined the church'?"

"Why, just that," Evelyn said evenly. "Presented herself for baptism."

"That's what I get for going to the Episcopal church." George scowled at the smug smile on Celia's face, the smear of mayonnaise across her cheek. "What the hell do you know about joining a church?"

"Well . . . you just walk down the aisle . . ."

"The 'sawdust trail,'" George interrupted.

"Is that what you call it?"

"See?" George muttered to Evelyn. "Yes, and then . . . ?"

Celia faltered. ". . . uh . . . and . . . and then you confess your sins . . ."

"Sins? What sins?" George struck the table again.

"I . . . uh . . . I . . . that is . . . it's . . ."

Ethel hurried from the kitchen with more steak hash for George's rice; Sallie spooned more gravy across his plate. Evelyn merely smiled, watching the lifted chins of her daughter and her husband.

"Go on," George insisted. "Just tell me. What the goddamn hell do you know about sins?"

Celia's chin rose a notch higher. "I've got just as goddamn many sins as you do."

Sallie found a sudden laugh-choked necessity to check the pantry for staples while Evelyn fled to oversee helpings of custard already spooned into serving cups.

"I won't have it!" George was saying when they returned. "I simply will not have it. You sit there and mouth inanities about 'evil spirits,' and god-knows-what, and tell me that's the reason you're joining a church . . . I won't have it."

90

"I have found it a necessity in my life-span to be washed clean by the blood of the Lamb," Celia announced imperiously, giving him a word-for-word phrase from the back of her Sunday school folder. She rose from her chair, trying to ignore the buckle on her best dress that had hooked under the table top. With heavy-footed tread, she marched away from the table, making mental note to pick up her dessert a little later.

"Now what did all that mean?" George stirred his coffee furiously. "One Sunday you can't get her out of bed. Today she's got to be 'washed clean.' And after all that bathing this morning? What the hell's the matter with her?"

Evelyn's voice was over easy, infuriating to her irate husband. "I was twelve when I joined."

"But Celia's—she's—"

"Going on twelve."

"She's going on eleven."

"That's close to twelve."

"Evelyn, if she had any idea . . . any inkling of what she's doing . . . but she doesn't. She's blundering into a preconceived, asinine ceremony—"

"Oh, George!" Sallie protested. "That's not—"

From the hallway steps, Celia listened in furtive glee as the argument raged. For once, just once, no one could accuse her of wrongdoing, and it amused her to hear the heated discussion based on her having done something normally considered right and morally correct. She was well aware of her father's afternoon visit to Reverend Dowde, and managed to get within easy hearing when he returned to the house.

"Well?" Evelyn asked. "What did he say?"

"Precisely what I predicted—'Suffer little children to come unto me.' He is nothing but a pompous old far—"

"George!"

"Uh . . . foop!" George amended for Sallie's benefit.

Seated on the stairwell, Celia made a mental note. "Foop" was a pretty good word, and no one could take exception to that.

6

THE SUNDAY of their Baptism was a foggy drizzle of rain, profoundly disappointing to Celia; a day as mindless and pointless as the sermons of Reverend Dowde had appeared to the increasingly distraught girl. Perhaps, Celia thought, once someone was marked, the Evil Spirits would keep "the good word" away from her. Cynthia suffered no similar doubts. She moved about in serene anticipation of her coming initiation into "the church" and to the total security it would afford against any unforeseen evil and/or peril. Cynthia gave Celia endless mini-sermons on their unsaved status, accusing her sharply for her doubts, ranting on as to the difference their salvation would bring. "Aw, shut up!" Celia snapped in a seizure of nervous pique on the Sunday morning of their prospective induction. "Just shut up."

"Oh, honestly, Celia. Sometimes I don't think you're ready for such a–a momentary decision."

"Momentous," Celia corrected her with a giggle that she later thought must have marked the entire day, along with her own indiscernible marking.

They arrived at the church a half hour before the service and were swept into the Sunday school building by two old-maid friends of Agnes's. Agnes sat in one corner of the heavily shel-lacked "lesson room," daubing at lugubrious tears as the girls stripped their clothing and were draped in oversized white choir robes. "Oh, my!" Agnes commented again and again. "Oh, my —I never thought I'd live to see this day. Oh, my!"

As they were being readied, Celia felt only a cold, icy chill, directly due to a drafty door and the endless winter sea wind whining in across bare tiled flooring. Cynthia later insisted it was the "hand of the Lord." Celia maintained a private conviction that any "hand of the Lord" would be a warm and friendly one. She was suddenly trembling violently and was secretly glad that her mother had decided to remain out in the church with her father, unable to witness her distress. George, at the last minute, had reluctantly agreed to attend the "barbarian ceremony" and was dressed in his best new suit for the occasion. At length, tennis-shoed, white-draped, and shivering, the girls were led to the glass side doors. Celia glanced into the church and darted back behind Cynthia.

"Go on!" Cynthia gave her a shove.

"No. He's in there."

"Who?"

"That Mr. Brown."

"What about it?"

"If he belongs, I don't want to."

"That's silly. All kinds of people belong. Go on in."

"But what if he is the Evil Spirit?"

"All the more reason for us to get baptized — go on."

"No. I—I want to go home."

"You can't."

"Yes I can. I don't want him to watch us . . ." Celia backed away, ramming into the soft black-suited belly of Reverend Dowde.

"Come along, girls." He opened the door and thrust them across the front of the church to the first pew.

Brown was seated directly behind them. His whiskey smell and wheezing breath swept Celia's neck, encompassed her breathing, enveloped her thoughts. Apprehension settled in her stomach, and she could taste the bacon she had eaten earlier.

The sermon began. Damned old foop! Celia thought, as Reverend Dowde rambled on and on about the evils of gambling, lust, envy, and attendant vices. Finally, with an upturned, glazed expression, he announced his joy at "welcoming two lost lambs to the bosom of the eternal church."

"Lost lambs, my foot," Celia muttered fiercely. "Bullshit. I've never been lost in my life. I'd like to see that old foop follow us on one of our bike trails, or—"

"Shut up," Cynthia managed to hiss, without opening her mouth.

Celia lapsed into silence, wishing she had followed her father's advice and discarded the entire notion of baptism. However, at the given signal, she dutifully arose and stood waiting by Cynthia's side. They were left waiting through four full stanzas of "Brighten the Corner Where You Are," rendered in puerile manner by a lethargic congregation and choir. During that interminable span of time, Reverend Dowde disappeared to don his baptismal rig: trout wading boots pulled up tightly beneath a flowing white robe that covered all of his other garments. Meanwhile, four clamp-jawed, dark-suited deacons stepped up to remove the platform cover of the baptismal font. The Belmont Baptist Church, "one of the oldest functioning institutions in the nation," as Reverend Dowde reminded them Sunday after Sunday, had a raised preaching platform across the entire front of the church. Normally, the preacher spoke from the precise center of this four-foot prominence. On baptismal day, his pulpit was thrust to one side, while the choir and soloist-soprano were crowded behind the railing that fronted the organ at the right edge of the font.

Today, in a tittering shudder, Celia realized belatedly that Mrs. Beezely was ensconced in the soloist's chair. She smiled and nodded to them, her black and ragged teeth showing clearly in the dull morning light.

The moment of their "washing" approached. Celia tried to eliminate mental pictures of washing machines, hand-soaked laundry, dog-baths, dirty dishes, car sprays. Unbelievably, she and Cynthia were about to be totally inundated in the pit opened now before her overanxious gaze. Inundated, prayed over, and sent home as "cleansed," after enduring the curious stares of family and townspeople. Yet she had to admit with her father that she would never be more thoroughly cleansed than after the four baths she'd had again that morning. If the Evil Spirits could see her after all that— What in the hell was she doing, offering herself freely—her body, her mind, her privacy—simply offering it to such an embarrassing situation? And what did Reverend Dowde know about her sins? He, after all, had not witnessed the Evil Spirit in the funeral home. Nor even guessed they had seen one. Too late it occurred to her that Reverend Dowde had never even told them what all this rigmarole meant, much less asked why they wanted it. Celia looked around in blind panic, contemplating a dash for the door. Cynthia sensed her impulse and took Celia's clammy fingers in her own sweaty hand.

The music droned on, a number of false notes obstructing the comforting tonal flow of the hymn. The organist, a high school girl with crisply curled blonde hair, managed an aloof expression that transcended most of her clumsy chordal errors, the foot pedal notes that trailed a full bar behind the right-hand melody.

Reverend Dowde emerged from his study and Celia pressed the back of her knees against the hard seat of the wooden pew. Oh, God, she thought obliquely, Oh, God—please help me— what am I doing here today? How could you do this to me? How the goddamn hell could you get me into this mess? Please get me out of this. An earthquake . . . or a fire maybe. Anything. Please? Nothing happened except that "Brighten the Corner Where You Are" wailed to an end, bass and treble finding each other in final triumphant blare. Fighting a sensation that she was going to fall, or throw up at the very least, Celia shifted from one foot to the other and pressed her back against the high wooden arm of the pew.

Reverend Dowde rose from his platform seat, raised a hand

dirt-mired from his small turnip patch. "Suffer little children to come unto me," he recited mindlessly.

"Again," Celia whispered.

"Shut up."

Celia began to understand the "suffer" part, her backside a flat compress against the wooden pew.

The organist shifted the organ's pitch and tilted into a spirited version of "Shall We Gather at the River?" Eyes amist, hat askew, Mrs. Beezely rose and took her place for the highlighted solo of the day. Her copy of the hymn was neatly spread across a music stand, canted to face the director-organist. Mrs. Beezely was automatically placed in profile to the congregation, most of whom were kind enough to overlook her quivering double chin, her even more quivering falsetto soprano. Mrs. Beezely adjusted her glasses, sliding them down along the bridge of her nose, and waited for the organ to slither through the introductory passages.

The congregation coughed, shifted in their seats, checked watches, subsided to listless attention. "Goddamn!" The whisper came from her father two pews behind them as he realized Mrs. Beezely was the soloist for the ceremony. Celia smirked and stifled a giggle.

Mrs. Beezely peered over her glasses at the glut of musical notes and notations spread out subserviently before her. Clasping her hands, turning to smile again briefly at the two girls, she began her musical delivery. "Shall we gather at the river, the bew-utifullll . . . bew-utifullllllrrrrrrrr-ihver, geyawather with the say-ints at the rrrrivv-ver . . . that flows by the throne ov-vo . . . Gawd . . ."

With no musical training and even less feeling for music of any type, Reverend Dowde stood patiently through one verse, then lowered himself gingerly along the marble steps into the lukish-warm, waist-deep water.

Mrs. Beezely still had three verses spread before her on the music stand. The young organist recognized the minister's watery predicament and ducked her head vigorously in his direction. Mrs. Beezely, her back to the font, interpreted the girl's

96

head nodding as enthusiastic approval of her rendition of the old hymn. She raised her shoulders and her voice, throwing all her wispy energy into the chorus.

Shivering, embarrassed, and intimidated, Reverend Dowde folded his hands and attempted to look benign and humble through the seemingly endless verses with chorus. Waiting in the rapidly chilling baptismal font, his clenched teeth chattered, his knuckles showed blue. Only Cynthia's persistent pinches kept Celia's snickering silent.

Twisting ecstatically, exuberantly, Mrs. Beezely reached the final chorus. Her voice cracked, wavered and cracked again; her enthusiasm remained consistent. "Yass, we will gather at the rrrivurrrrrr—the bewytifulll, bewytifulllll rrrivurrrrrrr . . . geyather with the Say-ints at the rrrrivurrrrrrrrr, that flow from the throne ov-uvvvv—" The final note was to have been the highest, "a spiraling, inspiring ascension toward the feet of the Deity Himself," according to the annotated notes accompanying the score. Flexing her entire frail strength through a new up-thrust of her shoulders, Mrs. Beezely made a valiant attempt to pluck down the last word of the hymn. With her uptilted head, with out-thrusting, clenched hands, she reached for that note. She took two steps backward in her efforts, caught one heel in the shaggy rug edging the baptismal font. For an instant her arms windmilled frantically; then she simply disappeared from the sight of the lethargic congregation in a soft slushing splosh of water. "Ass over tin-cups," as George was later to describe it. "Just ass over tin-cups." Her unexpected immersion caught Reverend Dowde squarely across the back of his shoulders. He was thrown to the marble steps, and both of them vanished into the depths of the font. In the shocked silence throughout the building, the only sound was baptismal water bubbling into trout wading boots. Then Reverend Dowde reappeared. His ministerial collar was undone; his hair hung down into his eyes. As he stood up, a loud bloop of air was released from his trout boots, immediately beneath his robe. The lightweight material bubbled softly and floated to the surface of the font, revealing Reverend Dowde's loudly checked orange-and-red undershorts. Simultaneously, Mrs. Beezely found her footing and emerged from beneath the water, staring in astonishment at her stunned fellow church-goers, at the young organist sitting stiffly upright with hands frozen above the keyboard in preparation for Mrs. Beezely's final note. Queasily, Mrs. Beezely folded her hands, shook her head. Her little hat with its tattered dark blue veiling loosened from its mooring of hat pins and slid across her forehead; her glasses hung from one dripping ear. ". . . Gawd . . ." Mrs. Beezely dutifully finished the last note of the hymn. Uncannily, for once, she was full-toned and right on key.

There was a slobbered, belching snore from Mr. Brown.

"Heee . . . he . . . . heeeeee . . . . ." Celia's nervousness exploded in shrill, unleashed giggling that split the silence. No amount of pinching from Cynthia could stop her. The next explosion came from her father, equally unaffected by fierce jabs from Evelyn, by then fighting to control her own mirth. The organist simply lowered her head to the keyboard, and the amplified instrument emitted a long, continuous hoot from the bass clef. And the congregation began to laugh. Merriment bounced, whooped, beamed through the church; universal laughter hurled the breath of life through the staid, stiff building. Even Mrs. Beezely went into a fit of laughter, leaning against the edge of the font and beating her arms on the dull rose-print carpeting that had been her undoing.

Only Reverend Dowde was unamused. He raised his arms imploringly, his brightly colored shorts even more clearly visible in the holy waters. "Brethren . . . sistern . . . uh, sisters . . ." New bursts of laughter drowned his intended lecture. "Quiet. Quiet, please! These blessed children are here for the explicit and serious purpose of baptism."

"These blessed children" were giggling fiercely, lying prostrate along the skimpy cushions of the pew seat.

Reverend Dowde abandoned any thought of baptism and retreated a soggy withdrawal to the comfort of the gas stove in his study. "The deacons can damn well clean up and fish out that

98

stupid old bitch," he thought in an unaccustomed flash of rage. Horrified, he subjected himself to an hour of fervent prayer for forgiveness. But nothing he had to say to the "good listening Lord" then or in the succeeding week could regain the attention of his two "lost lambs." They tried, he had to admit in all good conscience. They certainly tried. Through long lectures in the parish house, they were dutifully attentive. But Reverend Dowde had only to mention "baptism" and the two girls were off into convulsions of laughter. He finally admitted to George and Evelyn that he was forced to agree with George. It would definitely be wiser if the girls waited a year or so for their formal baptism.

It was two Sundays before Celia missed Mrs. Beezely at church. The first Sunday, over Evelyn's protests, George took Celia and Cynthia out in the boat, sparing them the harsh jibes he knew would be forthcoming from some congregation members. He had already cut short one of Alan's attempts at joking when Alan started to turn the garden hose on the two crestfallen girls.

"I'm jus' gonna wash 'em good and clean," Alan had insisted, his breath a musk of afternoon whiskey with beer chasers. He laughed and swung the hose toward the girls.

With one swift stroke, George knocked the hose from Alan's hands.

"Who are you to be so flipping high-handed?" Alan swayed, going to shut off the water. "Nothing but a friggin' outlander."

Watching Alan's inept attempts to coil the hose, George stifled his angry retort. "Come on, girls," he said quietly, and they had continued their walk to the beach.

Through the following week, Celia and Cynthia threw themselves wholeheartedly into school activities, arriving home late in the afternoons and usually attending some meeting or party at night. Too exhausted to be concerned about their "marked" status, they began sleeping peacefully through the nights, and within days both managed to thrust the spectre of the funeral home from their conversation.

99

The second Sunday, Celia realized that Mrs. Beezely's absence removed all spice from the dreary church proceedings. There was nothing to giggle about; there was no secret anticipation of musical disaster. The service progressed normally, which was to say dully, from start to finish. Celia squirmed impatiently through thirty-three minutes of sermon and ten minutes more of Reverend Dowde's ". . . and so in conclusion . . ." "Old foop!" she murmured to Cynthia, and ran for the exit at the first allowable instant.

"Is Mrs. Beezely sick?" Celia asked later, over Sunday dinner.

"In a way." George put down the drumstick he was eating, eyed her over his coffee cup. "You haven't gone by to see her?"

Celia was annoyed at the easy way her father had of turning a question into an accusation. "I've been busy. Real busy."

"I see. Hope Mrs. Beezely has, too."

"Why? What do you mean?"

"Oh, come now, Celia. How do you think she must be feeling about that Sunday?"

Celia rankled under his continuing gaze. "I-I was planning on going to see her today."

"Good." He went back to his drumstick.

Later that afternoon, Celia slipped from the house and walked the two short blocks to Mrs. Beezely's. The back yard of the store was empty, sun-filled silence underscoring the monotony of Sunday life in a small town. Even the switchboard was silent. Celia hesitated by the gate, fingering rough-end strands of wire fencing. She didn't know what to say. If Mrs. Beezely was taking a nap, she wouldn't have to stay. She eased across the yard, peering through the screen door. Inside, Mrs. Beezely was seated on the horsehair sofa, her Bible open in her lap. With the magnifying glass held at a cocked angle, she was reading one of Eben's ancient letters, smiling and bobbing her head to some unheard strain of music. Through the door behind her, Celia could see Miss Effie at the front end of the store. She had pulled her wheelchair into the warm sunny window and was dozing while she sat bolt upright in her seat. Celia smiled, feeling unaccountably tender toward them both. She would come back later, she decided.

She had made no sound. But before she could turn to leave, Mrs. Beezely glanced up intuitively. "Why, Celia. Come in, child. How are you?" Her voice was misty, remote.

"Oh—fine. Just fine, Mrs. Beezely. I—I was just leaving."

"No, don't go." Mrs. Beezely set aside the Bible and the letters, a gesture that returned her instantly to the world of the present. "Come in! Come in, come in, Celia. Just opened a new barrel of pickles, and some crackers I want you to taste."

"Thanks. But I just ate. And anyhow, I didn't come for a pickle." She edged through the screen door. "I came to say— well, I don't honestly know why I came, but—"

"Hush. Hush a minute." Mrs. Beezely raised one hand, clean and raw-knuckled from a vigorous Sunday bath. "Listen."

"I don't hear anything."

"Shhhhhh." Mrs. Beezely was motionless. "Effie —isn't that Donald?"

Effie was immediately awake, seizing her binoculars and turning them on the bridge. "Why, yes, Emma Ellen. It certainly is."

"Something must be wrong. He never runs poor old Marigold like that." She rose and trotted through the screen door to await his arrival.

Only then did Celia discern the wild rattle and screech of Donald's oxcart. Normally the wheel and harness sounds were spaced in a sedate, measured pace; today they blended in a frantic overlapping cacophony. She followed Mrs. Beezely into the back yard as Donald's cart rounded the corner and shot into the short alleyway. Marigold was heaving long drools of saliva; his great oxen carcass was dripped and matted with blood. Donald leaned halfway across the driver's seat, his face a mass of cuts and bruises.

"Oh, my God, my God—what has happened to you?"

Marigold halted at the sound of Mrs. Beezely's voice and stood at rest, his great head drooping, exposing moist, wildly rolling eyes.

"What is it?" Miss Effie called from the doorway. "Emma Ellen, what is it?"

"I don't know yet." She ran to help Donald from the cart, half-supporting his weight to the doorway. "Come in. Come in, Donald."

He shook his head, refusing to leave Marigold alone, and sat heavily on the doorstoop. Head back against the screen door, he muttered his story, wiping blood across the sleeve of his jacket and pointing again and again to the wounded ox.

"Effie! Call Dr. . . . ."

"I already have." Effie was back behind the screen door. "What's he say?"

"Some of those derned bridge workers got themselves all liquored up and were fishing down off his pier. He came in from his crab traps and they asked him something. 'Course he couldn't hear them and he doesn't know what they wanted—but they chased him up and down the beach until he fell onto an oyster bank." She was dabbing the slashes on his face and hands with her handkerchief. "Then they saw Marigold in the yard and chased him back and forth, hitting him with boards and broken bottles. Just look at that poor old ox. Just look!"

Marigold was standing over droplets of his own blood, his emaciated rib cage still heaving with exertion.

"Outlanders!" Miss Effie said.

"I'm afraid so." Mrs. Beezely was quick to catch Celia's cringe against the side of the store. "Normally I don't approve of that word, Celia. But everybody in town knows about Old Deaf Donald and Marigold. Nobody'd harm either one of them. The bridge crew are mostly from out of town, and I've never in my life seen such a mean, rotten bunch."

"But why would they pick on poor Donald and Marigold?"

"Oh, child. You put a little liquor in some men and they'll—"

She stopped as Dr. Phelps's car stalled in the driveway. After two attempts to restart it, he swore mightily, left it halfway across the sidewalk, and hurried to Donald's side. Donald pushed

102

away his helping hands, jabbered incoherently. "What's he saying, Mrs. Beezely?"

"He's not worried about himself—he wants you to treat Marigold."

"I'm not a vet, for crissake." He made another attempt to examine Donald's face. Donald brushed him aside and stumbled across the yard to soothe his stricken ox. "And I wanted to be a small-town doctor." Dr. Phelps fumbled through his black case and brought out a large bottle of vile-colored liquid. "Here, Emma Ellen. Donald'll trust you. Swab down that poor animal with this stuff while I take Donald over to my office. He's going to need some stitches. Got any cotton you can use on the ox?"

"I'll get it," Miss Effie called from the doorway, and rolled away toward the drug counter. "Be right back."

Not until he saw Mrs. Beezely begin to tend to Marigold would Donald consent to follow Dr. Phelps to the stalled automobile. With another oath, Dr. Phelps raised the hood, tinkered with the engine, and finally backed the car out into the street.

"Celia!" Mrs. Beezely called sharply. "Go get Marigold some water."

Under Mrs. Beezely's direction, Celia managed to fill the water bucket from an unwieldy pump. She was struggling to lift the heavy load to Marigold's reaching tongue when she smelled a welcome whiff of pipe tobacco. "Daddy!" Celia whirled, water splashing over her. "Daddy, Donald was—was—"

"I know. Miss Effie called." He took the bucket from her. "You help Mrs. Beezely."

Moments later, in answer to other frantic calls, Harlan arrived in his Sheriff's uniform, followed by Johnson Miles, editor of the *Bugler*.

Since Martha's arrest, Celia had viewed Harlan with awe, as some legendary creature from another sphere. Unlike other numerous relatives scattered around the Beldon township, Harlan never dropped by to visit Sallie. And he was never seen loafing along Buzzard's Roost for the regular coffee breaks shared by Beldon's merchants. Harlan had the reputation of a man totally dedicated to his work, and his name appeared constantly in the *Weekly Bugler* in connection with one case or another. Celia wrinkled her nose in distaste at the sickly sweet hair oil Harlan wore. She much preferred the rancid odor of Marigold's antiseptic.

Tiptoeing to lather the lacerated spine of the ox, Celia paused in awe, finding herself face to face with Johnson Miles. He was six feet six inches tall, a wiry man of forty-one, supercharged with nervous energy. He was already bald, and his shiny head showed a deep indentation from an automobile accident that had almost cost him his life and had marked him unfit for military service because of an artificial plate replacing part of his skull. "You would be Celia." She nodded. "Give me that." He took the reeking cotton swab. "I can reach the top better than you can. You get his legs and belly."

She nodded again, darting for more cotton.

George set down the bucket and stroked Marigold's nose. "What are you two doing here?"

"Because I called them, of course!" Miss Effie thrust her chair forward, forcing the screen door open. "It's high time we did something about that bridge crew. Past high time. We let them tromp through town, wreck our picnic grounds, just—just take over—and nobody lifts a finger. They ought to be arrested. Every single one of them." Miss Effie's eyes blazed, regal furies in her emaciated face.

"Now, hold on. Hold on a minute." Harlan grunted, fighting to extract a silver pocket knife from overly tight uniform trousers. Opening one blade, he began methodically cleaning his fingernails. He was the first man Celia had seen with manicured nails, and for some reason it troubled her. After lengthy, pointless questioning, Harlan determined that "the incident" had taken place across the bridge. "Well," he said, snapping the knife shut and forcing it back beneath his bulging stomach, "why didn't you say so? That's different. That's out of my jurisdiction." He lifted one hand, drowning their immediate protests. "Nothing I can do. Nothing at all. Sorry about old Donald, but then everyone knows he ought to be in some institution or other." Harlan yawned, stretched. "Ruined my nap. And to think Gertrude made me put on my g.d. uniform for *this*. Hell. Gotta get on home. Gertrude's expecting company for cocktails."

Silently, they watched him go. Johnson went back to swabbing Marigold, whistling between his teeth.

"Oh. That—that creature!" Miss Effie, for once, was numbed to silence by her indignation.

"No, Miss Effie. He's a good man."

"But, Johnson—"

"If it's out of his jurisdiction, who's going to protect Donald? There's no one living between Donald and the new bridge. Not a soul. And some of the crew's quartered out there. If Harlan tried to do anything—another drinking party and they might burn Donald out—or God knows what."

"How about a story?" George asked.

"Same holds true."

"Guess you're right," George admitted reluctantly.

They finally agreed the best thing they could do was to pay Dr. Phelps and send Donald home with extra bottles of antiseptic for Marigold.

Celia spent a restless night in a confusion of dreaming that brushed by Harlan's oil-slick, reeking hair and mixed with the whiskey odor of Mr. Brown; mixed somehow with Marigold's drooling mouth and rolling eyes, with the eyes of Martha standing on her front porch, with Donald's bleeding face. Celia woke with a stifled cry and again examined her body before the wind-rattled mirror. "Marked," Ethel had said. Somehow, she was marked, and she brought sorrow to everyone around her.

"Don't be silly!" Cynthia later dismissed her fears. Cynthia's energies had turned from the "blood of the Lamb" to the forthcoming school Christmas pageant, and she had no desire to be drawn into the vortex of Celia's new problems. "Ethel said 'you and yours,' and Donald's not one of yours."

"No. I—I guess not." You and yours. Celia stood blinking in pale sunlight, glancing around the schoolyard. The kindergarten swings hung limp and empty, unused at this hour since Martha had departed. Martha. Celia shivered. Martha wasn't "one of hers," either. So why was she still haunted by the memory of liquid eyes boring through her, first from the swing and then from a squad car?

"Celia—come on, will you?"

Deeply puzzled, Celia followed Cynthia up the hated pink steps and into the auditorium for their pageant rehearsal.

7

FOR GEORGE, the winter days crept along in an unmarked progression of waking and eating, puttering and sleeping. Evelyn stayed busily preoccupied with the constant interchanging visits of relatives, and George found his greatest enjoyment was taking Celia, Cynthia, and Jim out in the boat. Since their bogging experience, Mary had refused to go with them and had busied herself with Future Homemakers of America. George was delighted. She bored him, as much as her younger brother and sisters infuriated him. It was a relief simply to forget about them, and he gained additional insight to "The Club." Jim and Cynthia were a constant pleasure and surprise. Jim was proudly teaching George his native lore of tides and marshes, and Cynthia led Celia on forays across mid-stream sandbars in search of crabs and fiddlers. George noted happily that Celia had lost her prim mannerisms and was becoming as free and agile as her two cousins. The boat expeditions kept the children too busy to hang around Alan at the store, and George told himself he was content.

Then, one chilly morning, George, Evelyn, and Sallie were having their second cups of coffee in front of the living room fire and settling back in drowsy comfort when the phone rang. It was the pulsating, unbroken shriek of Miss Effie's personal alarum, and the entire household sprang to life. Celia came stumbling half-dressed down the steps as Ethel, still in her knit wool hat and new red overcoat, ran in from the back door.

Sallie was already answering the ring, and they hovered around her, each trembling as much with tension as with cold.

"It's Alan," Sallie said at last. "He's gone beserk or something and is trying to shoot up half the town. Annie wants us to come right over."

They scattered to yank on whatever warm clothing was at hand, and ten minutes later converged on Alan's house. Annie greeted them at the door, teary-eyed and slightly hysterical. Her yellow robe was buttoned askew, and hair hung around her face in uncombed strands. She reeked of brandy. "I don't know him! My god . . . I never met this man in all my life . . . Oh my god— what is happening?"

There was the sharp crack of a .22 rifle from the front of the house. Commanding the women to stay in the kitchen, George ran through a clutter of crushed beer cans in the musty living room. He found Alan in the front yard, seated in an old rocking chair, his rifle cradled in his lap. Although there were no trees across the street, the electric company was trying to cut the limbs from Alan's ancient live oak tree to install a new power line. Each time they made a move toward the tree, Alan stopped them with a well-placed shot, scattering sand in front of their feet or dropping tree twigs across their hands. In answer to George's questions, Alan merely shrugged, rocked, and hummed "The Old Rugged Cross."

"You're crazy, Alan. Crazy as hell."

"Mebbe. But no goddam outlander is going to chop up my tree." Harlan was arriving, and a delegation from the power company. In disgust, George rounded up Evelyn and Celia and went home for breakfast.

To Evelyn's worried queries, George shook his head. "There'll just be a lot of discussion, and then they'll go ahead and cut that tree. You'll see."

But by the end of the working day, the new power line ran to the edge of Alan's property, zigzagged across the street around the sweeping limbs of his tree, then returned to his side of the street to cut a swath through shade trees the remaining length of the block.

By nightfall, Alan's actions had assumed legendary proportions. Grown men swore they had personally seen him shoot off the heel of the foreman's right shoe. Two high school boys related in detail how Alan's single shot had twice severed a coil of cable the crewmen were holding. And everyone agreed Alan was perfectly justified in shooting out the engine of the company's truck. For the next week, George found it impossible to lure Celia, Jim, and Cynthia back out in the boat. They spent all their free time down at the store, trailing behind Alan's moments of glory and drinking in his obscene comments about the light crew. To George's dismay, Celia even began to mimic Alan's swagger and the funny way he had of hitching up his jeans. "I suppose any day now she'll start spitting the way Alan does," George grumbled to Evelyn. He was not amused by her laughter.

Saturday morning, George was awakened earlier than usual by the smell of coffee and the sound of Sallie's laughter from the living room. He came shuffling down the steps, puffy-eyed and tousled, his robe knotted carelessly over heavy pajamas. "What's so funny at this ungodly hour?" He licked his lips, hating the sour taste in his mouth from the scotch he'd drunk to smother his insomnia.

"Alan."

"What now?"

"We're talking about last week."

"Oh. That."

"I think he's just great!" Celia was dunking sugar cubes in a saucer of creamed coffee, eating with loud sucking noises.

"Celia, please, stop that." Louder sucking noises continued. George decided against an argument at that hour of the morning and sat down, hoping to conceal his annoyance.

Evelyn poured his coffee. "Every time I think of Alan dragging that old chair out in the yard and plopping down with his gun ..." She laughed again. "And Annie drunk as a lord. What a hangover she had all next day. And—"

"My coffee."

"What?"

"Please give me my coffee."

"Oh. Sure." Evelyn handed it to him, and he slid back into the leather armchair, his feet stretched out toward the fireplace, his head turned away from Celia and her sugar cubes.

Evelyn hitched her chair closer to the flames, shaking with merriment. "And I don't blame him. There was no reason to cut those trees when there wasn't a dern thing growing across the street. Why, I never heard of anything so—"

"For god's sake, Evelyn. Stop it. Will you, please?" The fire crackled in a sudden updraft.

"Why, George! I-I was only—"

"Does this family absolutely have to rehash every stupid little incident twenty or thirty times?"

Sallie tactfully occupied herself with the morning headlines. Celia sucked another sugar cube, and George stirred his coffee needlessly. Evelyn was sarcastically polite. "I happen to think it's a funny story."

"It was. The first fifteen times you told it. But that's all anyone in town has talked about for days, and now—here you go again. Truth of the matter is your brother-in-law behaved like some kind of a psycho, and it's a tribute to the years your family's been in this town—not to mention the minor fact of Harlan being a relative as well as being sheriff—that Alan wasn't jailed, or locked up in some mental institution. Where, incidentally, I happen to think he belongs." George set down his untouched cup and went upstairs, slamming the bedroom door.

Fire popped again in dancing flares of yellow, and Sallie leaned forward to brush a stray cinder back to the hearth.

"I think Daddy's jealous of Uncle Alan."

"Hush up, Celia. You hear me? ... Mother, I—I'm so sorry. He's usually bad-tempered in the mornings, but—that was inexcusable."

"That's more than bad temper, honey. That man's fretting quiet."

"That's silly."

"Maybe so. But I'm an old woman, and I know what I see." Sallie pushed herself to her feet, her balance momentarily shaky on her stiff ankles. "Believe me, Evelyn, George is a man used to doing. He needs something to occupy his time besides taking walks, going to the library, and sitting around the house."

"But he has his new boat, and the camera, and—all sorts of things to do."

"Um-hm. Excuse me for putting in my two cents. I—uh—I'm going to get dressed."

Celia began still another version of Alan's "hunting party," as he called it.

"Celia, you're giving me a headache. Please go get dressed."

Celia left the room, making an angry face at her mother's back. Evelyn sat thoughtfully a few moments, then ran swiftly, lightly up the steps. Their room was silent. Thinking George might have gone back to sleep, she eased the door open and peeked around it. Hands clasped behind his head, he was lying on top of the bed covers, staring blankly out the window at bare and empty pecan limbs. His face was as wistful as a child's, and Evelyn's breath caught in her throat.

He turned his head, and seeing her, snatched up the morning paper folded at his side. "You finished early. What's the matter —run out of gossip?"

"I—I'm sorry, George. I didn't realize how we were irritating you."

"Not irritating. Boring."

"At any rate, I'm sorry."

"Thank you." He snapped the paper open. "Wish the *Bugler* was a daily. This damn, lousy, narrow-minded Charleston paper. Only thing their editorials are for is soil conservation and Mother's Day."

Evelyn accepted his brusqueness as apology and busied herself with dressing. Paper rustled as George fingered the pages in search of a marked want ad. "Listen to this, Evelyn. 'Forced to sell. One female setter, two years old, fully trained for field and show. Asking $125. Call for demonstration.' It's a local number."

"What about it?"

George rose, tugging on his bathrobe. "If she's any good, I'm going to buy her."

"Whatever for?"

"I think the kids would enjoy learning to hunt, don't you?"

"Oh, George." Evelyn went to him impulsively, gently pressing his arm. "Dear George. What else are you going to buy to keep Celia away from Alan?"

George looked at her levelly. "Anything—everything I can. Even to another house in another town."

Remembering Sallie's admonitions, Evelyn bit her lip. "All right, darling. Whatever you decide is fine with me." George kissed her on the forehead, and she smiled back at him. "Think we could see her this morning?"

"You mean you'd go with me?"

"Sure."

"What about your Coffee Club?"

"I'll skip it today."

He smiled in pleased amazement. "All right. I'll phone right now."

After the usual convoluted gossiping conversation with Miss Effie, George managed to give her the number from the ad. To his surprise, he was directed to view a hunting demonstration at "Harlan's Headache," the sprawl of farmland Harlan owned twelve miles outside of town. Curious, George thought, then immediately decided the owner must be a friend of Harlan's. Before he could hang up, Miss Effie was back on the line. "What —you were listening?" George snapped, understanding Alan's standard obscene description of Miss Effie. "I would thank you, for once, to mind—" He rubbed the numbness in his ear as Miss Effie blasted him to silence, answering her in contrite amusement. "No, Miss Effie. I haven't the slightest idea how to get out there." To his dismay, he actually found himself agreeing to take Mrs. Beezely along on the expedition because the farm had once belonged to her husband's family and she always liked to drive back for a visit. He was feeling angry and disgruntled until Celia, in her wild excitement over getting a dog, completely forgot about the boating party Alan had arranged for "The Club." "Nevertheless," George grumbled to Evelyn, "we should open a passenger pigeon service. We'd make a fortune in this town."

Mrs. Beezely was quick to notice George's camera on the car seat beside him and chose a leisurely route through abandoned rice plantations. They drove slowly through live oaks drooping soft stalactites of moss, until they came to remnants of rice paddies deserted to myriads of duck, quail, and giant heron. George stopped to photograph the feeding birds, stalking them more cautiously than any hunter. Then, with easy chatter that George thoroughly enjoyed, they drove on to Harlan's sprawling cattle farm ten miles past the new bridge site. The farm was stocked with some of the finest game in the state, and stark signs warned casual strangers the land was posted and under surveillance. But "family" was welcome so long as they observed the generous bag limits Harlan set. A sweeping one thousand acres, it was a choice tract for cattle and game. The Inland Waterway surrounded the farm on three sides, leaving only a narrow neck of land to be fenced. Harlan's half mile of fence was an imposing barricade. It was stainless steel mesh, eight feet high, and topped a two-foot mound of earth dredged from the irrigation ditch running beside the road like a miniature moat. Local rumor maintained that the fence sometimes carried an electrical charge. Harlan smiled when confronted with the story, but he never denied it, and there wasn't a boy in town who could be tempted to sneak into his back fields for a quick bird or two, or even a squirrel. George drove along two ruts of sand in the waffle-iron shadows of the fence, heading for the gate at its far end. The heavy gate was open, and the car bumped across the irrigation ditch over horizontal iron pipes spaced far enough apart to prevent a cow from finding foothold and straying outside the fence.

A name plate of fine wrought-iron lettering hung from the gate-post. Set swinging by the car's vibration, it squeaked shrilly, metal biting against metal. "Harlan's Headache," it proclaimed, wry reminder that Harlan had purchased the farm as a gift for his wife Gertrude, but she had flatly refused to build "out there in nothing but wilderness." Instead, they had bought a new brick house crowded on a lot in the middle of town, where, as Harlan put it, "half the population knows it every time you belch." The farm's work crew drove in from the surrounding neighborhood, and the thousand acres remained untenanted, except for a herd of cattle and Morgan, the elderly Negro care-taker. He lived alone in a two-room whitewashed shack set well inside the gate. Spiraling a thin column of smoke, a brick chim-ney leaned away from the house at a precarious angle. Morgan sprang to the front window to check on who had entered the grounds, and George waved, tapping the horn by way of greet-ing. Recognizing them, Morgan waved back and pointed to an antiquated truck parked by the barn. A swarthy, filthy man was lounging against the truck bed, swilling wine from a quart bot-tle as he caressed the magnificent setter standing beside him. The man's leather jacket hung loosely around his bulbous paunch and was cracked with age, greasy with dark stains. He reeked of chewing tobacco, sour whiskey, and unwashed socks. George fought back a strong aversion and was tempted to drive away.

Celia gasped. "Daddy—that's the man that—"

"Yes? That what?"

Celia blushed. How to explain the way he'd acted with Mar-tha; the way he'd showed up at the Funeral Home; in church; the way he kept showing up from noplace?

"You the Major what phoned me?" Brown asked, lurching over to the side of their car.

"Yes. You Mr. Brown?"

"What the hell you think. Ready to see Adelaide work?" Reaching into the truck cab, Brown pulled out a double-barreled shotgun and began moving off across the field, still drinking from his wine bottle. The rangy English setter bounded around him in ecstatic circles. The dog's silky black-and-white coat was combed and brushed, feathering from her legs and tail like spun glass. Liquid brown eyes and moist, flaring nostrils showed her to be in the peak of health, and it seemed altogether impossible she could belong to the filthy man beside her.

"I'll be damned," George muttered, then climbed from the car. "C'mon. Let's go."

"Major!" Mrs. Beezely tapped him on the shoulder. "I've got one of my feelings—a strong feeling—there's something funny about this."

"I agree, but long as we're here, let's see the dog work out."

Brown turned, waiting for George. His eyes were set too close together and were almost lost in the fat of his cheeks, but they widened perceptibly when Celia, Evelyn, and Mrs. Beezely followed George across the roadbed. "They going, too?"

"That's right."

Brown waved them toward the pasture with the spilling wine bottle, weaving foolishly and clutching his shotgun by the barrel. Celia started to skip by him, but George caught her arm and pulled her back. "Go ahead," he said to Brown. "We'll stay behind you—and behind the gun."

With a grunt, Brown shouldered his gun upside down, setting off into the field at a brisk pace deliberately intended to discomfort the women. On sudden impulse, George took his Leica from its case and slipped it into his jacket pocket, hurrying to catch up with the others. George momentarily forgot his apprehensions when he saw the dog at work in the pasture. She was trained to respond to whistle signals pitched so high they were unheard by human ears, and Brown put her through her paces with occasional pauses for a swallow of wine. The dog sat by his side, quivering with eagerness, until he released her with a hard, silent blast on the whistle. With a joyful leap, she was off across the field, running effortlessly, her long hair rippling in flowing plumes. "Two blasts, she covers to the right. Three, to the left." Brown demonstrated, sending the setter back and forth in random alternations of direction until the dog halted, frozen into an attenuated point directed toward a clump of woods and corn shucks. Brown released the safety catch on his gun and lurched away after the dog.

"This'll be interesting," George commented. "How the hell is he going to shoot with that bottle in his hand."

By way of answer, Brown set the bottle down in a furrow and fumbled the shotgun to his shoulder. When he was certain Brown's attention was completely occupied, George took the camera from his pocket, delighted he'd left the telescopic lens in place. He made four quick pictures, catching the setter's majestically controlled shifts of stance as she eased closer to the corn shucks. It was luck that he snapped the last shot at the instant a covey of quail shattered the empty air with wildly flapping wings. Brown tried to anticipate their flight. With swift arc of body and gun, he fired toward the birds. His upward motion carried him stumbling backwards a step, and his foot caught the wine bottle. Brown vanished from George's viewer, ending up in a stupid-faced sprawl on the plowed furrow. In the adjoining field, cows bellowed and ran, scattering away as the quail had done. By sheer luck, Brown's wild shot had brought down a single bird. George returned Brown's wave of triumph, furtively slipping the camera back in his pocket, wondering at his strong urge for secrecy about the pictures. Celia giggled in uncontrolled merriment at Brown's predicament. After several attempts, Brown managed to get back to his feet and came weaving toward them, dragging his shotgun and waving the nearly empty, dirt-clogged bottle. "Bet you didn't think I could do it." He leered at George.

"Well—for a minute there, I thought we were going to see a setter retrieving a prize cow."

Brown blinked, too drunk to absorb fully George's sarcasm. He started to raise the shotgun for a drink, looked at it blankly, and then finished off the wine. George swiftly eased the gun from his hand and turned it away from the women to empty the second chamber before handing it back.

The dog bounded to Brown with the quail, holding the carcass tenderly in her enormous mouth. At Brown's command, she laid the bird at his feet and looked up, alert to fulfill his next signal. Brown pocketed his kill, the bleeding bird making an additional stain down the front of his jacket. "One more thing to show you." He sent the dog running across the field to the edge of the woods, where once again she froze into a point. Brown took out his battered whistle and held it between his teeth as he spoke. "S'metimes you—accidentally got inna post'd lan'. But she'll come back, even when she's got a sure scent." He gave six hard puffs. Slowly, reluctantly, the setter wheeled from her quarry and trotted back toward them, leaving a flurry of escaping quail.

Watching her sinewy gait, George coveted the dog with all his heart. He had to force himself to logical thought, taking time to fill and light his pipe.

"You train this dog yourself?"

"Yes."

"Then you know she's worth a lot more than you're asking."

Brown's cap came off with an obsequious hunch of his shoulders that made George totally despise the man. He began a shuffling, whining account, his eyes constantly shifting. ". . . and me and Mrs. Brown, we was all set to buy us a place hereabouts and start up a kennel. Then her Ma took sick and we have to go up to Boston to look after her and her store, and there's no space for any dog. 'Specially hunting dogs. So I'm having to sell out. Adelaide here, she's my favorite, so I'm mostly interes'd in gettin' her a good home . . ." He stopped as abruptly as if someone had turned off a record, and his fat-knuckled hands dropped to his side.

Celia's eyes moistened with sympathy. "Can we get her—can we?"

"Maybe."

Absorbed by the dog, none of them noticed the quick vitriol that crossed Brown's face at George's delay.

George stood with folded arms, puffing on his pipe and looking at the dog. He felt no sympathy for Brown's account but had to admit that his list of troubles would account for his drunken, unwashed appearance. The setter whined, nuzzling impatiently at Brown's palm, and George was filled with a fierce desire to free the beautiful animal from the stench of her trainer. And Celia obviously liked the dog. "I'll take her." He reached for his check book.

"Was hoping you'd say that." Brown took a deep breath, settling his greasy cap brim along a heavy indentation it had made across his forehead. "Only one thing—no checks."

"I have identification."

"No—no. It—uh—I-I got no bank account and no credit, and I need the cash real bad."

Brown was whining again and George was tempted to call off the deal, but the thought of hunting trips with Celia and the cousins was too strong a temptation. He capped his pen and pocketed the checkbook. "I don't carry that much around. How—"

"I'll bring her to you. Always make it a point to check living quarters before I let one of my dogs go. Tomorrow soon enough?" His hand went to the setter's head in lachrymose benediction; his voice shook with emotion. "That'll give me one last hunt with Adelaide."

George looked to Evelyn, who nodded quick approval. "Sure. And it'll give us time to buy a dog bed and some food and stuff."

"One thing—" George said quickly. "Where do I find one of those whistles?"

"I supply you one, along with the dog."

"O.K. Done." George jotted their address on the back of an old envelope and handed it to Brown. "I'll have the cash for you by noon tomorrow."

"See you then." Brown reverted to his surly attitude and pocketed the paper. Seemingly sobered, he strode into the woods, with the setter racing away in front of him.

"I'll be damned." George knocked out his pipe and angrily ground the ashes underfoot. "The bastard—think he'd at least say thanks, or—"

"Oh, Daddy. He looks like he's about to cry."

George grunted and took Mrs. Beezely's arm. They walked slowly across the field to the car. Mrs. Beezely was shaking her head, talking to herself, and George smiled down at her. She said nothing until they were all seated in the car. "There's something mighty peculiar going on, Major. I've just got one of my strong feelings."

George, too, was suffering from a sharp sense of something being amiss, but he said nothing, enjoying Celia's ecstatic comments about the dog's well-trained behavior.

But George spent half that night in restless pacing, unable to read or to write letters. He was regretting his decision to take the dog, and furious with himself for being unable to think of a reason to change his mind. "Like a damned old maid," he told himself, finally giving in and pouring another scotch.

"Daddy . . ."

Startled at Celia's sudden appearance, George almost dropped his glass. "What are you doing up at this hour?"

"I just wanted to tell you—I don't like him a bit, but I really did feel sorry for Mr. Brown." She came to his chair and knelt beside him, cradling her head against his knee in her former childish fashion. George let his hand drift across her hair, and for a moment time receded to long-ago, happier days.

"Guess I do, too, honey."

"There's just one thing."

"What?"

She looked up at him. "I really do think 'Adelaide' is an asinine name for a setter."

In her intensity, she reverted momentarily to her British accent and George burst into laughter, tears of mirth squeezing down the gray stubble on his cheeks. His laughter subsided when he realized the total seriousness of Celia's expression. "You know, I think you just hit the spot on what's been bothering me about the whole deal. We'll give her a new name."

"What?"

"I don't know—yet. Not now. We need to have her around and find out what she's like."

Celia snuggled her head against his knee and George put down his glass, smiling at the long straggle of her hair. He wouldn't need another drink to sleep tonight. No. Not tonight.

Promptly at noon the next day, Brown arrived in front of the house, announced by a loud series of backfires and by squeals of excitement from Celia, who had been hovering in front of the windows since ten-thirty. "He's here. He's here, Daddy."

"So I gathered." George rose and stretched. "Come on. Let's go welcome Adelaide."

Brown alighted from the truck cab, wearing the same filthy clothing he had had on the day before. With a snap of his fingers, he commanded Adelaide to his side. Man and dog climbed the steps to the porch and noncommittally followed George into the living room. Without troubling to remove his cap, hands on hips, Brown surveyed George, Celia, Evelyn, and their comfortable surroundings. "It'll do jus' fine for Adelaide."

"Thanks," Evelyn said dryly.

"How about yard space?"

George took Brown through Sallie's kitchen to the back steps and pointed out the area he intended to fence for a runway. Celia danced ahead of them, trying to get the setter's attention. The dog whimpered and cowered away from Celia's hands, going to sit at Brown's feet. Brown rubbed Adelaide's ear and stared around without comment or suggestion. With the setter following closely, they went back into the kitchen. Brown poked his toe at the mattress of the new dog bed Evelyn had set beside the wood stove, then leaned over to sniff a pan of icing Ethel was stirring at the back of the range. "Smells good." He lifted his dirty hand and sampled a heavy white globule on the rim of the pot.

" 'Scuse me, sir. Needs beating." Ethel snatched the pot away, and his knuckles brushed the boiling-hot stirring spoon.

"Owwww ... dammit."

Ethel snatched up a dishcloth and scoured the spot his finger had touched. The implication was not lost on Brown. "Why, you—"

George stepped quickly to Ethel's side. "Nobody in the family is allowed to touch her cooking pots. It's one of our rules," he said easily. "Now, about your money—it's in the living room."

Brown relaxed with an unpleasant smile, wiping off the hot smear of icing along his jacket front. "Don't taste no good anyways." He obeyed George's gesture, walking ahead of him to the hallway with Celia and the dog following closely.

Ethel muttered softly to herself as they were leaving, and sank to her knees to wipe up crumbles of icing Brown had let fall to the floor.

Brown stopped in the hall, breathing heavily, his hands clenching and unclenching. "Sassy nigger you got working for you, mister."

"She's not a 'nigger,' " George said with his ominously sharp authority of command. "And it's Major, not Mister. And don't you forget it in either case. Now take your money—or the dog—and get out."

"O.K. . . . Major." Brown's lips curled around the word as he looked back at Ethel's crouching form. "And—sir—believe me, sir, I won't forget. Major, sir."

"Move. Now!" George followed him into the living room, dimly aware of Celia watching from the hallway.

Brown took the envelope of bills George extended to him, and with an insolent twitch of his mouth, stood in the center of the room to check and recheck the total. Spittle bubbled on his lips as he wheezed through his laborious counting. Finally he pocketed the money, threw down a small box containing a new whistle and a grimy page outlining "Adelaide's Dyit." He strode heavily to the door.

"Wait a minute." George held up a typed sheet.

"What's that?"

"A bill of sale for the dog."

"I don't believe in signing no papers."

"Then give me back the money and take the dog."

Brown wavered, a growing hatred for George pinching his eyes into deeper porcine slits. At length, after glaring around the comfortable room, he took the paper and George's pen. Leaning against the wall, he signed his name in heavy block letters with a fiercely scrolled underline that slashed the neatly-typed sheet and broke the pen nib. He flung the shards on the coffee table. At the front door, Brown turned with his hand on the knob. "So long—Mister Nigger Lover." He was gone with a great slam, rattling windows across the front of the house. The truck engine choked, faltered, backfired, and roared away.

Adelaide rose with a soft whimper. "Stay, girl." George caressed her head, scratching one ear. The dog sat down gingerly, her sad eyes riveted on the front door.

Evelyn sank to her knees on the other side of Adelaide and stroked her long arched neck. "Thank goodness we're shut of that man. I don't know how even a dog could love him. He's—" She looked up to see Celia standing outside in the hall. "Hey— come see our dog. Isn't she beautiful?"

Celia nodded, swallowing heavily.

"You're not scared of her, are you?"

"No. 'Course not." She came a few steps into the room. "I—I just think it's awful the way Daddy spoke to that man. He'll tell it all over town, and people already say terrible things about you two being outlanders and all."

George looked at Celia a long moment. "Did you hear what he said?"

"Yes."

"And you didn't mind?"

"Well, Ethel didn't hear, and besides, it's only a word."

George turned away from her in contempt and disgust. Rising, he snapped a new leash on Adelaide's collar and walked swiftly out of the house.

Evelyn rose from her knees. "Why do you deliberately pick a fight with your father? Why?"

"But it was him picking the fight, not me. He made that man real mad." Celia's lower lip protruded, her eyes narrowed in self-righteous protest.

Evelyn fought back an engulfing wave of dismay, understanding one reason for George's silent depression. What was happening to the child? . . . Child? . . . Not for much longer. She studied Celia's chubby, burgeoning figure. Celia trembled under her mother's thoughtful scrutiny, but stubbornly held her own silence. They continued their stance of mutual distrust, both breathing unevenly. Evelyn's mind was teeming with ancient memories, early ambitions for her daughter. But Celia stood in an empty shell of determination, filled with wordless, growing resentment for her mother.

Evelyn broke the impasse, brushing angrily at long white dog hairs on her skirt. "You stupid little girl. By now, I hoped you would have learned the difference between picking a fight and standing up for what's right when it's not the popular choice." She saw Celia edging toward the hall and forgot her carefully chosen words. "Where do you think you're going, Miss? I'm talking to you."

Celia spun around, her cheeks flaming. "I'm sick to death of being lectured all the time."

" 'All the time'?"

"You're both old, and mean, and hateful . . . you—you just want me to say what you want . . . do what you want . . ." Her voice trailed thinly in the big room.

Evelyn held back her anger, determined to let Celia have her say. "And?"

Celia fidgeted before her, fingers nervously plucking nubs of wool from her blue sweater. "Well . . . I . . ."

"Yes?"

Celia took a deep breath, her words jumbling out. "I just don't see why Daddy has to make such an ass of himself. People—people laugh at him behind his back. They call you both 'outlander shits.' "

Evelyn's tone was scathing. "You are welcome to whatever opinions you and your—friends—have. Or think you have. But I will not tolerate your rudeness in our home."

Celia's face clouded and she breathlessly mouthed words of defiance.

"What did you say?"

Celia licked her lips, knowing she had gone too far. But like the suicide who feels the horror of rushing air, she was irretrievably committed and it was too late to turn back. "I—I said . . . the only 'discussion' is you two telling me to think like you do and you can . . ." Hot tears gagged her.

"Go on. Finish it."

". . . b-both . . . gotohell . . ."

Evelyn's temper came with a rush and her hand flashed out with a stinging slap across Celia's cheek. "Dress like your friends, think like them. Run in a pack, if you must. But when you are at home, you will remember the manners we've taught you. And you will extend to us the courtesy we extend to you. Now go to your room and stay there until I call you."

In cold fury, Celia crept up the stairs, forcing what she hoped would sound like heartbroken sobs. She lingered long at the top of the steps, poking one finger at the binding of a new book George had received in the mail that morning, wishing she had the nerve to snatch it from the bookcase and throw it at her mother. Why take up for her father, when he'd been so rude to Mr. Brown? And what the hell did her father know about anything? He didn't care what people said, so long's he had his nose in some dumb old book. "Mein Kampf," the lettering read. Who but a stuffy old man like her father would read a book with a title that didn't mean anything? Despite Celia's retching sobs, her mother heartlessly did not call her back and apologize. "I hate you both," Celia whispered, and shut herself in her room, taking the wise precaution of not letting the door slam behind her.

Downstairs, Evelyn was berating herself for losing her temper. Leaning against the small upright piano, she peered at a framed photograph she had sent to Sallie from Shanghai. It was Celia's third-grade class portrait. Fifteen grinning youngsters included a Japanese boy, two Chinese girls, an East Indian, Turkish, Tahitian . . . nine different nationalities in all, momentarily united in a small private school. Evelyn concentrated on Celia's face, remembering the happy tumble of children. She sank into the

124

rocker and snatched up her knitting, jabbing at the wool with fierce clicking thrusts of steel needles until she heard George's brisk step on the porch. She threw the knitting aside as he opened the door with a cheery whistle. "George, we've got to—"

"Hey! You should have seen the hit this dog made downtown. She walks right at my heel, and when I stop, she stops. Gus the Greek let two hamburgers burn up on the griddle, he was so excited. And Len was running a special order but he just shut off his printing press and came all the way across the street. I think when she gets used to me I won't need a leash, and—" He talked on, his eyes alive with delight, his silvery hair wind-tousled and boyish. Evelyn listened absent-mindedly. It was months since she had seen George so happy. No, she would postpone any discussion of Celia.

George was wildly impatient to take Adelaide out in the field, but a chilling rain swept in from the ocean, and for the next nine days they were trapped indoors. The whole family devoted themselves to trying to win Adelaide's affection. But while the dog obeyed each of them without hesitation, nothing they did elicited a single wag of the tail or a friendly nuzzle. For hour after hour, Adelaide lay before the fire, her great head sunk between her paws, her eyes watching the door through which Brown had disappeared from her life.

"God," George commented. "She's breaking my heart."

Sallie paused in her knitting, pulling a long strand of wool from the basket at her feet. "She's an adult dog, George. It's going to take a long time for her to love you."

"If ever." He crouched before the dog and stroked her head. "Poor thing. This morning an old truck went by that sounded like Brown's, and she almost tore my arm off trying to run after it." George rubbed his chest, hoping to loosen the sharp pain. "Damn this rain. Won't it ever stop?"

By way of answer, Tuesday dawned sunny and cloudless, with the saccharine unreality of cheap calendar landscapes.

George brought the new whistle with him to breakfast and set it by his coffee cup. Eating large servings of eggs and bacon, he recited the signals Brown had taught him, laughing at Celia's chirped imitations. Evelyn bit back her comment about Celia missing a day of school, stacked dirty dishes in the sink, and ran to join George and Celia in the car. The three of them set off for "Harlan's Headache" with Celia making inane cooing and chucking sounds, trying to get Adelaide's attention. But the setter remained leaning against the side window with its nose pressed to the glass. "Stupid dog." Celia quit her badgering and retreated to the opposite corner to stare out across the roadway.

When they reached "Harlan's Headache," Celia pointed to a truck that was crawling along in their wake of sand clouds. "Look, Daddy . . . just like Mr. Brown's."

George chuckled. "Yeah. So's every other old beat-up truck in the country." He eased the car through the gateway and tooted cheerfully to Morgan, then drove well beyond the fenced pasture area along a bumpy work road that rounded a sharp bend and came to a cleared field beside a swamp bog. Barbed wire kept the cattle out of this area. While George had never accidentally shot a cow, after Brown's near miss he preferred not to take any more chances hunting near Harlan's prize herd. He halted the car in the midst of five acres of dead cornstalks, harsh umber sentinels clacking beneath the sea wind from the marsh. Adelaide let out a long howl that set goosebumps prickling along Celia's arms. George's excitement and the dog's continual howls dissolved into the chilly air.

"Well," George said. "Here we are." He leaped from the car and slammed the door to keep Adelaide inside. Celia and Evelyn slithered cautiously after him. "Feel that air!" George was saying. "Wonderful . . . just wonderful."

"Um." Evelyn was dreading the winter chill after the warmth of the drive. George already had his shotgun out of the trunk and loaded. With the new whistle in his mouth, he stood at the back door of the car, waiting for their attention. "Ready?" They nodded, and he swung the door open wide. "Now, Adelaide!"

With another long howl, the dog was out of the car and off across the field. Running into the wind, she held her head high,

letting her long legs carry her effortlessly through dead cornstalks. Without a falter in her headlong gait, she sprang into
the air and soared across the barbed wire into the adjoining
pasture, running and running, straight as a shot. The sheer exultation of her freedom made George laugh with delight. "God.
Look at her. Look at her go."

"Look, Mother. Look."

"I I'm looking." Evelyn's teeth were chattering and she
thrust her hands into her sleeves, clamping her arms across her
chest. "Shouldn't she—shouldn't she come back?"

"I guess so." George fondled the whistle, hating to check the
dog's headlong exuberance. But Adelaide was nearing a thick
stand of woods. He put the whistle to his lips and blew six
blasts. Adelaide continued her unchecked running. "Guess she's
been penned up too long." George blew another series of six
blasts. And a final, sharper six. Without turning her head, Adelaide bounded into the woods and disappeared.

They never saw her again.

After an hour's search, the only signs of Adelaide they found
were the long white hairs on the back seat, the prints of her wet
nose all over the car windows.

8

FOR OVER A WEEK, George searched "Harlan's Headache" with Morgan's help in the mornings; with Celia and the cousins in the afternoons after school.

"Stupid dog!" Celia muttered the last day they searched. "I despise Adelaide."

"I think I do, too," George agreed with some surprise. "When we find her, we'll sell her and start over."

On the way home, they stopped briefly at Morgan's shack. Morgan was a gaunt, tired man in his late sixties. His hair was still jet black, his face unwrinkled. He shook his head with quick sympathy, his bony hand straying to the head of the large red hound beside him. "No. Still no sign of her, Major. And I don't think she can get out the gate without old Peaches here letting me know."

"Could she get around the end of the fence?" George asked.

"Yessss . . . she might could." Morgan was silent a moment, mentally tracing the land. "There's that path, comes in down there. But it goes through a lot of swamp. Seems to me she'd be more likely to come this way. I'll keep my eye peeled."

Finally convinced the dog had somehow slipped from the grounds, George went to the town newspaper to place an ad. The offices of the *Weekly Bugler* were in a small brick building located almost geometrically at the center of town, with the tiny Catholic chapel on one side, the one-room jail on the other, and the town's maniacal fire siren mounted on a four-story tower across the street. George made three futile trips before he caught anyone in the office. Each day, he arrived just as the siren announced the noon hour and its own excellent working condition. Its banshee shrill was deafening at a two-mile radius; it was cataclysmic in the immediate area. At any hour other than noon, the siren warned of danger, its fierce coded blasts denoting when small craft warnings were posted, when a hurricane was expected. But the siren's fundamental purpose was to give the location of a fire for the Volunteer Department. It was a haphazard system but the only one the town could afford, and it depended entirely on the efficiency of the siren. The town had no choice but to tolerate a daily test, and a vote had determined that it be held precisely at noon. The test began with a low, unresonant growl that grew higher as it grew louder, rising to a full-volumed shriek and holding it for ten seconds. Dogs howled; infants wailed; birds flew wildly, seeking relief in every point of the compass. Once a day the siren sounded; seven days a week; three-hundred and sixty-four days a year. Christmas was the exception, as there were usually at least three or four fires in badly heated, overdecorated shacks and everyone in town had positive knowledge of the siren's working order.

The first day George arrived at the *Bugler* office the siren sounded, according to his watch, at 11:46; the second day, at 12:39; the third day, at 12:14. George left the locked *Bugler* office and went straight to the jeweler's, leaving his watch to be adjusted. He made a point of going back to the *Bugler* at 8:30 the next morning. It was Saturday, and Celia skipped along at his side. George tried the front door of the *Bugler* office and was relieved to find it unlocked, with no attendant wail of siren. To his embarrassment, he found himself confronting Johnson Miles. "Hell, Johnson. You being editor, I think this is too minor to trouble you. I only want to place an ad."

"Shoot. We all take them when we're in."

"I'm not sure how it should be worded." George began to explain the circumstances surrounding Adelaide's disappearance.

Midway through his account, Johnson tore up the standard ad

form. "Wait a minute. Come with me, Major. I want to get this down in detail."

They walked through gray-tiled hallways to Johnson's office, a large pine-paneled room furnished in Sears and Roebuck colonial. George sat down in an uncomfortably stiff armchair with Celia leaning across his sore shoulders. Johnson slipped a sheet of yellow legal paper into his typewriter. He loomed over the machine, dwarfing it beneath long, slender fingers, and began typing furiously.

"There's no particular rush, Johnson. If the dog's been found, she'll—"

"It's a bigger story than you think, Major. It's happened four other times this year I know of, in a tri-state area. And always an English setter. I think—damn!" He paused, aligning the sheet of paper. "This goddamn machine hates paper . . . anyhow, I think it's the same dog, being sold over and over. You still got that high-pitch whistle?"

"Yes."

"Good. We'll get it checked—see if it has any whistle at all. Meantime, I want to get this front page in Sunday's issue." He checked the time, a quick jab of his arm releasing an expensive gold watch from his shirt cuff. His right hand had already grabbed up the desk phone, and he cranked vigorously for Miss Effie, cutting her inevitable socialities with a curt, "Urgent, Miss Effie. Get me Len."

"Len Finch, on Main Street?" George asked.

"Yeah. He prints us."

"I didn't know that," George said around lighting his pipe.

"He's the best in this part of the state." Johnson pressed the receiver to his ear. "What? . . . Now, Miss Effie. You know perfectly well I can't tell you. Read it in the paper like everybody else. And no listening in, or I'll report you!" He covered the mouthpiece. "Goddamn that woman. If I didn't love her so much, I'd get her bounced out of there tomorrow. But she's a thousand times more efficient than the dial system, and God knows, this town needs her. Offhand, I can think of three people who'd be dead, except for Miss Effie. And who knows how many houses might have burned down." Johnson toyed with his pen, doodling on the legal pad with strokes as sharp and quick as his comments. "But she does goad you, if you know what I mean."

"Amen! She—"

"What?" Johnson interrupted. Across the desk, George and Celia could hear Miss Effie's high voice explaining to Johnson that Len had "stepped across to the bank—but if you'll tell me what it is you want him for, I'll give him the message."

"No, I will not tell you. Ring the bank."

"I can't. They're busy."

"Miss Effie, you know well as me all the bank lines are not busy at this hour of the morning."

"Johnson Miles! Are you doubting my word?"

"Miss Effie," Johnson's voice was pleading. "Please ring the bank. And I'll bring you the first paper off the press. I promise you."

"Wellllll . . ."

"Before anybody else sees it."

"If you promise . . ."

"Yes. Promise! Scout's honor."

"Ah! A line just happened to open up."

Celia's quick giggle was stifled by George's hand placed gently but firmly across her mouth.

There was a sharp clicking sound, and within a few seconds Miss Effie had Len on the line. Swiftly, Johnson outlined the changes he wanted in the front page, checking politely on each step to be certain Len could manage the format upheaval. "And maybe a sketch of the dog," Johnson added. "I mean if I can track Buddy down before lunch . . . Right—be there in an hour." He threw the receiver into its cradle, simultaneously sliding back in place before the typewriter.

"Daddy took a picture of the dog."

Johnson's head came up sharply, sending his glasses halfway down his nose. "You did, Major?"

"Yes—at least, I took four, but the roll hasn't been developed, so I don't know what I've got."

"Great!" Johnson rubbed his hands happily. "We'll develop

them at our expense—if you'll let us—and run a shot with the story." He went back to typing swiftly, asking George for specific details as he went along, curbing his impatience at Celia's interspersed comments. In minutes the story was finished, and he plucked it from the machine. "Can I get that film now, Major?"

"Sure."

In spite of Miss Effie's promise not to listen in, Sallie's phone had begun to ring before they got to the house. Miss Effie had observed the courtesy of phoning Evelyn first to fill her in on the forthcoming story. When George and Celia came in the front door with Johnson, Evelyn had pulled the kitchen stool out to the high wall phone and was handling a friendly stream of inquiries from her comfortable perch, with an inevitable cup of coffee at hand.

"Goddamn that old bitch!" Johnson bellowed.

George pointed to the top of Sallie's head, barely visible over the top of her chair in the living room. "Be right back with that film."

"And don't forget the whistle." Johnson snatched off his soft wool cap and went into the living room, Celia trailing close behind in hangdog admiration. "Excuse me, ma'am, for swearing. I beg your pardon, Miss Sallie. But that confounded Miss Effie has beaten me to five big stories all in a row, and I don't know how to stop her."

"Easy," Sallie said.

"How?"

"Put her on the paper."

Celia snickered. "Miss Effie?"

Johnson flashed Celia a quick appreciative look, then realizing Sallie was in earnest, bit back his sardonic quip. He had never conversed with Sallie, and she surprised him by coming directly to the point.

"Let Miss Effie do a society column, in letter form. Lord knows she hears everything going on around town." Sallie rose with her stiff, room-jolting walk, opened a drawer in the marble-topped table, and handed Johnson a letter.

"What—what's this?"

"Letter from Miss Effie, of course, when I had the flu. Been meaning to send it to you."

"What for?"

"Read it. She's a pretty good writer. And you can use a woman's section—especially with her kind of humor. You're in a real stale rut with your feature stories." His face and bald head reddened, and she added kindly, "Oh, you've got a fine little paper, Johnson. But womenfolks get tired reading nothing but fishing and farming."

He waited for Sallie to continue, struggling to frame his automatic defense. But Sallie was a woman who knew the wisdom of silence, once a point was made. She leaned back, folded her hands, and smiled, waiting for him to digest her criticism.

"Honestly, Grandmother—that's the dumbest thing I ever heard. Miss Effie on the paper . . ."

"Celia, I don't recall asking for your comments."

Secretly, Johnson agreed with Celia, and he was astounded when Sallie had nothing more to say. With nothing to argue about, he found himself forced to admit she was right. Well, damn her soul, she was a sly one. His only objection to a woman's feature was the thought of dealing with any woman on a regular business schedule, and as for Miss Effie . . . He seized at the straw for rebuttal. "It might make it worse, Miss Sallie. If Miss Effie was around the office, she'd have the whole derned paper to talk about."

"She'd have to work at home. You know that, Johnson. And she's mighty loyal. You know that, too. You of all people. You can't beg beans-turkey out of her about the phone company."

"By golly, you may be right. All right. Let me take the letter along and read it."

George hurried in with the whistle and roll of film, and Johnson rose from his crouch before the fire. He bent down to take Sallie's brittle hand and press it warmly. "And thank you for your comments. I'll try to see what we can do about the features."

"I didn't mean to sound quite so harsh, Johnson."

He ran his hand across his head in a lifetime habit of smoothing down hair he no longer had, and put his cap in place with a sardonic smile. "You weren't harsh. I just don't like to hear any-one say anything except what they like. Never learn anything that way. Major, I'll give you a ring and let you know how these turn out." He shook George's hand and left with a cheery wave to Evelyn, who was still answering the telephone. The front door closed behind him, immediately reopened, and Johnson thrust his head inside. "Major—on second thought, I'll drop by on my way back to the office. That derned Miss Effie can prob-ably copy photographs over the phone."

George laughed. "See you later."

The phone was still ringing late that afternoon when Johnson came in with a handful of damp photographs. Though Evelyn and Sallie had taken turns answering, they were both getting hoarse, and their arms ached from holding the receiver.

"Johnson? Come on up and have a drink," George called from the top of the steps.

"Just a minute." Johnson went to the hall phone and took the receiver from Sallie's cold fingers, having to crouch to get his face on a level with the mouthpiece. "Hello, this is Johnson Miles. Who's speaking? . . . Oh, afternoon, Reverend . . . Yes . . . Well, would you please wait until Sunday and read it in the paper? These folks are mighty tired . . . Thank you, sir." He hung up and gave the bell crank a hearty whirl. "Miss Effie, this is Johnson. No more calls—Miss Sallie and Evelyn need a rest . . . I don't care how many you got waiting. Tell them to read it in the paper . . . I know you're busy, but after all, you started this . . . O.K. Thanks. And Miss Effie, I want to talk to you first thing tomorrow . . . NO! . . . Don't phone me—I'll come by there. Thank you, ma'am." He returned Miss Effie's letter to Sallie with a small peck of a kiss on her cheek. "That's not bad writing. Not bad at all."

"You going to hire her?"

"Maybe." His eyes twinkled mischievously. "Read it in the paper."

"Johnson." Sallie stopped him at the foot of the steps, twisting the letter in her hands. "I—uh—I don't suppose Miss Effie will earn enough to quit the phone company?"

His chin tipped back in an unrestrained guffaw that began at his head and traveled down his body to terminate with three heavy stomps of his foot. "So that's what you were up to! Well, I'm afraid not, ma'am. But she will earn enough so she'll be listening in on all your calls, instead of only half."

"Well . . . it was a good try." Sallie pocketed the letter with a rueful grin, and Johnson's laughter carried him up the steps three at a time.

He joined George and Celia in the upstairs living room in a swirl of motion that made all his movements appear to occur simultaneously. His coat and cap came off as he barreled into the room, stepping over Celia where she lay on her stomach studying a history book. He patted her head, handed the photographs to George, took the proffered drink of bourbon, and slugged it in one long draft while dropping into an empty chair. "Jeez, that's good."

Crazy bastard made you tired to watch him, George thought, mixing him a second drink. Johnson sipped it slowly, watching George as he sat down at the desk to study his photographs.

"What do you know, Johnson. They're all good."

"Sure are. Damned good. We'll use the top one." At the moment of trying to fire his gun, Brown's face was lifted into strong sunlight, and in the enlargement under George's hand, every feature of his face, every marking of the dog appeared in vivid detail, outlined against the dark forest behind them. "And, Major—on a hunch, I took some copies by Harlan's office. He thinks that may be the fellow who's been passing so many bad checks around town. He's part of the bridge crew Harlan gave permission to hunt his farm." Johnson took another sip of his drink. "By the way, that whistle he gave you? It doesn't."

"Not at all?"

"Not a peep, not a cheep." Johnson pulled the whistle from his pocket and tossed it to George at the desk. He leaned back in his chair, his legs seeming to stretch halfway across the room, and began tapping the soles of his fleece-lined suede boots together with an uneven, exasperating rhythm. Celia looked up from her book, twisting a strand of hair around and around her finger, staring at him with unmasked curiosity. Oh, Lord—he'd forgotten she was there. Ugly little monster would probably turn out to be another blabbermouth. Johnson scowled at the passing spectre of a newspaper staffed entirely by gossiping girls and women. The nightmare yanked him to his feet. "Gotta get back to the office."

"This late?" George reluctantly pulled himself away from admiring the pictures. "Can't you stay and have some supper?"

"No, thanks. I want to look through some old feature sections." Johnson already had his coat on. "I'll find my way down, Major. Oh. Almost forgot. The photo lab's going to print the rest of your negatives as soon as they get a lull. Two or three days, maybe. I'll bring them by."

"Thanks very much."

"Least we could do. Goodnight." He was gone.

Without the constantly ringing phone, the house seemed idyllic in its silence, and George was relieved to be rid of Johnson's frenetic presence. He poured himself another drink and examined the photographs with unabashed pride and delight. He'd only had a dozen lessons a few years back, but all four shots of the dog and Brown were as clear as an etching, framed and balanced with deft sensitivity for the subject matter. And he had shot without time to plan. He was impatient to see the rest of the roll, when he'd had the advantage of light meter and filters.

"Daddy..." Celia was still watching him, the book untouched before her, the single strand of hair twisted now into a hard rattail. "Daddy?"

"What."

"Is that Mr. Brown really a crook?"

"We don't know yet. And until we do, you are not to discuss it outside this house. Understand?"

"Yes." She fingered her book, sinking into melancholy. If Mr. Brown was a crook, then he must really be one of the Evil

Spirits. And if he was, then she should flat out despise him. Instead, she was sitting there feeling sorry for him. And she couldn't figure out why. Her father said she was "not to discuss it outside this house." She couldn't even discuss it inside the house. Certainly not with her father, who'd been cheated by that awful man. So why did she feel sorry?

Thoughtful and subdued, she let her gaze drift to the fire. Flickering light played across an expression timelessly sad and aged, totally out of place on her unwrinkled visage. George gagged on his drink, hastily added more soda. What was she thinking? Curious how children's faces always had that quality when caught unaware in some reverie.

To Celia's delight, Sunday's *Weekly Bugler* carried a blurry copy of George's photograph of Brown and Adelaide in a two-column spread under the headline, "Have You Seen This Man or This Dog?" The story credited George with the picture, and Celia read and reread it until she could recite it from memory. Johnson's writing was concise and compelling, and included the fact that five storekeepers had identified Brown as a bad check artist. AP and UP picked up the story because of its tri-state implications, and Brown's picture with the by-line credit to George stared out from every newsstand in the state. Not only did the phone begin ringing again, but telegrams and letters flooded the house. There were inevitable false reports of people having sighted the dog in every state from Florida to Oregon, and there were dozens of suggestions for retrieving the setter. One man recommended a well-cooked marrow bone "fastened to hang from the car's rear bumper and be dragged from the point where the setter disappeared to your own backyard." One woman cryptically wrote: "Consult 'Lady,' the psychic horse, Richmond, Va." In spite of Evelyn's insistence that there might very well be a psychic horse in Richmond, George refused to read any more of the letters.

But with all the uproar, there was no trace of Brown or the dog.

The setter's brief presence in the house had awakened George's boyhood love for pets, and he began scanning newspaper ads, determined to find a dog of his own. He was sprawled across the couch checking the Sunday city papers with Celia when Evelyn came in. "It's Johnson," she said, barely getting out of the doorway before he burst in. Johnson began pacing the rug and launched immediately into the reason for his visit.

George thrust Celia aside and sat bolt upright, sending newspapers flying, sheepish to be caught in so relaxed a position by a man who seemed incapable of rest. Son of a gun . . . probably slept standing up. No. He must lie down sometime. He did have children, after all. Or perhaps he made love standing up. A smirk stole to his lips as Johnson halted before him, one arm frozen in the midst of an excited gesture.

"I—I hope the idea doesn't offend you, Major."

George stammeringly admitted he had not been listening. "I'm sorry, Johnson. It's a bad habit of mine. But I get to thinking about other things."

Celia covered her face in embarrassment for her father's stupidity. Letting everybody in town know he was deaf. Or senile. Or both.

"My fault—I talk too fast," Johnson was saying.

"Take off your coat. I'll fix us a drink."

"No, thanks. Promised Irene to get home early for a change." He sat down on the arm of the red leather chair, pressing his fingertips together, concentrating on them as if they were forcing him to slower speech. "Those photographs of yours our lab developed. I thought you got those shots of Brown by luck—but, Major, that entire roll is excellent. Every single one of them. And what I wanted to ask you was this—see, we've been shooting pictures just any old way, with a cheap flash camera, or mostly using sketches. But the paper's getting too big for that, and I was wondering if you'd work with us. Be our official photographer. I don't mean all the routine calls, but big things—like weddings, graduations, cattle fair awards." Johnson's smile was sardonic. "Things you could schedule at your convenience. Besides which, I've decided to enlarge our feature section. I am going to use

Miss Effie." He paused and nodded to George's knowing grin. "But we've got room for more. Something to interest the ladies. And I'd like to run one of your scenic shots each issue, under your name. That could be anything at all you'd care to let us use. Human interest, or comic, or—you know. I can't pay too much." He looked at George with a self-conscious smile and thrust his hands into his pockets as if he expected to ram his fists down to his knees. "Hell. It was just a crazy idea. Guess you wouldn't be interested."

"The hell I wouldn't! I'd do it for expenses."

"Oh, we can manage a little more than that." Johnson stood up. "Can you come in tomorrow and talk about it?"

"You bet. What time?"

"Any time before eleven. We're closed from eleven to one. Because of that damned siren. We never know exactly when it's going to signal noon. And the noise gives us all headaches."

"Why the devil is that siren so erratic? Who's responsible for sounding it?"

Johnson spread his hands despairingly. "Miss Effie. She forgets about it when she gets to talking."

George laughed.

"What is it?"

"How about that for my first feature? A shot of Miss Effie sounding it? Maybe if she gets enough publicity she'll be pressured into sounding it on time."

Johnson let out one of his foot-stamping guffaws. "Deal!"

They shook hands and Johnson darted out, leaving George in a slow spreading warmth of excitement.

"Are you really going to be in the paper, Daddy?"

"Yes. Every week."

"Golly," Celia said, in obvious awe.

"What?"

"It's just—just—amazing . . ."

"What do you mean?"

"Somebody like Johnson Miles hiring an old man to work on his newspaper."

"Thanks," George said dryly. He rose, hurrying through the hall, with Celia following close behind. George found Evelyn peeling potatoes at the sink and pounced on her, hugging her hard, pulling Celia in between them.

"What's happened? Did Johnson find the dog?"

"No. But he's hired this 'old man' for a regular job on the paper." He told her Johnson's offer, pleasure and pride bubbling into amazed laughter. He talked excitedly through her congratulations and was still talking as he pulled on his coat and started down the stairs.

"George? Where are you going?"

"Look at the fire siren tower and figure out what time the sun's best to photograph it. Going to try superimposing Miss Effie over the tower."

"Can I come, Daddy? Can I?"

George smiled up at her from the stairwell. "Celia, I hereby appoint you my official assistant and camera carrier. Get your coat."

Celia scrambled into a heavy jacket, and the two of them vanished down the steps. Evelyn smiled, her own excitement beginning as she heard George for the first time in months singing a bawdy military marching tune. She dried her hands and went downstairs to tell Sallie.

"That's right fine," Sallie said immediately. "Then I guess Johnson will be around a good bit?"

"I guess."

"Then maybe we should think about redesigning the house."

"What?" When Sallie had a joke in mind, her expression was so provocative that Evelyn felt an inclination for laughter even before she knew what was funny. They were both laughing as Sallie merely pointed above her head, where Johnson's foot-stamping guffaw in the upstairs living room had produced a jagged crack all the way across the newly plastered ceiling.

9

NOTHING George or Evelyn said could convince Mrs. Beezely she was not personally responsible for George's loss of the setter and one hundred and twenty-five dollars. "I had one of my feelings!" she kept repeating. "I knew! I should have warned you not to take that dog."

Harlan's official investigation revealed nothing beyond the obvious fact that Brown seemed to have vanished along with the setter. "But I can guarantee you one thing," Harlan said cryptically. "Your pictures and Johnson's stories have made it impossible for Brown to operate any more in this town—in fact, the whole damn state."

"Maybe," George said. "I hope so."

"I know." Harlan twisted his hat uneasily. "And if he ever does show up around town, I would strongly advise you not to tangle with him, George."

"Thanks." George tapped ashes from his pipe. "That's a big help."

Embarrassed by George's quiet sarcasm, Harlan slammed his hat down across his eyebrows. "Shit. Guess I might as well tell you—I do know he's still working with the bridge crew. 'Course, long as he stays over there, there's not a damn thing I can do about it. It's—"

"—out of your jurisdiction," George finished for him.

When Mrs. Beezely heard Harlan's summation of the situation, she grumbled a lengthy phone call to Evelyn. "This just makes it worse. Brown sitting right over there, and Major without his money or his dog. And it's all my fault."

"No—it is not," Evelyn insisted gently. "George doesn't blame you in the least."

"But I had one of my feelings," Mrs. Beezely repeated.

That afternoon, in a burst of guilty inspiration, Mrs. Beezely phoned her distant cousin Edwin, who raised setters. After some involved dickering, she agreed to replenish his tackle box, and Edwin agreed to give George the dog his son had just finished training. Jubilantly, Mrs. Beezely put up a "Back in 10 Minutes" sign and hurried over to tell George about the dog.

George was evasively polite. "Hold on a minute. That's very kind of you—and of Edwin," he added swiftly. "And I—uh—don't want to hurt any feelings, but—I mean, I'm looking for a good hunter."

"Why, Edwin says Bertram's one of the finest hunting dogs around!"

"Bertram?! A hunting dog named Bertram?" Celia shrilled.

Evelyn was quick to see the shadow cross Mrs. Beezely's face. "Now, Celia. It's not any worse than a setter named Adelaide."

Mrs. Beezely smiled again. "I should say not. Now, Edwin tells me Bertram's not too fancy to look at, but he's got a fine hunting reputation with men who come in my store."

"I-I'll certainly be pleased to take a look at him, but—well, it may not be the dog I want."

"Oh, dear." Mrs. Beezely bit her lip. "That'll put me in a terrible position. You see, the one man in the world they'd sell him to has already got himself another dog—because Edwin wouldn't let him have Bertram. And with his temper, Edwin may never set foot in my store again if you turn that dog down now."

"But look at the spot you put me in. I am not like the damn—" George stopped as Evelyn frowned warningly. "I-I mean—I'd be—proud to have—Bertram. It's an honor. A great honor."

Celia snickered at his scathing tone.

"How the hell did I get trapped like this?" George murmured

to Evelyn. "Stuck with some dog I don't know, might not like. This business of being polite sometimes gets to be a pain in the ass."

"Now, George . . ."

"—and he's a young dog, only about a year old," Mrs. Beezely was saying.

George groaned. "A puppy."

"No, no. Edwin always starts his own hunters young, and his boy trained Bertram himself. Edwin says you can come for Bertram any time after Wednesday, when his boy goes off to college."

"That's dandy." George licked his lips. "Just—dandy. Uh . . . thank you so very much, Mrs. Beezely. We'll pick him up Saturday."

"Fine! I'll go phone Edwin." Mrs. Beezely went back to the store smiling proudly. She'd done it. She had exonerated herself for not following up on her "feeling." And Bertram had just better be a good hunter, or Edwin was going to find himself with water in his gas tank next time he came in the store. She'd warned him good.

" 'Bertram,' " George grumbled. "Will you please tell me exactly how Mrs. Beezely talked me into this?"

"Oh, cheer up," Evelyn said. "You can always take him out to Harlan's Headache and give him to Morgan and swear he ran away."

The following Saturday morning, they rose at dawn, routed Celia out of bed, and drove straight to Edwin's farm. To soothe his anger, George whistled the Marseillaise through his teeth. Celia grinned and stretched out along the back seat in contented dozing.

Evelyn looked up from the map Mrs. Beezely had sketched for them. "I'm so sorry about all this, George, having to take a dog you don't know. But it'd break Mrs. Beezely's heart if you didn't."

"I know." He reached over and took her hand, squeezing it warmly.

Half a mile later, a fetid stink began wafting through the ventilators, and George cut off the flow of air. "Phew!" Celia stirred restlessly, pushed herself into a semi-sitting position. "What's that?!"

Evelyn wrinkled her nose. "Edwin runs a dairy–pig farm. No wonder Mrs. Beezely said we couldn't miss it."

Edwin's driveway wound through fields of green cropped to the ground by grazing cows and giving an appearance of sweeping lawns. "Look!" George caught Evelyn's arm in boyish excitement. "Those dogs are beauts!" Beyond the barn were a series of large wire runs. They could see a sleek red setter suckling her squirming litter of pups, and in the next partition, a heavy male English setter dozing in a sunny corner.

They found Edwin inside the barn shoveling manure into an open truck. He tipped his cap to Evelyn, recognizing her at once, and she introduced him to George. "Reckon you done come for Bertram."

"Right." George choked in the overpowering fumes of the manure pile, and Edwin smiled. A man no more than thirty-five, he was aged by weather and despair, and his placid resignation gave him an aura of authority. "Come on outside where you can breathe, and I'll show you your dog."

"I can't tell you how much we appreciate your generosity."

Edwin was self-conscious about his secret swap with Mrs. Beezely for new fishing tackle, and he cut George off with a wave of his hand. "It's me what's appreciative, believe me. C'mon." He rambled slowly out the side door, his loose coveralls and shirt flapping on his wiry frame with every move. George and Evelyn followed him in wordless obedience while Celia ran at his side with a tumble of questions about the dogs. They walked along a pathway between two rows of wire runways, each with a doghouse at the back.

"You raise dogs professionally?" George asked.

"Yep. Started as a hobby and just *litter*-ally multiplied on me!" He slapped his thigh in appreciation of his own bad pun. Celia groaned at her father's hearty laugh. "But I don't train 'em, 'cept for myself. Folks round here like to train their own. That's how come it's so hard to buy one. I mean, honestly," he added, in quick deference to George's misfortune.

George eyed the dogs avidly. None of them had Adelaide's spectacular lines, but they were handsome animals, all of them. "This is my lucky day," he was humming softly, when Edwin halted before the last runway and opened the gate. They stepped inside the empty enclosure, and something stirred in the shadowy doghouse. Out rambled an ungainly female dog of uncertain lineage and unlikely dimension. She had a thick, jet-black coat with a white semicircle around her nostrils and a white festoon on the very tip of her tail. She was ninety-eight pounds of heavily muscled frame, with hindquarters a good three inches higher than her forelegs. She ambled slowly toward them in a stumble-footed shuffle, her wagging tail rocking her rump from side to side in a clumsy rhumba, her heavy head hanging low in continual apology for existence.

"That's Bertram?" George asked, outraged.

On hearing George speak her name, the dog made a joyous self-introduction by galloping across the yard, rearing up, and planting her paws on George's shoulders. Off-balance, he tripped and stumbled backwards, sitting down hard on the bare ground. Bertram planted her paws on his chest and pinned him to the dirt, covering his face with slobbering licks of greeting.

"She does that when she hears her name, which is how come we named her something nobody's apt to call her accidental-like." Edwin hooked his fingers in the wire mesh above his head and laconically shifted his weight from one hip to the other. Evelyn and Celia clung to the gate beside him, convulsed with laughter as they watched George wrestling helplessly with the powerful dog. Celia clapped her hands excitedly, dancing around behind Edwin. " 'Course," Edwin continued thoughtfully, "she's still only a pup of nine months. She'll probably stop that when she gets her full growth. But for the time being, it's best to call her by her full name. Bertram-Down-Girl."

Bertram-Down-Girl wheeled and trotted over to sit at Edwin's feet, her oscillating tail sweeping dust back and forth over George's trouser legs. George crouched on an eye-level with the dog. "Good girl." He scratched the dog's ear, and to his astonishment, Bertram-Down-Girl's mouth twisted up into a grin. She had a heavy, squared-off nose and muzzle with ears that started at a jaunty angle just behind her eyes, only to end in a morose droop along her cheeks. George continued scratching her ear, staring at the dog's conformation in disbelief. "What in God's name is she?"

"Dunno." Bertram, it seemed, was the runt of twelve in an accidental litter produced by Edwin's prize red setter, who had gotten loose one weekend and come home complacently pregnant. Of the twelve dogs, some were red, some brown and white; one was mottled brown; one had curious tan stripes circling its body. And, of course, there was Bertram, the single black dog of the litter. Edwin had given the other puppies away for pets, but no one wanted the oddly marked, misshapen, and sickly runt. He had been about to destroy Bertram-Down-Girl when his son asked for her to practice up on dog-training. "He done a good job, too. Only excuse for the dog is she's a derned good hunter. But Lester's off to college. And Bertram-Down-Girl here ... well, she's so affectionate, we figured she ought to be in somebody's family."

"Um." George stood up and dusted off his trousers. "That's what Brown told me about the setter."

A quick flash of resentment crossed Edwin's face at the comparison to a man despised by the local community. "Tell you what, Major. If you take her and decide you don't want her, you just bring her back and let me sell her for you. No charge to you, of course."

"Thanks," George said, beginning to laugh. "But I think I do want her. Even if she couldn't hunt, she'd be a great conversation piece."

There was no need for a leash. Bertram-Down-Girl trotted proudly along the path between George and Evelyn, nuzzling first one hand and then the other, licking at Celia's fingers. At

146

the car, Edwin opened the back door and the dog bumbled into the rear seat, her hindquarters slipping clumsily to the ground on her first two tries. Edwin scratched her ear fondly. "Now, you sit quiet, girl, you hear me?" Bertram-Down-Girl instantly settled her great rump on the seat, rested her forepaws on the floor, and laid her muzzle on the back of the front seat. "Likes to see where she's going," Edwin explained.

Celia snuggled next to the dog, to be awarded with an enthusiastic lick on her nose. "I like him!" Celia said.

". . . Her . . ." George corrected.

"Whatever. I think Bertram's just great!" The dog pounced on Celia, until, shrieking loud giggles, she remembered the "Down-Girl" part.

"What do you feed her?" Evelyn asked as Edwin helped her into the car.

"Anything, ma'am. Anything at all."

"Well, thanks again," George said.

"I think you folks will like her. Frankly, she's got more common sense than all my so-called prize dogs put together. But I just don't have time to play with her." Edwin touched his cap in farewell, and the car rolled slowly along the drive.

Evelyn was watching George closely. "Honey? I know you said you didn't care if he was an elephant, but—"

"She," George interrupted.

"What?"

"Bertram's a female. Down-Girl!" he added, barely in time to avert the dog's leap across the back of the seat.

"Edwin did say he'd take her back. You could leave her right now."

"Nope. I like her. Already." Bertram-Down-Girl let out a great snort and settled her muzzle against George's neck. "Now I ask you—who could resist that?"

Bertram-Down-Girl's entry into the household was instantaneous and cataclysmic. Bounding up the steps, the dog dashed through the door ahead of George and Evelyn to assume enthusiastic command, her great tail lashing approval and, in the process, encompassing several vases, a reading lamp, the coffee service, and two potted ferns. George and Celia ran into the living room after the dog, following the wake of shards and Sallie's shrieks of dismay through the dining room and into the hall. The mammoth black form disappeared through the swinging door into the kitchen, and ominous silence descended.

"D-does it bite?' Sallie quavered.

"I don't think so," George said. Celia tentatively pushed the swinging door open and they peered into the kitchen. The dog was standing on her hind legs, forepaws planted amicably on Ethel's shoulders. "—and I'm glad to meet you, too, Mr. Dog," Ethel was crooning, nuzzling her nose against Bertram-Down-Girl's. "Only you stay around. None of that running away nonsense, you hear me?" Bertram-Down-Girl sank to her haunches, and Ethel held out a handful of tomato peelings. With gentle laps, the dog wolfed them down and settled contentedly into the dog bed by the stove. Ethel turned to George and Sallie, dropping her head back, her normally impassive face rippling with pleased laughter. "Major, the Lord done sent us a happiness. It make you laugh to see that animal walk through the door."

George turned to Sallie. "Funny. I didn't hear you laughing."

"No. But I think maybe I will after I clean up the mess and get a nap."

That afternoon, George found Evelyn curled on the bed, drowsy and lethargic. "Celia and I are walking Bertram-Down-Girl over to the store. Then we're going out in the boat. Want to come?"

Evelyn shook her head. "Don't you want a nap?"

"No." He picked up loose change from the dresser, thrusting it into his pocket. "Alan and I have a bet running on the new dog—if she'd obey me or not. He's been kidding the hell out of me about her name, and this is one bet I want to collect."

"But, George—he won't be there. Saturday's his fishing day."

"Usually. But he's working today. Some problem about the new bridge."

"Have fun. And please—don't argue with him about anything."

148

"Oh, go to sleep." Downstairs, George whistled to Bertram-Down-Girl. Celia joined him at the steps, and they set off for the store with Bertram-Down-Girl shuffling along behind them.

"Daddy, how does Bertram know she—" Celia was dropped to her knees by the dog's leap, and George rescued her, yanking the dog back and commanding, "Down-Girl." He pulled Celia to her feet. "You O.K.?"

"Sure." She stood up, her eyes alight. "Does Uncle Alan know about the Down-Girl part?"

"No, I don't think so."

"Let's get even with him for all his teasing about her name—don't tell him."

George's laughter was sheer exultation. "Deal!"

They shook hands conspiratorially and made their way down the street to the corner at the foot of the bridge, waving to Miss Effie as they passed beneath her window. The heavy panes at once shot open. "Is that the dog, Major? Is that him?"

"That's him. Her, I mean."

"My. I never. I mean, my! . . . now that is a dog. Yes, sir. He surely is. Has Emma Ellen seen it?"

"No. We'll stop by later."

"My!" The window slammed shut, and they could see her fumbling with the switchboard.

"Hm," George chuckled, hearing Miss Effie's shrill laughter. "It'll give her something to do all day, broadcasting Bertram-Down-Girl's arrival."

On Main Street the usual noonday lunch hour silence was broken by the mad clatter of the printing press, and George waved across the street to Len Finch, who was seated at the shop window talking on the phone. Len pointed to the receiver in his hand and then to Bertram-Down-Girl, and George cupped his hands, calling sardonically, "Tell Miss Effie it's a female dog, not a male." Len grinned and nodded, his mouth working frantically as he tried to interrupt Miss Effie.

George and Celia strolled slowly along. George whistled cheerfully, no longer disturbed by Celia's constant chatter as he anticipated their coming boat trip. Those were the hours he most enjoyed with Celia. Alone on the Sound with the great sweep of water and marsh isolating them from cousins and friends, she was again the child he knew, dreamily silent for long stretches at a time. Usually he took a book along and they would drift with the tide for miles, laughing over passages from *Alice in Wonderland* or lost in a volume of English poets. Lately he had taken to reading science fiction to Celia, and he had chosen the small leather-bound collection of H. G. Wells for this afternoon.

At the moment, Buzzard's Roost was vacant, deserted to pale sunshine and one bilious seagull that lazily flapped away as Celia approached. The tide was high, and water lapping against the seawall was a soothing sound in the empty nap-time street. Celia's step quickened when she saw Jim and Cynthia standing on the open back of the store truck parked alongside the loading platform. "We got him—her, I mean!" Celia yelled to them. They waved back, screaming excitedly for them to hurry.

Alan was behind the truck with Thomas. The two men had shed their shirts and were laboring side by side to wrestle a heavy barrel to a makeshift ramp of planking leading up onto the truck bed. Alan's bare back was mushroom pale and soft in the sunlight, contrasting sharply with the coppery black sinew of Thomas's shoulders and arms. He was arguing loudly with Alan. "I tell you, Mr. Alan, just the two of us can't do it this way."

"Shut up and push."

"You're going to bust your back again. Lemme rig us up a pulley."

"You and your dern contraptions. That'll take half the afternoon." Alan stopped to mop his sweaty face and grinned broadly, seeing George and Celia approaching with the black dog stumbling along at their heels. "Hey, Thomas. You see what I see?"

Thomas hooked his thumbs into his jeans pockets and began to chuckle. "That the dog, Major?"

"That's it." George smiled complacently and fumbled for his pipe with a quick wink to the giggling Celia.

"I don't believe it." Alan handed George a windproof lighter.

"Thomas, my brother-in-law must be the biggest fool in the county."

"Don't be so quick to criticize," George said mildly.

"The name is bad enough, but you sure that thing's a dog? Let's have a closer look." Alan squatted down. "Come on over here, Bertram."

The dog obliged him with one of her headlong lunges, and Alan was sent sprawling to his back. Bertram-Down-Girl sat squarely on his chest and began lapping his face.

"Is that close enough?" George asked with mock concern, bending over Alan's prostrate form while the children squealed with hysterical giggles and Thomas draped himself across the barrel with hearty guffaws.

"All right, all right, you son-of-a-bitch . . . call him off! . . ." Alan squirmed beneath the dog's joyful licks. "Call him off, George! 'Quits' . . . 'Uncle' . . . !"

"Down-Girl," George said gently, and the dog immediately trotted back to his side. He scratched her ear, and everyone laughed again at the grotesquerie of a smile outlined by the white fur on her large black muzzle. Enormously pleased with herself, Bertram-Down-Girl sank back on her haunches with her hind legs sprawled forward around her forepaws. George snapped his fingers. "Oh, I forgot to tell you, Alan. The dog's whole name is Bertram-Down-Girl. It's best not to forget the Down-Girl part of it. She's still only a little puppy."

"Well, by god, she does obey you, George. You sure win your dollar." He handed over a crumpled bill, and George pocketed it, with a broad smile to Celia. Alan stood up, grinning good-natured acknowledgment at being the butt of a joke. "But great gawdamighty, George. You call that thing a dog? Looks more like a knocked-up nigger."

Celia's giggles ended with a choked gasp and a startled intake of breath. She bit her lower lip, her cheeks flaming as she looked up anxiously at Thomas. George was the first to realize her embarrassment, and his quick turn in her direction silenced Cynthia and Jim. Thomas turned his back to the group and knelt by

Bertram-Down-Girl, stroking the dog's silky head. Bit by bit, laughter died and an awkward pall settled around them. Alan wiped his sandy mouth with the back of his hand, a quick movement, emphasizing his uneasy chuckle. "Why, 'scuse me, George! What I meant to say was—'a *pregnant* Negrah.'"

No one smiled, and Jim and Cynthia stood rooted on the truck. Caught by the contagion of embarrassment, Cynthia became absorbed by a scab on her elbow and Jim stared out across the Sound at a small fleet of shrimp boats passing by.

George was unable to turn away from Celia's distress. So, she could say "nigger" in private, but not to a man's face. George knew in the instant that, no matter what she might say for the benefit of her cousins, she had not lost all his training, and he was filled with quiet happiness.

Thomas interpreted George's silence for discomfort and smiled easily, continuing to fondle the dog's ears. "Don't pay Mr. Alan no mind, Major. He's just all shook up today, having to do a little honest work for a change."

Brushing sand from his damp back, Alan smiled fondly at Thomas. "You're damn right. It's Saturday, and the Lord says Saturday's a day of rest and fishing."

"Yeah?" Thomas squinted up at him. "I don't recall reading that no place. But the Lord sure didn't count on folks resting the other six days besides."

They were all grateful for the banter, and laughter bubbled up again. But Celia remained silent and wide-eyed, lost in a confusion of thoughts. Jim and Cynthia sat on the tailgate of the truck and opened a package of Juicy Fruit chewing gum, a soggy sweet lump extracted from the pocket of Jim's dungarees. Alan took advantage of the merriment to add an explanatory note for Celia's benefit and clasped Thomas's shoulders. "Boy, if you weren't so black, I'd swear you could be my own son. And seeing as how my bootlegger's just past your farm, you might be, at that. No telling what I won't do with a drink in my belly."

George coughed a cautionary warning. Once Alan started kidding, there was no end to his bawdy jibes.

But Alan was unnerved by Celia's grave, continuing stare.

Her expression surrounded him, stripping his attempted jokes to baldest cruelties. He gestured hesitantly to the dog. "Does she —does she hunt, George?"

"So I'm told. Haven't tried her out yet."

"Why don't you get Thomas here to go with you, first time you take her out? He's the best dog handler in the state. And if she tries running away, he's the only man I know who could outrun her." He went on extolling Thomas's many skills as a hunter, and George relaxed, leaning against the truck fender and enjoying Alan's Bunyanesque exaggerations of a hunting trip he and Thomas had made.

The humor was lost on Celia. She stood plucking at the seams of her slacks, feeling the red flush on her cheeks and wishing fervently that she could turn to dust and blow away. You just didn't *do* things like that, she thought, struggling to sort the chaos of her feelings. You just didn't. Not to Thomas. He was their friend. No—more. Thomas was family, almost. You didn't go around calling him a—a whatchacallit . . . only Uncle Alan hadn't really said Thomas was one. He'd said . . . What exactly was it he did say? . . . Celia scowled, feeling dizzy with the effort of concentration.

Alan ended his story and gave his trousers an irritable hitch when no one awarded him an appreciative laugh. Instead, George stretched and let out a smothered yawn. "We better get going and leave you to finish up your job." He gave the nearest barrel an experimental shove and whistled in appreciation for their efforts. "What you got in there?"

"Nails."

"Two barrels of nails?"

"That's right." Alan smiled again, hoping it was a story they would appreciate. "The state wouldn't give the new bridge job to any local folks. Oh, no. They send us these fancy outlander contractors, and I tell you, George, the damn fools don't know what they're doing. They forgot about the tide rising and falling seven feet, so what happens right off the bat? Yesterday they tied off their first supply barge on a three-foot slack, then took off to get themselves liquored up. Thomas tried to tell them when we were out there delivering some caulking, and you know what that foreman said?—that damn fool Albert Thatcher —well, he says, 'Get your fucking black hide outta here. Ain't nobody alive can teach me my job.' So I says, real polite, 'Thomas, it is time we were leaving.' But I go over and give Albert Thatcher my card, see, and I mark my home telephone number. 'What's this for?' he says, real nasty. And I just smile, easy-like. 'You'll find out,' I says. And we drive off. So in comes this fullmoon tide, and after the first four feet of water the barge hawser holds its nose under water, and swoosh! she's flooded and sinks before the night watchman sobers up to know what's happening." Alan's face crinkled with delight, and his laugh came in whinnied gusts of mirth. "They lost every single sack of cement they had—some girders—and I don't know what all. Plus which, when the barge sank, it smashed up the dock, and they've got to rebuild that before they can even start the bridge. That's why they want the nails in such a hurry."

George chuckled with him. "Celia and I are going out in the boat. I'll head over there and get some shots for the paper."

"Be at least a week before they can start the bridge. But if you want some pictures of one grand mess, you got them." Alan shook his head grimly. "Tell you the truth, I'll be glad when that job's finished. They're a pretty rough crowd. Yes, sir. I'll be glad for all of us when they're out of this town. They're a rotten bunch. Rotten. Drinking, fighting, whoring around . . . there's not one I'd trust as far as I could throw him."

"Oh, come on, Alan. I know some of them are rough, but they can't all be that bad." George spoke lightly, but his words had a sharp edge of resentment. "Not everybody can be born right here in town. Somebody has to come from somewhere else."

"Do tell. Now, that never occurred to me, George." Alan turned away abruptly to spit into the sand beneath the loading platform.

"Like I said—we better be going. Or do you want a hand pushing those barrels onto the truck?"

154

"No. No, thanks, George." Alan's smile was stiff and forced. "Thomas and I can manage just fine. We always have."

"All right. See you later. You ready, Celia?" He was smiling at her, his eyes bright blue in the sunshine with a look she didn't understand.

"Hunh?"

"I said we'd better be going or Uncle Alan and Thomas will never finish up their work. And we don't want to lose our high tide."

"Oh . . . yeah, O.K." She rested her hand on the dog's neck and followed her father back up the alley to the street, heading toward the boat dock. To her amazement, he began to whistle happily. Why, the old fool really was crazy. Uncle Alan had just said those things that usually made him mad as hinges, and here he was—whistling!

Alan followed them across the yard to the gate and watched them walk away. Licking sweat from his lips, he squinted his eyes against the sun, and a harsh expression crept across his chubby round face.

Thomas saw the slight twitching of his check and quickly silenced Jim's chattering comments about the dog. "Jim—Cynthia—hush up. You're bothering your Uncle Alan. You two go on and play at the house."

"No!" "We wasn't doing nothing!" Jim and Cynthia chorused. Jim jumped from the truck bed to grab Thomas's arm. "And we wanta ride out to the bridge wreck with you."

"Not this time."

Cynthia rattled the open tailgate in her pique. "Please, Thomas. We'll be quiet."

Alan whirled and strode to the heavy barrel, pounding the top with his fist. "You heard Thomas, didn't you? I'm tired of you kids messing around underfoot when we're working. Now, get. Both of you."

"O.K." "Sorry, Uncle Alan." Jim and Cynthia scuttled across the yard and out the gate.

"What got into him?" Cynthia asked indignantly.

Jim thrust his hands into his pockets and swung a vicious kick at a pebble in the driveway. "Aw, Uncle George makes him mad."

"That's no call to take it out on us."

"No. But Uncle Alan does, and that's that."

Their voices carried clearly in the deserted street, and Alan struck the barrel another angry blow. "Damned spoiled brats. Come on, Thomas. Quit wasting time." He threw his shoulder against the barrel staves and Thomas hurried to help him. Straining together, they managed to force the wobbly barrel two feet up the ramp before it slipped from their sweaty hands and rolled to one side with a heavy crash. Alan swore loudly, a stream of invective covering the new bridge, the construction workers, outlanders, and the necessity of working on a good fishing Saturday.

Winded and panting, Thomas was unmoved by his outburst, waiting quietly until Alan was silent. "Mr. Alan, why don't you just rest a minute and have yourself a Coke. I'll get us a pulley rigged by the time you've finished."

Alan agreed, going to yank a Coke from the cooler. He didn't recall falling asleep. But long moments later he was sprawled on his back along the loading platform and he stirred slowly, reluctant to move his aching shoulders from the sun-drenched planking. Alan stretched, wincing at the ache in his back. "Guess I dozed off."

Thomas laughed. "Dozed, my foot. You were snoring like a bullfrog."

Alan's eyes lighted on the two barrels of nails already loaded on the truck bed and lashed firmly to the side railings. He sat up hastily. "Why didn't you wake me up to help you?"

"Wasn't any trouble with the pulleys." Thomas shook out his T-shirt and began tugging it over his head. "Mr. Alan, why don't you go on home? I'll drive this out."

"Unh-unh. No sir." Alan stood up and searched for his shirt. "I'm not letting you go out there by yourself—not with that mean bunch of bastards."

"They don't bother me. I just don't pay them no mind."

"Thomas—you were right about that barge, and their smart-ass foreman was wrong. That's the worst thing you could have done to a man like that."

"I know, Mr. Alan." Thomas kicked softly at the tire truck.

"I don't want you going out to that bridge by yourself—today or any other day. Understand?"

"All right, Mr. Alan . . . and thank you."

"Aw, shut up and help me find my shirt."

Thomas plucked it from the top of the Coca-Cola machine, holding it for Alan to slip into without straining his back. Alan nodded his thanks. Let George talk, he thought. Let him. But he, Alan, did something about things, and that was what counted. The only thing that counted. He grunted again. Let George talk.

10

W HEN THEY REACHED the boat, Celia automatically took her place at the tiller. Without hesitation, Bertram-Down-Girl gently jumped in beside her, settling easily at her feet and placing her muzzle on Celia's hand, which rested on the steering rod. "Well, that dog's sure used to boats," George commented. "Hard to say which one of you is driving." Amused at the picture the two of them made, George took a couple of quick shots as Celia skillfully steered the boat through the narrow creek and headed across the Sound for the new bridge. But on the opposite shore, the position of the sunken barge made the light wrong for George to get any clear shots from the water, and there was no safe landing spot in the broad expanse of marsh and mud. "Damn," he grumbled. "Celia, I'll have to go home and get the car, and postpone our long boat ride until tomorrow." When he saw the sharp disappointment on her face, he suggested that, as his official assistant, she should come along with him. George was touched by her swift smile and chuckled as she chattered loudly all the way back to the dock. They tied off the boat and headed for the garage with Celia skipping along beside the dog, wildly excited over seeing the wreck at close hand.

Johnson intercepted them at the edge of their yard. "Alan said you got pictures of the barge?"

George shook his head, explaining the light problem.

"And you're taking Celia? Over there?" Johnson asked softly.

George bent closer to him. "I'd rather she see these 'outlanders' from my point of view than from Alan's!"

Johnson joined them in the car and the three of them rode over together, with Johnson laughing heartily at Bertram-Down-Girl's ludicrous expression. The drive along the temporary work road was hot, jolting, and monotonous. Bored by the men's conversation, Celia curled herself against Bertram-Down-Girl and was half asleep when they arrived at the construction area. Laughing, George shook her awake. "Front and center, Celia, on the double. And leave Bertram-Down-Girl in the car. Hurry, honey—we're losing the sunlight fast."

Celia grabbed his camera and the lens bag and stumbled out of the car, running to catch up with Johnson's swift stride.

The bridge site was, as Alan had put it, "one royal mess." The barge was nose down in the mud. Remnants of a trellis of bridge-work hung foolishly sideways into the Sound, and the work dock was a jumbled jackstraw confusion of palmetto pilings and slivered planking. The snarl of metal and wood and the angry atmosphere among the workers awoke Celia from lethargy with a hard sense of trouble, echoing from the tenseness of her father and Johnson.

"What the fuck do you two want?" the foreman, Albert Thatcher, asked.

"Nothing," Johnson said cooly, hands spread. "Just out to get a story and a couple of pictures."

"Oh?" Thatcher stood with his legs apart, his thumbs hooked in his jeans pockets. "Seems every time some of you town people come around we got trouble."

Johnson smiled easily. "Wasn't any townspeople caused this fiasco. If anything, I understand Alan and Thomas tried to warn you about the short tie-off on that barge."

"If you mean that friggin', high-tone nigger—"

"Watch it." Johnson nodded toward Celia.

"You had no cause to bring a kid out here."

"You got no cause to say she can't come."

Celia hugged the camera strap around her neck, feeling un-

159

accountably naked and exposed under the eyes of the surrounding workers.

George was lighting his pipe, a gesture Celia recognized as determination to keep his temper, as there were only a few dead ashes in the bottom of the pipe bowl. "We'll get a few pictures and leave," he said, seemingly self-assured.

"I don't think so," Thatcher began.

"We won't get in your way. Just go ahead with your regular work and I'll get some candid shots."

"I said no."

"Now, look," Johnson interrupted. "It's my home state paying for this bridge—with my taxes—not to mention taxes my subscribers pay. This is our bridge, and if we want pictures, we'll damn well take them."

"Celia," George said softly. "I'll need the 'cloud lens,' and clean it for me."

She nodded, fumbling through the lens bag. Her attention was diverted by a sudden, surreptitious movement. "Daddy!" she said sharply.

He recognized her panic and turned quickly. "What?"

"Over there. It's Mr. Brown."

George followed the foolish point of her finger, to accost the full hatred in the face of the man.

"That's him!" Brown announced. "That's the one that spread me over three states." He strode to Celia, who was still carrying George's Leica. "Give me that goddamn camera. I'll show you what to do with it." He reached for the strap, accidentally grabbing her breast.

"No!" Celia shrieked, fighting away from him and the inadvertent memory of his hands on Martha's body.

Without thought or hesitation, George knocked Brown sprawling to the ground. "Don't touch her. Keep your filthy hands away."

Johnson was close behind him, crouched, waiting. Brown remained on the ground, his eyes riveted resentfully on George. The rest of the crew was immobilized, shocked, silent. George pulled Celia to his side. "We are taking our pictures," he said, and began adjusting the camera setting. Without interference, they moved through the muttering crewmen, photographing the fallen dock, the destroyed bridge pilings, and the sunken barge. Thatcher refused to answer Johnson's questions as to the estimated amount of damage. Johnson shrugged easily and made detailed notes to caption George's photographs. "I'll get the rest of the information from their main office in Columbia," he told George as they finished getting close-ups of the soggy heap of cement bags lying uselessly melded together on the rear of the barge.

In the car, Johnson congratulated George on his calm and his control of the situation. George grinned at him. Just above the seat, out of Celia's view, he held out his hand. It was shaking violently. Johnson whistled softly. "Back to the office. Got some 'coffee' there that'll take care of that."

After two coffees laced with stiff shots of bourbon, George left his roll of film with Johnson, and he and Celia drove toward home. Midway along the narrow blocks, Celia's hand crept across the back seat to touch his shoulder, and Bertram-Down-Girl gave his neck a soft nuzzle. George smiled away the swift lump in his throat.

It began raining that evening and rained steadily for two weeks, a cold gray drizzle that pounded the Sound until ocean and air embraced in a sheet of dancing mist. Dampness permeated sealed storage bags to lay down a sickly coat of mildew. Rain bounced off overflowing gutters, and a puddle beneath the gutter spout expanded to rivulets that glutted drains and backed up knee-deep water into the street. Cars stalled and stopped, to be left standing akimbo in the middle of every intersection. All bridge construction work ceased, and the town was thrown into further turmoil by the crewmen venting their boredom in drunken rampages through business and residential areas. To Celia's chagrin, George insisted on driving her to school, and she was forbidden to go downtown alone through the working lay-off of the bridge crew.

Each night Sallie insisted to Ethel that she stay home the next day, but each morning Ethel arrived at the back door promptly at seven. "It's not so bad as it looks," she would say, shaking out her soaking red coat. One morning Sallie helped her smooth it out on a hanger, fluffing the fur collar into line. "These cuffs are already frayed," Sallie remarked.

"They jus' fine."

Sallie's fingers plucked at the seams. "Before we have it cleaned for storage, I'll turn them down."

"Turn them down?" Ethel clutched the fur possessively and Sallie laughed.

"Just a little bit, to hide the worn places. Anyway, some of the seams need mending. Look." She pointed out a ripped place below the armpit.

"All right, Miss Sallie, if you're sure it won't change the looks none."

"It won't. I promise you." Sallie watched Ethel changing into dry shoes. "And Ethel, truly there's no need for you wading through all this water. We can manage fine until the rain stops."

Ethel tied on her apron. "Tell the truth, Miss Sallie, I enjoys walking in the rain."

"Oh, my. I used to. How I used to!" She looked longingly out the teeming window, envying her romping grandchildren but afraid now to risk her balance in any slippery footing.

Evelyn yawned, logy with boredom. "Lord. Many more days of this and I'll be a raving maniac."

Sallie smiled. "Just remember, it's washing away winter. Spring will be here when it stops."

"Hunh. I'll believe that when I see it," Evelyn grumbled.

But, as Sallie prophesized, spring came overnight to Beldon in explosive puffs of pastel. Three mornings later, an abruptly hot sun came out, and migrating birds hopped and pecked around mud puddles, their brilliant plumage peppering the lawn with shades of red, yellow, wine, and blue. One yellow crocus made a beginning splash of color by the fence post.

The following Sunday, George came home from an afternoon's walk with a handful of travel folders. Sallie's door was closed for her daily nap, and he sauntered through the hall to the empty kitchen. It smelled faintly of pound cake and fried chicken. "Evelyn?" A scuttling movement in the back yard by the shed caught his attention, and he went to the door, thinking he saw someone edging behind the storage shed. "Celia? Is that you? . . . Celia?" There was no answer, no sound. One of the other children, probably, with their endless games of hide and seek. He found Evelyn in their upstairs living room. She was on her knees beside Celia, trying to let out the seams of a light-weight dress. Bertram-Down-Girl lay on the floor beside them, her great black muzzle resting mournfully on a discarded pile of clothing. Celia fidgeted impatiently while Evelyn sat back with a rueful scowl. "This one won't do either."

It was the dress Celia had worn home the day their plane landed. George remembered it with a shock, seeing how much Celia had grown. Not up. Out. Where the silk had hung loosely around a child's skinny frame, it now clung snugly, outlining beginning breasts, a chubby stomach, and ballooning hips. "Puppy fat," Evelyn called it. Ugly, George thought, whatever you call it. So Celia was going to be a fat adolescent. He felt unaccountably sad. "What?" he said, suddenly noticing Evelyn's questioning look.

"I said, what have you got?"

"Oh." He dropped the handful of folders on the coffee table. "Thought you'd want to start thinking about a vacation."

Celia's face puckered, a foolish childlike expression. "We don't have to go anywhere do we? I mean . . . hell . . . we just got unpacked."

"It's entirely up to your mother. I was not speaking to you." George had not intended to sound so severe. He went to the desk for his favorite pipe, looking out the window to the Sound.

Evelyn rose and caressed his shoulder. "Do you really want to go away?"

"As a matter of fact, Evelyn, Johnson was talking to me about running a series of vacation pictures on this area. You know, sailboat races, surfing, and so on. But I thought you'd rather take a cruise or something."

Evelyn looked around the cool white room and touched the glowing black wood of the coffee table. "It would be nice to spend our first summer at home."

"Done," George said, obviously relieved. "We stay home. Maybe take some time in the mountains in August. That satisfy you, Miss Celia?"

She nodded, her face so transfused with joy that George was filled with guilt. "I keep forgetting travel's no novelty for you, either." He cleared his throat. "Would you like to go fishing?" She nodded again. "O.K. You pick out a book while I rinse off and get changed. Want to go, Evelyn?"

"No, thanks." She picked up the pile of clothing. "I'm going to take off this hot girdle and stretch out in bed with the paper."

"Now, that's what I call a thrilling afternoon."

"You would, if you had to wear this derned girdle."

"Way this household feeds me, I may have to." He patted his stomach and headed toward their room. Yawning, Evelyn followed him, tugging off her tight garments. Standing idly at the cool window, she saw a form moving swiftly away from the chicken shed. Odd she thought, glancing automatically at the clock. Ethel is late leaving today. She started to call down and offer her a ride home, but the idea of having to dress again stopped her. She pulled on her favorite robe, a soft pink Japanese kimona with flowers of watercolor hues billowing around the hem. Kicking off her shoes, she stretched across the bed and let herself go limp, reveling in the sensuous luxury of silk and fresh salt air.

There was a hard rap on the door. "Daddy? Are you ready?"

Evelyn stirred reluctantly, routed out of her reverie by Celia's impatient tone. "Come in, honey."

Celia came charging through the door, holding up a book. "I chose *Don Quixote*. That O.K.?" She blinked. "Where is he?"

"Shaving and showering."

"But the tide's going to change in half an hour. We'll miss the—"

"Stop shouting!"

"Well, I don't see why he has to take a shower now. He'll just have to take another one when we get back."

"He can take two showers if he wants to. Or three, for that matter. Now sit down and be quiet."

Celia flopped down in a small wicker armchair, draping one leg over the armrest, letting the crotch of her dungarees cut sharply across her plumping bottom. She knew her pose was one that irritated Evelyn, and she remained stubbornly in the uncomfortable position, riffling the pages of *Don Quixote*.

Evelyn picked up a section of newspaper and folded it back with a sharp snap of irritation. "Where are your shoes?"

"I'm going barefooted."

"On that hot pavement? You'll blister your feet."

"No, I won't. Jim and Cynthia said if you start now, you can toughen your feet so you can walk on nails and ground glass. Soon as school's out, we're not going to wear shoes all summer. Then next fall, before we start back, we're going to put some nails and ground glass in a pit and try walking on them. So we made a pact. No shoes, not even for church or parties."

"We'll see about that."

"Not once. Not for anything."

"Oh, lord." Evelyn put down the paper and pushed her hair back from her face. "In the first place, you are not going to—" She was interrupted by the gentlest of taps on the door. "Dammit, I knew it. Just let me take off my girdle and somebody drops in." The tapping was repeated, scarcely audible over George's boisterous whistling from the bathroom. "Who is it?" Evelyn called politely.

"Cynthia." She was almost whispering.

"Oh." Evelyn sank back on the pillows. "Come in, dear."

The door eased open, and Cynthia's squat frame tumbled across the sill. She shut the door carefully and leaned against it, fingering a lock of her straight blondish hair. "Sorry to bother you, Aunt Evelyn, but I didn't want to wake up Grandmother."

"That's all right. What is it?"

". . . Aunt Evelyn, if . . ."

Evelyn waited, watching the chubby-faced girl. Her face had lost its chin line in a heavy wreath of flesh, foreshortening her plump neck. Evelyn involuntarily glanced down at her own plumping stomach, at Celia's fat behind. They should all go on diets, the whole family.

". . . Aunt Evelyn? . . ."

"Yes. I'm listening." Evelyn spoke wearily, wishing Cynthia would hurry. Get to the point and get out, she thought in exasperation. She surely must hold the world's record for deliberation.

"Aunt Evelyn, how do people turn in fire alarms?"

"What?!"

"I mean, if there was a fire, how would you turn in an alarm?"

"It would depend on where you were." Evelyn smiled. Children. You never knew what the little devils were thinking. "For instance, some cities have alarm boxes on the street. Or you could phone the fire department directly from home."

"But suppose it was just a town. Like Beldon. I mean, you couldn't call the station, because the Volunteer Firemen wouldn't be there."

"In that case you would call the Operator."

"Oh. Thank you." Cynthia edged the door open.

There was a growing duskiness in the haze of pecan limbs outside the back window, a shimmering haze of blue that was several shades denser than blue-green new leaves. Evelyn thought she smelled a wisp of woodsmoke and sat up sharply. "*Why?*"

Cynthia's bland face reappeared in the doorway. "Ma'am?"

"Why do you ask, dammit?"

"Grandmother's shed is on fire. But don't worry. I'll phone Miss Effie." She was gone.

"Oh, my god!" Evelyn shot from bed, scattering sheets of newspaper. From the window she could now see vivid tongues

166

of flame lapping at the back of the tin-roofed building. The chickens in their adjoining cage began to cackle wildly, running back and forth in their wire enclosure. Celia had flung her book aside, racing for the door. "Celia! Where do you think you're going?"

"To fight the fire!"

"Not in your bare feet."

"But, Mother—"

Evelyn rapped on the bathroom door. "George?" The shower was running full blast and he was caroling "On the Road to Mandalay," his deep bass reverberating full volume in the metal shower stall. "George! . . . George, there's a fire, honey . . ."

". . . And the dawn comes up like thunnnnnnnderrrrrrrrr . . ."

"Dammit it to hell!" Evelyn knocked again.

"Mother, I can't put on shoes. I told you—I gave my solemn oath!"

"Goddammit." Evelyn swung her arm back and whacked Celia's behind, putting every ounce of her strength into the blow. "Shoes! Now!"

Convinced she meant it, Celia ran to her room.

Evelyn paused with her hand on the bathroom doorknob, listening to Cynthia downstairs on the telephone. "Yes'm," Cynthia repeated for the fifth time. "Miss Effie, I wanted . . . Ma'am . . . Oh, yes. Uncle Alan's fine, thank you. He just sprained his back this time . . . Yes'm . . . Uh, excuse me, Miss Effie, but Grandmother's shed is . . . What? . . ." There was a long pause; then Cynthia continued politely, "Yes'm . . . uh . . . Miss Effie . . . Miss Effie, please—Grandmother's . . . What? . . . No'm. All Mama's rental cottages are full . . ."

Evelyn tried the bathroom door and found it locked. She swore lustily, scrambling frantically through the sheets of newspaper she had knocked to the floor, searching for her slippers. They seemed to have vanished. She swore again, and grabbing up a pair of George's ankle-high gardening boots, ran for the hall with shoes in hand. Sallie's door flew open as Evelyn reached the steps. Immaculately dressed, her face freshly powdered, Sallie hurried to the phone and took the receiver from Cynthia. "Miss Effie, it's Sallie. Our shed's on fire . . . What? . . . Of course I'm sure. In fact, I'm positive . . . No—not the one you can see. I'm talking about my storage shed out back . . . Oh. I'm sorry. I should have told you, I'm not calling from Annie's house. I'm at home . . . Yes, yes, that was Cynthia who called you, but she's at my house, and it's my shed that's burning, so would you please call the . . . yes . . . fire department. We'd appreciate it . . . Yes, thank you. Goodbye . . . What? . . . Well, how the devil am I supposed to know if we've lost it or not? Call me back later, after we get the fire out." Sallie hung up with an exasperated puff of breath and tucked a stray wisp of hair into place, watching Evelyn struggling to tie George's large shoes around her slim ankles. "The smell woke me up. Looks like a good-sized fire. Have you seen my keys?"

"What?"

"Keys. I've got a fire extinguisher in the canned goods pantry, but I can't find my derned keys." She hustled into the living room, and Evelyn could hear her opening and closing drawers, emptying cigarette boxes, picking up picture frames.

Cynthia clasped her hands as the fire siren began its rising whine. "Listen, Aunt Evelyn. It's for us!"

"Do tell," Evelyn said sardonically. "Go help Grandmother find her keys."

"Yes'm." Cynthia trotted placidly after Sallie, and Evelyn ran out through the kitchen as Celia came pounding down the outside steps. Flames had engulfed the back of the shed and were creeping around the far side, fanned by the steady sea breeze. A blast of heat stopped Evelyn at the foot of the back steps. She realized in dismay that the key to the padlocked shed door was on Sallie's missing key ring.

Johnson Miles, necktie flying, came vaulting over the back fence, followed by two young Marine Corps privates.

"Oh, Johnson. Thank God!"

"What's in there?"

"Trunks. Clothes—extra furniture. But I don't have the key."

Johnson glanced around the yard, seized a shovel from Sallie's flower bed, and prized the padlock loose. The nails gave easily in the dry wood, and the door swung open. One of the young Marines was leaning over the fence, whistling shrilly up and down the street. "Hey, Marines! Fire! On the double!" Under Johnson's supervision, the blond boy already had a broken-seated rocker out of the shed and was hauling a trunk through the door. His friend ran to help him. Johnson opened the door to the hen house, and chickens rocketed past them, squawking wildly as they scattered across the yard. A group of Marines joined the first two, some running in and out of the storage shed helping to empty it, others throwing sand at the flames and trying to beat out the fire with green branches torn from the pecan tree.

The fire siren sounded again in another staccato series of alarms. Two long blasts, three short bursts. The coded signal for their block gave Evelyn a sharpened sense of danger. She began to tremble, mentally measuring the distance from the shed to the house. The breeze was from the back of the shed, and as the flames grew higher, they licked out toward the outside steps of the big main wooden building.

The sidewalk was beginning to echo with running feet. Townspeople had pinpointed the location of the fire, and the yard filled with eager helpers. The cousins materialized, a tight cluster of goggle-eyed children standing squarely before the open door of the shed. Evelyn herded them sternly away, pointing to the most distant corner of the yard by the garden hose. The garden hose! Dragging the nozzle toward the shed, Evelyn shouted for Celia to turn on the water. The hose jerked and writhed in Evelyn's hands and water gushed out, only to recede to an impotent trickle. "On the road to Mandaa—laaaaaayyyyyy ..." George was singing; then he segued lustily into "Give me ten men, who are stout-hearted men ..." "Celia! Go tell your father to turn off the water!"

"I wanta watch!"

"We don't have any water pressure as long as he's showering,"

Evelyn screamed. "Run! Holler in the window from the back steps, so's he'll hear you—hurry, before the house catches." She pointed out the scorch marks beginning to appear on the back steps, the rising blisters of paint on the house siding. Celia sprinted up the outside back steps two at a time.

Inside the house, Sallie had located her keys in the medicine cabinet. However, a quick search of the canned goods pantry failed to yield the fire extinguisher, and Sallie neatly relocked the door. With Cynthia's help, she methodically searched through the china closet, then the jam and jelly pantry. Celia came through the hall with George. He was soaking wet, wrapped in a beach towel, his bare feet thrust into his good shoes, and he was trailing soapsuds over the hall rug. "I found it!" Sallie told him, but he was gone. Plucking the fire extinguisher from a pile of pickle jars, Sallie stood up, rubbing her sore knees. The extinguisher was a cardboard cylinder eight inches long and three inches in diameter. Heedless of the fact that the contents had long since corroded the cardboard into a soggy, useless glob, Sallie grasped the cylinder in her hand and hurried to the back porch. She stopped at the top of the steps, looking around the yard. Aided by neighbors, Johnson and the young Marines had completely emptied the shed, and its contents were strewn across the yard. Arms folded, the group stood silent and motionless, awed by the searing flames. The steady sea breeze had died down. With an angry roar, the shed roof collapsed, and fire engulfed the wooden siding and the chicken coop, leaping two stories high, straight up into the still air.

Johnson smiled up at her. "You're lucky the wind stopped, Miss Sallie."

"Yes. Thank the good Lord." Sallie looked up at the towering flames and back to the miniscule cardboard cylinder in her hand. "Well." She smacked her lips decisively. "I'll just save this until next time." Wheeling around, she trotted back inside the house to wrap the extinguisher in its frayed tissue paper and lock it away in the pantry.

George had turned the garden hose on the big house, playing

the thin stream of water across the back steps and rear wall to keep the heat of the burning shed from igniting the hot wood. Water cascaded down the siding, raising wavering clouds of steam.

Over the crackling flames, Evelyn heard the chugging wail of the fire engine. Pulling her robe around her legs, she picked her way past the broken rocker and a doll's bed and pushed through the crowd of people to wave the engine on. She reached the front walkway in time to see the fire engine coast to a stop for the red light at the corner, although the streets were deserted. Howard Magnum sat behind the wheel. He was wearing pink-toned pajama bottoms, and his Fire Chief's helmet made a semicircular shadow on his bare chest. "Howard!" Evelyn shouted, waving frantically. "Hurry!"

He waved back and clanged the truck bell reassuringly. The light changed and the truck moved forward, stalled and moved again, rounded the corner and roared off in the opposite direction. "Picking up the others!" Howard shouted back to her, and disappeared toward the Bay Shores section of town, where most of the Volunteers lived.

Evelyn stamped her foot, howling with rage, but she masked her frustration when she caught sight of Ethel running heavily along the empty sidewalk. Ethel was gasping for breath, her shoulders heaving with effort, and tears streamed along her face. "Do, Jesus! Don't let them burn up, please, Jesus!"

Evelyn ran to meet her, throwing her arms around her. "Shhhhh. Ethel, it's all right. It's not the house—just the shed."

"You sure? You sure nobody's hurt?"

"Nobody. You catch your breath, then come see for yourself."

Ethel ran past her to the back yard, where she counted and recounted the family members. Satisfied at last, she sank down on the wet back steps and rocked back and forth, keening her dismay to the Good Spirits.

"Now, now, Ethel." Sallie patted her shoulder. "You know how I've been saying for years I wanted to rebuild that old shed thing."

171

The flames had died down to bonfire proportions when the fire truck finally returned with its siren wailing and its bell clanging wildly. Four Volunteers clung precariously to the back, hanging on to the long chrome bar under the ladder and shouting encouragement. Alan was standing on the right running board, held in place by Len Finch's firm grasp on the belt of his pants. Alan had been repairing Harlan's boat engine. His hands were too slippery with oil to risk the back rod, and he was taking advantage of his forward position to shout unnecessary directions. The alarm had caught Gus the Greek in his garage gymnasium, and despite the heat, he wore a fleece-lined gym suit and tennis shoes. Harlan was in his swimming trunks, while Dr. Phelps sported garish madras shorts and knee socks. The truck careened around the corner, bounced up onto the sidewalk, and cut straight across the front lawn. Evelyn eyed the deep ruts from the tire tracks, muttering under her breath.

Sallie shrugged. "They're just trying to help."

"Be calm!" Howard Magnum was shouting to the quiet group of spectators. "Everybody be calm! Stand back! We'll get it under control!"

Gus the Greek and Len Finch attached the fire hose to the corner hydrant, yelling to each other and to Howard. Alan yelled back, unwinding the hose. Harlan and Dr. Phelps ran with the nozzle to the edge of the smoldering shed. They braced themselves for the water's rush, shouting to Gus the Greek and Len Finch, "Let 'er go!—let 'er go!" A heavy rush of water belched through the hose and blasted the dying fire. Water bounced and gushed. Hissing steam swirled up from red-hot embers.

Dancing up and down, Howard Magnum waved his fire chief's helmet. "That's it! That's it! Now we've got it!" In his excitement, he planted his heavy bulk squarely on the fire hose. The nozzle went limp in Harlan's arms as the stream of water diminished, cut off by Howard's heavy weight on the old and badly weakened hosing. "Turn 'er up!" Dr. Phelps yelled. "Give us more pressure!" Blocked by Howard's weight, the new surge of water backed up in the antiquated hose. A weak spot swelled to football size and the hose exploded, sending the broken end dancing across the lawn. Howard screamed at the rush of cold water pounding on his bare back. The force of it knocked him headlong into a thick tangle of blackberry vines. Chickens cackled and ran wildly back and forth across the lawn as water sprayed across them and across the crowd of onlookers. Alan and Harlan leaped for the writhing hose end, their screams of confusion obscuring Gus and Len's call for help. Johnson saw that they had jammed the fire hydrant wide open, and he went to their assistance, throwing his wiry frame against the wrench with theirs.

The gush of water slowed and stopped.

Someone turned off the garden hose and there was silence, broken by occasional cluckings from the chickens and the heavy breathing of the panting Volunteers.

The three trunks the Marines had safely hauled from the shed were drenched, and the side flower bed was six inches deep in water. Alan looked at the ruptured hose dripping across his hands. "Sorry—about all this water."

"Oh, well," Sallie said resignedly. "That pansy bed needed a good soaking."

Alan dropped the hose, and it landed in the puddle with a heavy squish. "Anyhow, we sure did get that fire out."

Johnson gave a contemptuous sniff. "Damn shame you didn't get here any later. You'd have had it out sooner."

There was a shout of laughter, and the crowd surged around the Volunteers with good-natured remarks about their assorted outfits. Johnson pushed his way over to George, who was tightening the beach towel around his bare midriff. A gift to Celia, the towel was lace-fringed and hand-embroidered with a border of garden flowers. George's face and hands were darkly tanned, but his stocky chest and bare legs were sickly white. Evelyn stood at his side in her delicate kimona and the oversized gardening boots. Johnson eyed the two of them. "You both look darling," he said. "Absolutely darling."

"You're a fine one to talk," George grinned back. Johnson's suit was glued to his lanky frame by sweat and water, and his bare skull was covered with soot smears. "You look pretty darling yourself."

The Volunteers finished packing their gear, and the crowd began to drift away. The yard emptied quickly.

Johnson lit a cigarette and leaned against the banister. "Damn thing's still hot."

"George nodded. "Thought for a bit there we'd lost the house."

"Me, too. Hope you got some good shots."

"What?"

Johnson flipped the burnt match to the ground, grinding it into the wet sand. "George, you don't mean to tell me you didn't take any pictures?"

"Oh, my god. I-I didn't think—" He brushed a soapy strand of hair from his forehead as he caught the twinkle in Johnson's eyes. "You crazy bastard—you really had me going."

Sallie, Annie, and Evelyn began unpacking the waterlogged trunks. With Celia at her heels, Ethel had already filled the clotheslines with winter dresses and sweaters. Seizing another load of wet garments in her strong arms, Ethel picked her way around the back of the smoldering shed site to drape the clothing over the wire fence. She started back to the trunk but stopped and sniffed, her sharp nose detecting a familiar scent. "Jus' a minute, child."

"What is it?"

"Don't know for sure." Ethel made her way cautiously along the two-foot clearance between the fence and the hot embers to the point where the shed had joined the chicken coop. Stooping down, she seized a charred stick and poked at the ruins. With a wild shriek, Ethel rose and stumbled back, her hands across her eyes. "No, Jesus! No, no Jesus! Please . . . no . . ."

"Ethel?" Celia reached for her, only to be thrust away.

"Ethel?" "What's the matter?" George and Johnson ran to

174

Ethel, and the three women stopped unpacking clothes, frozen in watchful attitudes.

Ethel was mumbling unintelligibly, pointing to the ground. Johnson took the stick from her and stirred back the ashes from the spot she indicated. He caught his breath sharply. "George. Look here."

George knelt beside him. There was a broken whiskey bottle that reeked of kerosene. It lay beside burned remnants of a heavy wadded ball of cotton waste and a two-foot pile of newspapers. The papers were badly charred around the edges, but they had been stacked against the outside of the shed, and the unseen brick foundation had trickled water in a puddle that prevented them from being completely destroyed. "I'll be damned," George said, remembering the stealthy movement he had observed at the shed earlier that afternoon. "If one of you kids was playing back here with matches, I'll—"

"Unh-unh." Johnson stopped George. "Look at the paper's banner."

Ethel sobbed as George bent closer. "*Flaming Crosses,*" he read. George stood up. "What the hell is that?"

"KKK. Official publication in this area."

"What's a KKK?" Celia asked. No one heard her.

Johnson looked from George to the three women at the trunk. "Seems to me someone set your fire on purpose. But why?" Johnson snapped the stick in two and flung the ends into the shed embers. "Get dressed, George. We've got work to do. Meet you at the office in half an hour."

"Where we going?" Celia asked.

"You're not going!" "No!" "Certainly not . . ." ". . . no . . ." "No, indeed." "You're staying home." It was a simultaneous chorus from everyone there.

"Why? Why can't I go?"

Ethel pointed at her. " 'Cause the Evil Spirits done marked you and this family . . ."

"But—but what's happening? Why is everybody so excited

about a bunch of old papers?" Celia looked around in bewilderment, tears in her eyes. "And why did Ethel say that? All I did was ask what a KKK is."

Evelyn rose. "Come on. I'll explain it to you upstairs."

Relieved that for once no one had said "later," Celia obediently followed her mother into the house, wondering why she moved so slowly, so sadly. At the top of the steps, Evelyn rested against the banister and Celia twisted impatiently. She must really be getting old, too. Couldn't even make the steps any more.

Evelyn was sifting through her thoughts, searching for words to tell Celia the truth without terrifying her. Celia tugged at her robe hem. "Let's go, Mother. I want to know about KKK."

"All right." Evelyn walked slowly toward their living room. Innocence, she reflected bitterly. It always seemed to get lost in the goddamndest ways.

11

WHEN EVELYN LEFT the living room, Celia sat in stunned silence, staring at nothing, twisting her fingers in Bertram-Down-Girl's soft fur. All her limited experience rejected the brief facts Evelyn had outlined to her. "Bullies," her mother had called those Klan people. But running around in costumes, that was kid stuff, not the way grown-ups acted. She didn't believe it, she told herself. However, back down in the yard, Celia met her father and Johnson returning from the news office with grave, troubled expressions. She edged into the shade of the cedar tree, chewing a fingernail and staring at the now ominous ruins of the fire.

"Don't touch anything around the shed," Johnson cautioned Celia unnecessarily. Even though she kept insisting to herself that she didn't believe any of it, at the moment she could almost see Ethel's Evil Spirits in rancid smoke spirals curling up from blackened timbers.

Ethel stayed in the kitchen, too terrified even to glance in the general direction of the smoldering shed. She refused Sallie's suggestion that she go home, and took refuge in cooking a hot supper for the family "to put some heart back in our bodies." Pots rattled wildly in her shaking hands, and her muttered prayer soliloquy to her Good Spirits filled the back yard, obscuring Johnson's quiet remarks to George. "—but first of all, I'll go get Harlan around here," he concluded.

"You're welcome to use the phone."

"And let Miss Effie get wind of it?"

George nodded acknowledgment of Johnson's wisdom and began setting up his tripod. Celia moved mechanically to help him, too numbed to feel his appreciative hug. George was taking some close-ups of the charred stack of *Flaming Crosses* when Johnson came back with Harlan. They walked swiftly along the driveway, their feet stirring up swirling puffs of white sand. Harlan had again put on his uniform, marking his appearance as an official visit. His hat sat squarely over his eyebrows, and his hair was oiled flat to his head. Celia fought back the intense nausea that Harlan's odor always seemed to cause her. He nodded to Annie and Evelyn, who were hanging out the last wet clothing, and knelt by the ruins, his swarthy cheeks streaking red when he saw the broken bottle, the kerosene-soaked cotton batting, and the stack of newspapers.

"Well?" Johnson watched impatiently, yanking out a handkerchief and dabbing at soot on his face and hands. "It was set, wasn't it?"

Harlan stood up quickly. "Hold on, Johnson. Don't go flying off the handle for the sake of a good headline."

"What the hell, Harlan!" Johnson touched his toe to the whiskey bottle and the blackened rags. "What else could it be?"

"Don't know yet. But I'm not jumping to any conclusions."

"Somebody dragged these papers in, and—"

Harlan held up one pudgy hand to check him. "Those papers could have been stored out here."

"Oh, sure." Johnson smiled his contempt. "Miss Sallie's a charter member of the KKK."

Harlan turned his back on Johnson. "Where is Miss Sallie?"

"Inside," George said. "Resting, I hope."

Pulling a notebook and pencil from his pocket, Harlan went into the house, gesturing to them to follow. "You ladies, too, if you don't mind," he called to Annie and Evelyn. "And Celia, of course."

"No!" Sallie snapped to Harlan's insistent questioning. "I did not store newspapers, or rags, or kerosene out there. And cer-

178

tainly not in whiskey bottles. You know perfectly well I do not drink." Her body ached from her labor with the trunks, and the aftermath of tension had begun to sweep over her in waves of exhaustion.

"Now, Miss Sallie, don't get excited."

"Don't you 'Now-Miss-Sallie' me, Harlan. I may have gray hair, but I'm nobody's fool. I knew about spontaneous combustion long before you were ever born. Hot as that shed gets in warm weather, only a jackass would store rags and kerosene anywhere near it."

Harlan took a deep breath. "Annie, how about you? Did you have any newspapers out there?"

Annie's fat chin quivered with indignation and she shook her head, sending her tight curls bouncing. "Why, Harlan, don't be stupid. That is not my shed. I don't even have a key."

"But this stuff wasn't in the shed. It was behind it. Now, you could have thrown some papers out back of the shed from your side of the fence, couldn't you?"

"I could have. But I didn't. I happen to be a very neat house-keeper." Having been a regular in her home for years, Harlan knew better, but he did not pursue the point, and Annie folded her plump hands into her lap and sat back in her chair.

"What about Agnes?"

Annie laughed. "She never keeps a paper five minutes after it's read. And she wouldn't know what *Flaming Crosses* was if all of us explained it."

"Where is she, by the way?"

"Migraine," Evelyn said. "You know how any excitement up-sets her."

"And Fred?"

"Funeral," Sallie snapped. "You know that well as me. It's your men directing traffic."

"Oh, yeah." Harlan chewed his pencil again. Celia was slouched against the piano, listening intently. But she straight-ened up hastily when Harlan's attention turned to her. His face took on the same prurient grin he'd had when he arrested

Martha and her mother, and Celia trembled uneasily. "Now you're old enough to play behind that shed with a boyfriend. Were you smoking back there while you were—let's say playing around? Playing 'doctor,' maybe?"

Celia's mouth twisted, unsure as to how she should answer.

"Oh, for Christ sake, Harlan!"

George's anger silenced him, and he mouthed the end of his pencil again, apparently lost in thought. Johnson was striding around the room, and George and Evelyn shifted restlessly on the couch. It had been well over an hour since Harlan began his questioning. Evelyn was beginning to feel hungry and was getting a bad headache. George toyed with his Leica, wondering at the aimless drift of Harlan's inquiries. He was startled to hear Johnson voice his thoughts. "What the devil are you trying to prove, Harlan?"

"Shut up, Johnson, and let me finish." Harlan shifted his cap and notebook from one stocky knee to the other. "Annie, have you ever seen one of those *Flaming Crosses* before?"

"Oh, yes. Many times." Her casual smile turned to confused stuttering under their startled reactions. "I—I mean—I think that's what they were called—those—those papers."

Johnson stopped pacing, irritated by Harlan's smile. "Where did you see them?"

"Why, Alan brings them home every now and then."

Harlan snapped his notebook shut. "See? It doesn't necessarily mean some outsider brought those papers into the yard. Let's go talk to Alan."

Celia started to follow them, then hesitated, looking to her mother. She was relieved to see Evelyn slumped against the couch arm, her head buried in her hands. Celia tiptoed out, running across the lawn and instinctively staying hidden behind the shrubbery.

The three men left the house through the back, taking the short cut to Alan's house. They found him on the front lawn, stretched at ease in a string hammock slung between two young live oaks. There was an empty beer can in the grass beneath him. Hands folded behind his head, Alan swayed slightly in the shade, enjoying the sweeping view of sound and marsh. He hooted at the sight of Johnson, still dirty and disheveled. "Hell's pecker, Johnson! Water turned off at your house?" Johnson silenced him, blurting a swift account of Ethel's discovery. Alan got out of the hammock. The smile vanished from his round face as Harlan questioned him about possessing copies of *Flaming Crosses*. "Well . . . well, yes. I've brought them home every now and again. So what?"

"Where do you get them?" Johnson asked.

"Why—I-I find them. Just find them, lying around . . . Lately, I-I've been running across them all over town. Picked up a couple somebody left down in the store. And—uh—one, folded up on Buzzard's Roost. And fished one out of a trash can . . ." Alan was stopped by their silent accusation. He glanced from George to Johnson, the muscles of his cheek beginning to twitch. "So what the hell's the matter with that? I was curious to see what they said, that's all."

Johnson shrugged and crouched down to tear nervously at the tufted grass. George leaned against one of the live oaks and stared out at the Sound. Alan scooped up the beer can, crushed it between his palms, and flung it hard, watching it soar over the seawall and drop into black mud with a soft plop. He chuckled at their obvious disapproval. "Lemme tell you something, George. I don't owe you, or Johnson, or anybody else any explanations. I'll read any goddamn paper I want to, anytime I want to. And I'll think any goddamn way I please. And I'll tell you something else—some of those articles made more sense than you and your fancy foreign ideas. You think you can come into town and change things around to suit yourself—but you can't. You're nothing but an outlander, and you always will be an outlander, and don't you forget it. So you just put that in your imported pipe and smoke it. Now excuse me. I need some fresh air." Alan swung on his heel and strode across the lawn to the dock, disappearing into his boat. The engine caught with a roar, and he gunned the cabin cruiser through the channel and out to the Sound.

Celia's stomach knotted, and she covered her eyes in embarrassment. Dear God, she thought, why couldn't you let me have something dignified—like a migraine headache—when I get upset? Why did you have to give me a nervous stomach? Lost in self-pity, she longed to run somewhere. Hide. But the men's voices had dropped down to confidential tones and curiosity drew her closer. "Please, God," she whispered, "at least don't let me throw up." She crawled on her hands and knees to a stand of Spanish bayonet and crouched down within easy hearing.

". . . yes, I know, I know." Harlan coughed. "Alan's got a mean temper, George, but he don't mean half of what he says when he's mad." There was no reaction and Harlan coughed again, clearing his throat uneasily. "But you do see why I said go slow, Johnson? Miss Sallie's at the forgetful stage. She could have overlooked the rags and kerosene. And—and those papers —they could have come from here." He rolled his eyes from one to the other, searching for agreement and finding none. "Why —uh—why, the kids could have saved them. Out of curiosity. You know how kids are, they save any old thing." Harlan hitched up his trousers with a nervous yank. "Of course, I am going to conduct a full investigation, in case it was arson. But I—I hope you're not planning to run a story on this."

Johnson quit worrying the grass and frowned up at him. "I sure as hell am. Front page."

Harlan's fingers worked at his collar, loosening his tie. His tone was assured and confidential, but perspiration poured from his face. "See, Johnson, it's been my experience that this Klan business gets inflamed by publicity. It—it's best to ignore it." Johnson stood up and Harlan continued hastily. "It's been five years since we've had any problem in this county. Five years! I know it's been cropping up in other places all over the state, but it's nothing serious. You just leave it alone and it'll die out of its own accord, like a bad cold."

"Like the plague, you mean." Johnson dusted grass from his damp trousers with quick, angry thrusts.

Harlan spread his hands in a deprecating plea. "I've offered you the best advice I know how to give. If you don't choose to listen ... well ..." His voice trailed off helplessly. "I'm going to the office. Unless you need me around for anything." They remained silent, and Harlan walked slowly away around the big white frame house. George and Johnson were motionless, watching until he was out of sight.

"Lily-livered bastard son-of-a-bitch," George mouthed furiously.

"No. Harlan's a good man, George. I've know him all my life. As Sheriff, he has to consider every angle."

"Maybe." George lifted his head to look at the tangle of live oak limbs and Spanish moss making a canopy above them. As dense and matted and tangled as their own lives, he thought. He said aloud, "Harlan spends so damn much time considering, he never gets anything done."

"If he said he'd investigate, believe me, he will. And it'll be thorough. He's slow—not too bright. But he is thorough."

"Like he was with poor Old Donald?"

"Come on, George. You know goddamn good and well Donald was out of Harlan's jurisdiction. This isn't."

"Maybe."

"Well, Harlan or no Harlan, I am going to do a story. You game to let me use the shots you made?"

"Hell yes!" George said without hesitation, and Johnson smiled again. They turned and almost fell over Celia in the shadow. "Celia!" George collared her, ready to shake her, or spank her. "What in God's name are you doing?"

"Listening." Her face was sweaty and defiant, but he saw that she was weeping silently and relaxed his hold.

"What is it, honey?"

"You—you just stood there with Uncle Alan calling you an outlander and saying those awful things, and you—you didn't say anything back—you just stood there ..."

He looked down at her, disgust clearly showing in his face. "He's got a right to his opinion, Celia."

She had expected him to say something that would explain everything about the whole stupid day. Instead, he simply walked away with Johnson, leaving her in the shadowed shrubbery and in the shadowed confusion of her own thoughts. "Old fool!" She sobbed through clenched teeth.

Johnson ran the story on page one, under a headline reading "Mysterious Circumstances Surround Local Fire." It was a factual account of the fire and Ethel's discovery of the newspapers. But the editorial page was devoted to a history of the Klan's activities in the state. Scathingly, Johnson called attention to the recent outbreak of cross burnings and suggested legal action to end the Klan's activities.

Once again, Sallie and Evelyn were kept busy answering a flood of phone calls from friends and total strangers, offering sympathy and advice.

But to Johnson's disappointment, he received the merest trickle of correspondence in response to his editorial, five letters in all. Saturday afternoon he went back to his office and read them once again. The first one, unsigned, called him a "rabble-rousing son-of-a-bitch." Edward Jones, a self-appointed Baptist minister, informed him that the Klan represented the "fiery hand of God" and included forty-two Biblical quotes to prove it. Fire Chief Howard Magnum wrote a brief note insinuating Johnson was crazy. The Mayor responded with an official letter castigating Johnson for maligning the township with his "preposterous assumption" that there was any Klan activity whatsoever in the community. The one letter Johnson treasured was a second unsigned note written in pencil on a lined sheet of cheap paper: "God bless you for what you are trying to do." Johnson read the words over and over, sitting at his desk and toying with his silver letter opener. He was interrupted by the phone and grimaced when he recognized Miss Effie's voice. "Morning, Miss—"

"Morning. Excuse me for interrupting you, Johnson, but I have a long distance call waiting, so I have to come right to the point. You know how impatient people are when they're waiting for a call to go through."

"Yes, indeed."

"Why, you wouldn't believe some of the stories I could tell you. Do you know I've actually had a grown man to swear at me?"

"No!" Johnson said in mock sympathy, thinking, it was probably me.

"Well he did. And just because I accidentally disconnected him. My! He was surely mad."

"I can imagine!" Johnson heartily agreed.

"Now. What number was it you wanted, Johnson?"

"Uh . . ." Johnson's slender fingers automatically reached for his blank note pad. He chuckled. "Miss Effie—this time, I think it was you that called me."

"I did?" She was silent a moment. "Oh, yes! Now I recall what it was. That construction foreman out at the bridge—uh— what's his name . . ."

"Albert Thatcher?"

"Yes—that's the one . . . Mercy! . . . There's another rude man for you! . . . Well, anyway, he just called their main office in Columbia to say they were ready to start pouring cement for the bridge. And didn't you say you wanted to do a story about it?"

"I sure did! Thanks, Miss Effie." Johnson jumped to his feet, sending his desk chair rolling into the wall with a crash. "Would you please call—"

"I've got the Major holding on another line." She completed the connection with an efficient snap that left Johnson's ear ringing. He shifted the receiver to his other ear. "George?"

"Yes, Johnson."

"Sorry, I didn't know you were holding. You busy?"

"No. I was getting ready to take Celia fishing. Why?"

He quickly agreed to go with Johnson to the bridge site. Certain he would, Johnson had reached for his looped necktie from the coatrack and dropped it around his head as they were talking. Grabbing his jacket, he hurried to his car and drove swiftly to Sallie's house.

The family was sitting on the downstairs front porch, and Johnson joined them, settling himself against the banister rail to sip a glass of iced tea Evelyn handed him. George sat in the end rocker with the camera balanced precariously on his knees while he dusted the lens and film rollers. At the far end of the porch, Celia was rocking furiously in a petulant pout, not only because her fishing trip was postponed, but because her father refused to allow her to go on the bridge trip. She rocked harder. The wooden rockers made a thundering rumble on the floor, drowning out something Sallie was saying to Johnson. From the expression on her face, it was obviously something she was uneasy about. "Ma'am?" he asked quickly.

Celia's chair worked its way around in a semicircle, and the rockers began to bite horizontally across the grain of the flooring. The rumble became a sharp clattering.

"Stop that!" George almost dropped the camera in his irritation.

There was momentary silence. Sallie was squinting as she sewed the black fur cuffs back in place on Ethel's red coat. "Ma'am?" Johnson repeated.

She took several nervous stitches, bit off the short thread, and searched through the folds of the coat for a spool of thread. "Harlan was by," she said at last.

"Oh?" Johnson's voice was casual; his eyes were not.

"First thing this morning. He says a lot of people are very upset about your stories in the paper. And—" Sallie looked to George, who nodded quiet encouragement. "Harlan wants me to say the trash man dropped those papers and things. By accident."

"Accident? Twelve feet from the garbage can, in a two-foot space between the fence and the shed?" Johnson rattled the ice in his glass.

186

"Harlan says it'll save giving the town a bad name. And he wants me to write a letter for you to publish."

"Are you going to?"

"Certainly not! Tell the truth and shame the devil, I always say." Sallie's blue eyes glistened, and she made angry little jabs with the end of the thread, trying to locate the eye of the needle.

"Johnson." Evelyn looked up from the storage bag she had made for Ethel's coat. "Why would Harlan ask Mother to tell a lie?"

"I don't know. Unless he's keeping an eye on somebody and wants to throw them off the track. It could be something that simple."

George blew a final speck of dust from the camera. "I think Harlan's afraid that if that damned Klan business is starting up again, he can't handle it."

"Nobody can, except public opinion," Johnson said glumly. "And the public doesn't give a good goddam . . . excuse me, Miss Sallie . . . but they will before I'm through. The Klan has begun an all-out campaign for new members, and—"

"That can't be possible!" Sallie cried out in sharp protest. "I don't believe it. Not in this day and time."

"I'm afraid it's true."

"How do you know?"

Johnson thrust himself away from the banister and began his quick nervous pacing up and down the porch. "Something Alan said got me to thinking. Remember, George, when he told us 'lately' he'd been finding copies of *Flaming Crosses* all over town?" George nodded. "When I got back to the office, I started checking our clipping files. We get them from all over the state, Miss Sallie, and in the past half year, Klan incidents have almost doubled. Cross burnings, smashed windows, membership rallies, and so on."

Sallie finished one cuff and thrust the needle into the blouse of her dress. "But who would do things like that?"

187

"Wish I knew. If I could publish some names, some specifics, it'd help."

"Certainly no one we know," Sallie continued. "I don't think any normal person would care to associate with that sort of behavior, do you?"

"Hard to say." Johnson leaned on the banister again, reluctant to argue with her.

She sensed his disagreement and cocked her head up at him, her eyes bright and piercing. "There's not a single soul in this town who'd get mixed up in a vicious business like that. Not one. Or do you know of any?"

"No. No, I don't. Not by themselves, one by one."

"Well, then." Sallie felt she had made her point and relaxed again, sinking against the back of the rocker.

George lit his pipe, puffing as if he would finish it in the first instant, studying Sallie's soft gray hair and the sweet smile playing on her lips. Such innocence. And where the hell did she think that stack of *Flaming Crosses* came from? She could ignore that hard fact, just as she overlooked any unpleasantness that came into her life. Yes. He had seen her laying aside newspaper accounts of war atrocities, murders, riots, rape. She would throw the paper away—throw ugliness out of her life—and continue to sit rocking on the front porch, maintaining her belief in the essential goodness of man. He was relieved to finish loading the camera and snapped the back of the case shut. "I don't know when we'll be back Evelyn, so don't wait supper for me."

"All right."

"So long, honey," he said to Celia. "Tomorrow we'll skip church and go fishing."

"Maybe." She refused to look up.

George resisted a strong temptation to thwack her on the top of her head. Impatient to be away from the pervasive smell of talcum powder and the rattle of ice in tea glasses, he hurried after Johnson to the car.

Evelyn walked to the banister, watching them drive away.

188

"I wonder if Johnson is right about the Klan starting up again. I swear, it scares me."

"I don't think we have to worry. Not here. But it makes you feel so sad to think any human being anywhere could go around burning crosses, scaring people half to death."

"Hunh." Celia twisted sideways in her chair. "Who cares?"

"Celia!" Evelyn turned on her, genuinely shocked.

"Well, I mean . . . I think it's dumb, all this excitement over our fire because of a stack of old papers. And if anyone's stupid enough to get scared over some little cross burning in the yard, then—then . . . well, you know . . . who cares?"

"Celia, you are the most selfish, self-centered little monster I have ever—"

"Let's take Ethel her coat," Sallie said loudly. "She's been worried to death I was going to ruin it."

Evelyn was silenced, helping her button the coat on a hanger and slip it into the storage bag.

"Say!" Sallie clapped her hands, in the instant seeming younger than Celia. "After we drop off the coat, let's ride over to the ocean for a picnic!"

Celia was on her feet, all smiles again. "Could we? I'll pack the stuff."

"All right." Evelyn watched Celia stampede into the house, slamming clumsily against the doorjamb in her excitement. "I swear—she's impossible."

"Gently with her, Evelyn. Gently. This is the worst year in a young girl's life—neither fish nor fowl. Not out the door, but not in it either."

Evelyn patted her hand, and arm in arm they went to help Celia pack what Sallie called "the makings." Celia collected Bertram-Down-Girl, and they climbed into the car, driving slowly along the street past the schoolhouse. "Blahhhhhh!" Celia made her customary face at the pink portico and, as always, Sallie threw back her head with appreciative laughter.

Evelyn swung the car left onto Pine Street, a narrow unpaved roadbed of smooth white sand. It was a street that amused

George, being a checkerboard of Negro and white homes and businesses. "Can't sit by a Negro in the movies, but it's O.K. to live by one," George invariably remarked, and Sallie would as invariably reply, "Now, George, you know perfectly well—that's different." They passed the bakery, a brick dentist's office, Len Finch's stucco house, and slowed in front of Ethel's home. It was a neatly whitewashed cottage with dormer windows upstairs. The open front porch was bordered by profusely blooming flowers. A six-foot gardenia bush stood at one end of the house, and a thick red camellia at the other. Ethel was on her knees by the gardenia, digging chicken manure into the sandy soil. Her face glistened silky black with sweat, but she was crooning a happy spiritual that ended in a surprised shout when she saw the car. Evelyn slammed on the brakes, narrowly avoiding two squawking chickens that darted across the road and into Ethel's garden. "Shoo!" Ethel flapped them away from the porch with a flick of her skirt. "Don't know which smells the worst—the chickens, the gardenias, or the manure. But it surely—" She stopped, clasping her hands in delight. "Do, Jesus! You done brung me my coat."

"I want you to try it on." Sallie held out the hanger to her, and Ethel's brow furrowed anxiously. "Can you come in, jus' one minute, so's I can rinch off my hands? I wouldn't want to touch it with my hands so dirty."

"Of course."

Ethel ran up the two shallow steps to the porch, holding the screen door wide.

Celia jumped out of the car. "I'll carry it for you, Grand-mother."

"Why, thank you." She handed Celia the coat, hiding her knowing smile that Celia was using this as an excuse to see the inside of Ethel's house.

"You shouldn't have gone out of your way like this, Miss Sallie. I'd have come back for it. It's just terrible, taking up all your afternoon." Ethel kept up a running chatter of happy protests as she darted into the small kitchen at the back of the house.

Celia shifted the coat from one arm to the other, looking curiously around the spotless living room. Dotted swiss curtains hung at the windows, billowing with wind and sunshine. Ethel's ten-year-old gray cat lay dozing on one windowsill, his forepaws tucked together beneath his chest. Celia scratched his ear, pleased to hear his purring. She was standing on a rug, hand-braided in shades of green, that covered most of the floor. A deeper green couch filled the back wall, facing Ethel's brown easy chair and footstool by the crooked hearth of an open fireplace. "Look, Grandmother—on the end table. What a pretty Bible."

"Yes. Prettiest thing is, she reads it."

Oh, shit, Celia thought. Grown-ups sure could twist the simplest things you said.

Sallie was amused to note that Ethel had painted the walls since her last visit. White. Like Evelyn's. Sallie smiled. Evelyn would be pleased. Ethel hurried in and eased the coat from its bag, sliding it carefully over her muscular arms and shoulders. Once it was buttoned, she relaxed into pleased laughter. "It's better'n new! Better'n brand new." She took off the coat and began folding up the storage bag.

"No, that's for you. Evelyn made it for your coat."

Ethel burst into louder exclamations of pleasure and ran out to the car to thank Evelyn, then thanked Sallie all over again. "Yes, ma'am! Now it'll stay safe from moths. See, I keep my coat in my hall closet right by the front door." Ethel's forefinger jabbed the air, making certain they understood. "Summer and winter. Right by the front door. That way, in case there's ever a fire, I can be sure to grab it while's I's running out the door."

At length they managed to break away, refusing Ethel's offer of tea, Cokes, or coffee. They drove across the bridge and twenty miles to the ocean, following a meandering road that led them across a chain of narrow islands cleared for truck farming. At length, the paving ended and two sandy ruts wound around a deserted lighthouse. A spiral of windows marked the ascent of its steps to the circle of glass ten stories above them. Most of the windowpanes had been shot out. At the top, someone had knocked out the heavier glass encasement with an ax, and inside the jagged remains, hornets had taken up residence in the sheltered cone of the roof. Celia could see hundreds of them swarming around the papier-mache basketball of their hive. She shivered and rolled the car window shut against their imagined onslaught.

The road made an S-curve, a tunnel of green ending unceremoniously at a smooth strand of beach eight miles long. Celia slipped the collar from Bertram-Down-Girl's neck and kicking off her shoes, ran squealing after the dog down to the gentle ocean surf. Sallie and Evelyn sat in the skirt of shade thrown down across the strand by the trees that crowded its edge. Chatting idly, they watched Celia's ceaseless antics in the swirling edge of foam. It was almost sundown when they called her for supper. The evening star had come out, and a new moon floated in a cloudless, ice-blue sky. Celia came running up the strand to fling herself full length beside the dog. She held her arms wide toward the sky, her face a rapture. "Oh! It's such a glory sort of time!"

"What?" Evelyn glanced up from the ham she was slicing, expecting some sort of joke. "What do you mean?"

"Oh, you know. A—a—well, just a glory time, that's all."

Sallie crouched to pick up a minute seashell, her knees protruding clumsily to either side like stiffened frog legs. She rose with the seashell in her palm, its tiny cusp a mother-of-pearl replica of the luminous moon above them. "She means the sort of time you know you're going to remember, even while it's happening. And it's never the big, important days, somehow. It's the quiet ones. But there'll be something about some clouds, or the way the wind sounds, or the way a gull is flying. And you know that's a day you're going to carry in your pocket all your life. Like a perfect seashell." She tucked the shell into her sweater pocket and smiled at Celia. Celia leaned back, resting her head against Bertram-Down-Girl. That was exactly what she meant, she thought with some surprise. And how on earth could her grandmother have known? She lay still, smelling Bertram-Down-Girl's wet fur and feeling the prickle of salt drying on her legs. If only she hadn't seen the hornets' nest. It put a mark on things, somehow.

Although it was only eight-thirty when they got home, Sallie excused herself, yawning. "The ocean does this to me." Stacking the dirty picnic things in the sink, she unbuttoned her dress as she walked through the hall. She was in bed and asleep when George got home a little after nine. The hall lamp was off, signaling him that everyone was already home. George methodically locked the front door and tiptoed up the dark steps.

Evelyn had changed into a nightgown and her pink kimona and was lying on the bed flipping through a woman's magazine. Celia lay on her stomach on the rug beside the bed, reading a comic book, its pages shadowed by the strands of salt-sticky hair tumbling around her face. Engrossed in reading, they didn't see George standing in the doorway. He remained silent, proud of the picture of serenity and comfort they presented in the bright white-and-red room. And, by God, he had done that, all by himself. It was worth all the cold nights and searing days in military service. Evelyn threw aside her magazine to reach for another. Her eyes met his and she smiled, their silent gaze a warm embrace. She had turned a lot grayer in the past year, George saw, sitting on the edge of the bed and leaning over to touch Celia's hair.

"How'd it go?" Evelyn yawned.

"Rough! . . . g'night, honey." He blew Celia a kiss as she stumbled drowsily out the door. "They had some problem about the first batch of cement and had to dump it. Albert Thatcher wouldn't tell Johnson exactly what went wrong. Thatcher seems to think we're trying to get him fired or something." George set the Leica on the bureau, his arms and shoulders stiff with exhaustion. He went on, through a heavy yawn. "But in spite of Thatcher's bitching, I got some good pictures of the work, I think. Then we hung around for pay call, and I shot another roll on that." He shook his head. "They'll be one sad, hungover bunch tomorrow. Thatcher was getting up a party to celebrate starting actual construction."

Evelyn yawned with him. "Oh, well. It's Sunday tomorrow. Just be glad they're way out there where no one can hear them." She fell asleep without seeing George go to the living room with a book. He had a pounding headache, and the muscles in his arm felt cramped and tingling. He read until first light, skipping from a detective story to poetry to a new autobiography. Nothing caught his attention. At five-fifteen, he bolted three heavy shots of Scotch and fell into bed for restless, troubled dozing.

Sunday morning dawned foggy and cold, a momentary relapse into winter, and Sallie slept beyond her usual six-o'clock rising. The household was quiet when her eyes fluttered open at seven-thirty, and she stirred drowsily, stretching a little under the warmth of the covers. Seven-thirty? Ethel would think she was sick. She pulled her warm robe from the closet and hurried through the hall to the kitchen. "Ethel? Good morning." The kitchen was empty and silent. There was no scent of perking coffee, only a rancid odor from dirty picnic dishes stacked in the sink. A fat roach crawled through a smear of mayonnaise on one of the plates. Sallie dispatched it with a fly swatter and went out to the back yard. "Ethel?" The yard, too, was empty, and the chickens cackled their hunger. She threw them some feed and returned to the kitchen to begin making breakfast. "That's funny," Sallie said aloud. "Must be Ethel who's sick."

It was almost nine when Sallie finished cleaning the dirty picnic things and fixing Sunday breakfast for the family. She rang the brass gong, and Celia and Evelyn came stumbling down the steps in their bathrobes. "George is sound asleep." Evelyn gouged sleep from her eyes. "That trip must have worn him out. He—" She saw the apron over Sallie's robe. "Where's Ethel?"

"Sick, I guess. She usually calls first thing, or sends word, but maybe she's sleeping late."

"Wish I was," Celia grumbled, sliding into her seat at the table. "No sense getting up to go fishing when Daddy's still asleep."

"You are not going to wake up your father and that is that," Evelyn said firmly.

When they had finished eating and cleaning the dishes and there had been no word from Ethel, Sallie went to the phone and tried to call her. "No answer," Miss Effie reported after a number of vigorous rings. "Want me to call next door to Len Finch?"

"No, thanks, Miss Effie. We'll drive over and check up on her. She must be feeling pretty bad if she didn't come to the phone, and there may be something she needs we can get for her."

Evelyn insisted that Celia go with them, certain she would find some "accidental" way to awaken George if she stayed at home. There was a fine drizzle of rain when they went out to the car, and Evelyn drove cautiously along the slick pavement. The Methodist Church carillon pealed out across town, and Sallie sang with it in her high-pitched, quavering voice: "He leadeth me, O blessed thought; O word with heavenly comfort frought. Whate'er I do, where'er I be, Still 'tis God's hand that leadeth me . . ."

Pine Street was strangely deserted and silent. Evelyn noticed all the shades were drawn in houses along both sides of the street. Curious, she thought. There was a group of five young Negro men at the far corner. Hands in their pockets, they huddled together in the rain, staring across the street at Ethel's house. Evelyn was watching them as she stopped the car, when a startled outcry from Sallie brought her attention back to the house.

In the middle of the little plot of flower bed, there was a black and smoldering cross.

They sprang from the car. "Where's Ethel?" Evelyn yelled to the young men. One ducked his head toward the house. "Is she all right?" He shrugged.

The three of them ran to the gate. It hung open and awry, torn loose from the top hinge. They stepped inside the yard, staring in shocked disbelief at the smoking cross. Two metal pipes had been soldered together and wrapped with cotton waste wired into place and doused with kerosene. The sooty remains had the same heavy stench as the batting in the scarred embers of Sallie's shed. Ethel's flower bed was tramped into dust; the gardenia bush and the red camellia were axed down to the ground.

Sallie went up the steps to the front door. It stood ajar, and cautiously, she entered the silent house. "Ethel?" The white curtains were slashed, and every pane of window glass was shattered. Furniture was upended into jagged remains of vases and lamps. The couch upholstery was slit to ribbons, spilling padding in an erupting pus of white cotton. In glaring red paint, "Nigger" was spelled out on all the white walls, and the paint had dripped to the floor to be trampled into the green braid rug. In the kitchen, every plate, glass, and cup had been broken, flung against the stove, and the sink was pried loose from the wall. Evelyn looked into the little back yard. "Ethel—where are you?" The metal clothesline had been yanked down. One strand was attached to a small hanging blackened shape. It seemed at first no more than another lump of burned cotton, and Celia stared at it curiously. Another cross? But at the top, white teeth showed through a seared black mouth drawn taut in final agony, and Celia recognized the charred remains of Ethel's old gray cat. The clothesline had been wired to his neck before the animal was doused with kerosene and set aflame, and the sand and the wooden clothes pole showed the scars of its violent struggling. "Mother . . ." Celia gagged.

"I know. I see it." Evelyn shut the door easily, reverentially. The three of them went back through the living room and started upstairs.

The white wall above the staircase was filled with four-foot letters of gummy red paint. "Nigger-Lover's Nigger," the letters read, underlined by a bold, six-foot horizontal swirl that trickled

196

down to the paint can overturned at the foot of the steps in a coagulating puddle of scarlet. Darker red puddles led up the stairway, and Sallie tested one with her finger. She followed the trail up the steps. "Ethel!" she called fearfully. "Ethel, it's Miss Sallie . . . answer me, Ethel . . ." Her voice caught in a sharp cry as she saw four short lengths of steel pipe in the upstairs hallway. They were matted with kinky gray hair and more globs of dark red. Celia stepped beyond Sallie to go past the open bathroom door and let out a shrill, piercing scream.

Ethel lay crumpled in the far corner, trapped between the tub and the pink tile wall. One leg twisted from her body at a grotesque angle; her right arm showed an end of jagged bone. She stirred at the sound of Celia's scream and her left arm came up to ward off another blow. "Do, Jesus . . ." she mumbled inaudibly. "Do Jesus, help me . . . do, Jesus . . ."

"I'll go phone George." Evelyn ran down the steps.

Celia slumped against the door, immobilized by horror.

"Ethel! Oh, my Ethel! What have they done to you? Oh, dear God!" Sallie knelt beside her on the red-spattered tile.

"Miss Sallie?" Ethel lifted her head blindly toward Sallie's voice. Her eyes were swollen shut, matted with blood from gaping scalp wounds. "Miss Sallie . . . is that you?"

"It's me, Ethel." She sat on the floor and gathered Ethel tenderly into her arms, easing Ethel's heavy weight from the cold tiles to the comfort of her own warm, soft body.

". . . Miss Sallie . . ."

"Shhhhh. It's all right now."

Ethel torturously lifted her arm, uncovering a bundle she was sheltering in her lap. "Miss Sallie . . . look what they done to my coat . . ." She held up the ruins of red wool and black fur, knived into shaggy rags. "Why? . . . Why they want to do that, Miss Sallie?" She brought the pieces to her breast, cuddling them softly. "My coat . . . my coat . . . my red coat . . ." Her mouth twisted open with silent tears.

"Shhhhh . . . I'll make you another one . . . Sallie will make you a new one."

197

"... my coat ..."

Sallie took a piece of the silk lining, dampened by Ethel's tears, and began carefully wiping clotted blood from Ethel's face, crooning in a soft soothing tone. "It's all right . . . lie still now ... it's all right ..."

"... coat ... my coat ..."

"Sallie will make you another with a big, brand new fur collar. Maybe even a fur cape. We will drive to Savannah, and we will look and look in all the stores for just the kind of cloth you want. And we—"

"... my coat ..."

"... we will walk all over town until we find some brand new shiny buttons. And you will choose the silk for the lining, and we will buy a whole new bolt of red cloth."

"My coat ... my coat ..."

Sallie shut her eyes and lifted her head. "Why, God? Why?" she whispered, and her tears mingled with Ethel's.

Weeping, Celia stumbled back down the bloody steps in search of her mother.

12

WHEN EVELYN RAN down the steps, she searched the shattered living room for the phone, only to discover that it had been ripped from the wall, and she went slowly out to the porch. Following her, Celia sank down on the top step, turning her face away from the black and smoking thing beside her. The stench permeated her nostrils, searing into her mind the picture of Ethel lying helpless and alone in the blood-spattered, pink-tiled bathroom. She retched, struggling for breath. The drizzle turned into pelting rain, and the cross sizzled ominously.

The silent crowd of Negroes on the corner across the street had grown in size. Several women joined the men, one holding a nursing baby in her arms. They stood numbly, without umbrellas, rain pouring down across watchful faces. There was no one Evelyn knew well enough to ask for help. A curtain fluttered at one of the windows in Len Finch's house, and she turned her head to see a pasty ghost retreat furtively behind the shade. "Come on," she said to Celia. "Watch Ethel's house from Len's porch. If any stranger comes near, yell for me." Celia gladly followed her to the house next door. But even with a handkerchief clamped across her nose, she could not rid her senses of the smell of burned rags and kerosene. Unaccountably, she remembered the hornets swarming around the lighthouse, and nauseous fear shuddered through her.

Long minutes passed, and Len did not answer Evelyn's frantic knocking. "Open the door, Len!" she called, pounding on his door and simultaneously ringing the bell. "I know you're in there—I saw you. Open this door, you hear me!" The heavy oak door finally creaked back to a narrow slot, revealing Len's huddled form. The flesh of his cheeks hung in loose jowls, and his gray eyes were red-rimmed and watery. He clutched a dirty bathrobe over musty pajamas. Evelyn thrust the door wide. "I need your phone quickly. Emergency." When Len made no move to help her, Evelyn stumbled into the living room at her left, a cluttered cavern with heavy dark furniture smelling of mildew and stale cat's urine. Evelyn found the phone on the desk and rang for Miss Effie, her anguished voice silencing any curious questions. "Call Dr. Phelps first. Then ask Johnson to bring George over here. We could use Fred and Alan, too. And hurry!"

Len remained standing in the doorway, his arms hanging limply at his side. "Evelyn—is she—is Ethel all right?" He dropped his head in shame before Evelyn's scathing look, as full comprehension crept across her face. "My god, Len—you mean you heard it all? You did—didn't you? You had to hear it. Why didn't you at least call us? Why?" He made no answer, and Evelyn's hand shot out in a hard, stinging slap across his flaccid mouth. He had not moved when she and Celia ran down the steps and across the yard to Ethel's house.

Dr. Phelps was the first to arrive, his gray eyebrows furrowing when he saw Ethel's beaten, twisted form. He offered his hand to Sallie to help her to her feet, but she refused to leave Ethel alone on the cold floor, and Dr. Phelps knelt beside them to give Ethel a shot of morphine. He shook his head to Sallie's questioning look.

Minutes later, George and Johnson came running into the living room. Fred and Alan followed, having stopped by the store to pick up Thomas. The five men walked through the living room and kitchen, jolted into silence by the physical shambles of hatred. In the back yard, Johnson turned away from the dead cat and began to swear under his breath, a long stream of furious profanity. "I shouldn't have used Ethel's name in that story about the fire. But it never crossed my mind she wasn't safe, living right in the middle of town . . ." He was interrupted by

Dr. Phelps calling them to help move Ethel from the floor. It took all six men to lift her onto a blanket and carry her into the bedroom. Celia ran ahead of them, trying to straighten covers on the bed. The bed had been badly damaged by ax and steel pipe, leaving the headboard and footboard leaning in toward each other, a splintered parody of a bombed cathedral. Evelyn wrenched the mattress free and threw it on the floor, and Celia kicked aside bureau drawers and clothing to clear the way for the men and their half-conscious burden. Ethel's lips drew back in a moan as they laid her flat on the mattress, but she made no outcry. Evelyn took Celia downstairs while Dr. Phelps finished a swift examination, giving Ethel first aid to staunch the bleeding. Rising, he said to Sallie, "I'm going to have to send her to the hospital in Savannah."

"No, no!" Ethel shrieked in protest and struggled wildly to sit up. "No, please, Miss Sallie. I ain' done nothing, please don't send me away, please!" Dr. Phelps hurried to Ethel's side, calling for Thomas to help him hold her down. "No!" she was screaming. "No! Please—don' punish me no more . . ."

Sallie leaned across the edge of the mattress. "It's not punishment, Ethel. It's to take better care of you."

"Please, God, Miss Sallie, don' let him send me away. I ain' done nothing wrong, I swear I ain't . . ." She thrashed wildly on the mattress, fighting their helping hands and screaming incoherently as she felt the morphine overtaking her.

Dr. Phelps was perspiring heavily, holding Ethel's feet and legs. "When in hell is that shot going to put her out?"

"No!" Ethel screamed with a fresh outbreak of sobs. "Miss Sallie . . . please help me . . . please, please God . . . help me . . . Miss Sallie! I ain' done nothing . . . don' let them hurt me no more . . ." Fresh stains of red seeped through the bandages wrapped around Ethel's gray, frizzy hair.

Sallie brushed past Thomas and knelt to take her reaching hand. Ethel hung on to her with the clutch of a drowning child. "I'm right here, Ethel. Shhhhh. Lie still. It's all right, I won't let them send you away."

"Please, please, Miss Sallie . . ."

"I promise you, Ethel."

Ethel's struggling subsided at once. "Hones'?" Her tongue slurred, her eyes began to glaze.

"I promise. And I never broke a promise to you, did I?"

"...no'm..."

"Now you lie quiet."

"Miss Sallie . . ." She licked her lips. "I can't think so good. I feel the Bad Spirits taking hold on me."

"No, they're not. That's something Dr. Phelps gave you to help the pain. It's going to put you to sleep for a little while, but when you wake up, I'll be right with you." Ethel was fighting to keep her eyes open. Sallie smiled down at her. "I promise! Now go to sleep."

Ethel's lips twitched, trying to smile back, and she slid into unconsciousness, clutching Sallie's hand and a remnant of black fur cuff. Thomas and Dr. Phelps moved back from the mattress. "Good thinking." Dr. Phelps took Sallie's arm and lifted her to her feet. "I'll go phone Savannah."

"No." Sallie stopped him in the doorway.

"But, Miss Sallie—"

"I said no. I promised her."

He came back to the foot of the mattress. "I don't think you realize how seriously injured she is, Miss Sallie. I don't know why she's even alive, and I'm not at all sure she'll pull through."

"All the more reason not to upset her by sending her away."

"She's going to need constant care. That leg will have to be in traction, and she won't be able to stay here alone."

"Not here. My house. I'll put her in the guest room."

"Miss Sallie . . ." Thomas began picking up the clothing strewn around the room. "My mama's a good nurse. She could come stay with her during the day. And my sister could come at night."

"Fine." Sallie was deeply touched by the incongruous picture of the dark young man delicately folding Ethel's baggy pink bloomers. I'm getting to be a stupid, senile old woman, she thought, wiping sudden tears from her eyes. "See?" she said to

Dr. Phelps. "We've got our own hospital." She went downstairs to tell Evelyn.

"It's crazy!" Alan exploded when he heard Sallie's plan. "You can't do it! You know how people are in this town. What do you think they'll say?"

"People in this town?" Sallie lifted her head defiantly and gestured around the wrecked living room. Her blue silk dress showed bloodstains where Ethel's head had rested on her breast, and her hand was bruised by Ethel's heavy grasp. It was one of the few times Evelyn recalled seeing Sallie's hair disheveled, and she thought she had never seen her mother look more beautiful. Sallie stood in the midst of the group of men, her slight frame erect and dignified, her voice strong and purposeful. "People in this town, people-in-this-town! Where were they last night? Tell me that, Alan." He would not meet her gaze. "Now excuse me. I promised to be there when Ethel woke up." She stepped across the overturned paint can and pulled herself painfully up the steep flight of steps.

A hush fell across the room. Alan rammed his fists into his rear pockets and pushed the toe of his sneakers at some loose pages ripped from a book and strewn across the rug. "Sallie's taking this thing too personal. You all know I don't mean anything except that Sallie's too old to take on a heavy responsibility like this, and—"

Johnson touched George on the shoulder. "Where's the Leica?"

"In your car."

"Let's start with that burnt cross."

"I'll get your camera, Daddy." Celia darted away, and they followed her slowly.

Alan kept blindly pushing at the ripped pages with his dirty sneaker. "Evelyn, you can't let your own mother do this . . ."

"Excuse me." Evelyn curtly cut him short, rising from the tattered couch. "I'm going home and get the guest room ready."

"Wait for me." Fred shot a nervous glance at Alan. "I—I'll go get the ambulance." He set his hat in place and fled from

Alan's sullen glare, his thin form clattering quickly down the porch steps after Evelyn.

Alan was left in the living room with Thomas, who leaned in the kitchen doorway, waiting. His tall, lithe form was relaxed and casual, as if he were marking time waiting for a bus. But his bare forearms were clenched tightly across his chest, and a heavy knot of dark muscle stood out starkly against his white shirt. Alan ground his toe into one of the loose pages, mechanically reading the print beneath his feet. ". . . at home there is as death. They have heard that I sigh; there is none to comfort me: all mine enemies have heard of my trouble; they are glad that thou hast done it . . ." It was a page from a Bible, Alan realized with a quiver of shocked desecration. He read on, mesmerized. ". . . thou wilt bring the day that thou hast called, and they shall be like unto me." Alan's hairline prickled as the words reached out and commanded his full attention. "Let all their wickedness come before thee; and do unto them as thou hast done unto me for all my transgressions: for my sighs are many, and my heart is faint." The rest was obscured beneath a thick smear of paint. Alan withdrew his feet quickly. In a nervous sweat, he seized the remains of the Bible and threw it at the fireplace with all his strength. It fluttered wildly, like bob-whites in startled flight, and fell to the dirty hearth. Thomas remained immobile, unseeing. Alan rubbed his twitching cheek. "All right, Thomas. They're taking care of Ethel. Let's see what we have to do to clean up this goddamn shack of hers."

Those were the words Thomas had been waiting for. "For one thing, Mr. Alan, the kitchen sink will need some new pipes, and the—"

"Hold on, hold on. Don't rush me, dammit. First off, let's bury that poor old cat."

Out in front of the house, Fred hovered beside George and Johnson, uneasily twirling his hat. "George . . . if there's anything I can do . . . I . . . Darn it. I don't know how to say it. I—I just don't understand how this could have happened. Not here."

"Oh my god, Fred. It's so easy to run with a crowd," George commented grimly.

"I guess," Fred mumbled. "But if you need anybody to . . . to . . . Well, call on me for something. Anything. Money, or time, or—or anything. I . . . Oh, you know what I mean."

"Sure. And I will." George shook his hand. "Thanks, Fred."

Fred clapped his hat in place and strode away with his jerky, bouncing stride. Watching him go, Celia sat motionless on the steps, resting her head against the porch rail. "Run with the crowd," her father had said so often to her. The phrase stuck in her mind. Back from forgetfulness came the recollection of Martha standing on the steps of her house, half naked and alone, while a Deputy nailed shut the door of Martha's home and Celia herself stood gaping from the safety of the crowd across the street. Would it have helped Martha if she had crossed the street and spoken to her, even to say "I'm sorry," or "good-bye"? Maybe not. But she should have tried. Even worse, Celia thought again of that terrible moment when she had left Martha sitting sad and rejected, all by herself in the swing. Celia pressed her fingers tightly to her eyelids, trying to erase the picture.

With Celia carrying the tripod and lens bag, George and Johnson finished photographing the ruins of Ethel's house and sat down on the splintered couch to wait for Harlan's arrival. They talked idly, watching Alan and Thomas taking notes on repairs the house would need. They had worked their way to the stairwell and were staring gloomily at the smear of paint below "Nigger-Lover's Nigger." "Hell," Alan muttered. "Paint will never cover this. Guess we better figure on replastering. Wallpaper, maybe." Thomas nodded, writing rapidly on the back of an envelope.

George glanced at the inscription along the stairwell. Something about the underscored swirl caught his attention. Something . . . something . . . something. Wordlessly, he loaded the Leica with a new roll of film and shouldering his flash equipment, shot the vicious legend, first from one angle and then another. Johnson watched him curiously. "What do you want all those for?"

"Tell you the truth, I don't know."

"They're both getting queer as ticks," Alan commented, and led Thomas up the steps.

Half an hour later, Ethel was safely installed in Sallie's guest room. Without discussion, Sallie and Evelyn busied themselves the rest of the morning with trivial tasks. They made a lengthy list of sickroom supplies. Then they drew up a chart, dividing Ethel's regular cleaning chores between themselves and Celia, trying not to hear the soft unconscious moans from the back room as Dr. Phelps and a nurse worked to set Ethel's arm and leg. Only once did they come close to breaking their politely guarded façade, when Sallie reached into her sweater pocket for a handkerchief and pulled out the seashell she had picked up on the beach the day before. Translucent mother-of-pearl, it had the quality of a forgotten, golden era. "Celia's 'glory day,' " Sallie said bitterly, and broke the shell in two. Their eyes met briefly, and Evelyn quickly picked up her pen. "I forgot to list sweeping the front steps." She bent across the paper, brushing away fresh tears.

It was one o'clock before the Sheriff's car coasted to a stop outside Ethel's house. "About time!" Johnson went to the front door. "Harlan—where the devil have you—" He stopped, seeing a baby-faced blond deputy step out from the driver's seat. He was alone in the car, and he edged uneasily through the broken gate with his gun slapping loosely at his thin buttocks. "Where's Harlan?" Johnson demanded.

"On vacation." The boy's voice was thin as a girl's.

"Vacation?"

"It's all right,' the Deputy continued in his high, reedy twang. "Mr. Harlan appointed me to take over here and make a full investigation." They watched in disbelief as he began poking ineptly at the wreckage of the living room, making endless notations as to what was broken and where; how many vases; how many cups and saucers. "Looks to me like a drunken party," he announced, parrotlike.

"Why, you snotty-nosed little—"

George stepped between Johnson and the Deputy, loosening Johnson's grip on the terrified boy. "It's not the kid's fault. It's Harlan we need to see." Johnson nodded angrily, and George turned to Celia. "Come on, honey."

They drove swiftly to Harlan's brick home in the Bay Shores section of town. Drapes were drawn shut across the picture window, but Gertrude's Cadillac was in the carport with the trunk open. Johnson halted his car at the curbing, and they hurried up the walkway and rang the bell. At first, Gertrude refused to let them in the house. "We're busy packing," she insisted, barring the doorway with her scrawny body. "And we sure don't need any kids messing around." Celia had never seen her before, but despised her at once. She was a sharp-boned woman with pinched features that gave her a wary, angry appearance. George had never encountered her when she wasn't wearing earrings and high heels. Even now, in crisp gold slacks, her feet were thrust into wobbly, backless slippers with high spiked heels, and diamond pendants dangled from the pierced lobes of her ears.

"We'll only take five minutes or so," Johnson said in a deceptively mild tone. "I need his advice about something."

"I told you no!" she shrilled. "We don't have time for—"

"Ah, hell, Gertrude. Let 'em in," Harlan yelled from his study, his voice muffled. "I'll have to see them sooner or later."

"Make up your mind, you damned fool!" Gertrude shouted back. She opened the door wide and disappeared into the kitchen.

"Thank you so very much." Johnson bowed in her direction with ironic gracefulness and led George and Celia through the painfully modernistic house to Harlan's study. Harlan was spotlighted in a flood of amber sunshine. He sat slouched down in a captain's chair, his feet planted on a spindly black table. An open bottle of bourbon stood on the floor beside him, and he was rolling a silver shot glass between his palms. Celia hung back nervously as her father and Johnson walked to the edge of the table and stood there, waiting. Harlan stared out the window, rolling and rolling the shot glass. It made sharp clicking sounds against his wedding ring.

"Harlan?"

"Save your breath, Johnson. I'm quitting."

"What?"

Harlan poured himself another drink, drained it at a single gulp. "Quit. Quitting, quitted. Resigned, as it were."

"Why?"

"Tha's none of your goddamned—" He poured another drink, gulped it down. "I—I've been promising Gertrude a long tour abroad. And you know how Gertrude is. When she wants something, she wants it yesterday, and—" Harlan belched a sour drunken stench. "No . . . that's not fair, blaming her. It's me. I can't—can't handle it. I'm scared. That's all. Out 'n out scared."

Johnson leaned across the table. "By yourself, you'd have a right to be. But you're not by yourself. Help us, Harlan. Work with us so we can get the filth out in the open and clean them out."

Harlan's eyes glazed, distant and drunken. "Always have to be the glory boy, don' you? All them pretty words. Even so—you been a good—fren' to me. But you don' even know what you're running into. They're going to eat you up alive. And you know what? I wouldn't enjoy watching. I don' wanna see any part of it—be any part of it." The shot glass continued clicking against his ring, metallic heartbeats in the sunny room. "Now, get out. Jus' get out. Nobody invited you here—get the hell out of my house . . ." He hid his eyes from the two men. Only Celia could see the heavy tears dropping from behind his hands.

Gertrude was not in sight when they went back through the living room, but the front door slammed shut behind them before they reached the sidewalk. Johnson was pale, and his hands shook, searching through his pockets for the car key.

208

"I'm sorry, Johnson. I know what a friend Harlan's been to you."

Johnson looked back at the neat brick house. "There are friends and friends. Sometimes you know people all your life and don't know them at all. I'm going home for a nap. I'll be up all night trying to decide what to write, and how. Want me to drop you at your house?"

"Thanks, no. I'd rather walk. Frankly, I could use some fresh air."

Celia reached quickly for his hand. Johnson gave a sardonic salute and the two men parted, each one glad for the privacy of his own thoughts. George led Celia across a vacant lot to the Sound. They stood a moment on the seawall, scanning the blue bay and inhaling the fresh smell of marsh grass still wet from the morning's rain. A northbound yacht was cutting the glassy water, sounding its whistle for the drawbridge in long, melancholy hoots.

"Daddy . . ."

"Celia, I can't talk about it. Yet. I honestly don't understand it myself."

To Dr. Phelps's astonishment, Ethel began improving rapidly. "I've never seen anything like it," he said to Sallie after the third day. "Medically, I would have said it's impossible."

Sallie's smile was sad and knowing. "Lots of things in life are."

"Did you find out why she's so scared of the hospital?"

"I doubt if she knows herself. Probably some horror story she heard. And bless her heart, she's a woman who surely does confuse fact with fable."

The simple fact was that lying in the airy, well-known guest room, Ethel felt secure and happy. While Miss Sallie was close at hand, there was small danger of the Bad Spirits creeping in and snatching her away as she slept. And when she was awake, there was the style book of coat patterns Sallie brought her, and a shoe box full of red wool samples. Celia entertained her by the hour, reading new recipes from Sallie's *Boston Cook Book*. Ethel turned all her strength of body and soul toward getting well. No telling when Miss Sallie would need the guest room for company. She needed to be up and around. Anyway, she wanted to try some of the new recipes, and Celia promised to read them for her when she was back in the kitchen.

The household moved quickly into its temporary routine. Each morning Thomas brought his mother to stay with Ethel and took his sister home. They came and left so quietly, Sallie was sometimes startled to find they had exchanged places. And to Evelyn's delight, Celia never once complained about her cleaning chores. Instead, she began quietly helping Sallie with her share of the additional work.

After a hasty conference with George, called in the privacy of his *Bugler* offices, Johnson decided to go ahead with an all-out campaign against the Klan. "Frankly, George, since they've gotten away with one strike right in the middle of town, it bothers me to think of you having Ethel in the house with your family. Especially since we don't have a decent sheriff at the moment. You don't have any protection at all."

George was thoughtful, drumming his fingers on the arm of the easy chair. "I'll have to admit it scares hell out of me. But that's what they count on, isn't it?" Johnson nodded. "Evelyn and I have started keeping pistols by the bed. Loaded. She's a pretty good shot." George smiled and rose to leave. "After all, I taught her."

Again, Johnson's story adhered strictly to the indisputable facts of Ethel's attack. The one exception he made was to take the precaution of deleting Ethel's name from the final draft, referring to her instead as "a resident" of Beldon. He recorded, without comment, the series of events and Harlan's sudden resignation. His editorial castigated his readers for their apathy and called for "responsible citizens" to take action against the Klan. The response was immediate. Hundreds of letters poured in. One reader enclosed a fifty-dollar check to help with the reconstruction of Ethel's house and wrote: "I have been shocked out of my bland insistence that, while such things might go on elsewhere in the world, it was impossible for them to occur in a town of Beldon's cultural heritage." Smaller donations totaled one hundred and three dollars, and a steady procession of visitors filled the *Bugler* lobby with gifts of clothes, dishes, food, and a folding bed.

George was surprised by Johnson's gloomy reaction to the readers' response. With Celia in tow, they were sauntering along Main Street on their way to give Alan the cash donations for Ethel's house when Johnson stopped in the middle of the sidewalk and pulled out the *Bugler* check for the total amount. "One hundred and fifty-three dollars. One-five-three. There are thousands of people in this area." His long arm swept across an arc that included the town and the green fringe of islands across the Sound. "If everybody gave just one dollar . . . but no. They give some lousy old clothes they were going to throw away anyhow and congratulate themselves that they're doing something about the basic problem of the g. d. Klan."

"But it's a good beginning."

"No, it's not. It's an end. They feel absolved, and they'll forget about it now. You wait and see. They'll forget because I don't have any specifics, and until I do, it doesn't really concern them."

Celia looked up at him, wide-eyed in the bright glare of sun. "Maybe if a bunch of us kids went around door to door—you know, like Red Cross people—and asked—"

"No, Celia. You must not get involved in this. It's too dangerous."

"You heard him." George overrode her protests.

They walked on in silence and turned into the alley beside Villiers Hardware Store. Alan was sitting on the loading platform, swinging his feet and drinking a Coca-Cola while he enjoyed the spring sunshine. His round shoulders hunched over a soft paunch of belly, and his mouth sagged with exhaustion. He greeted them with a curt nod. Johnson extended the check to him, explaining it was from donations. "I know it isn't much," he apologized, "but I'm pledging the *Bugler* to match every penny that comes in."

"Hunh. That the best all your high-flown writing can do? You talk and talk, Johnson. You and George. Talk, talk, talk. But when it comes to proof of the pudding, doing is all that counts. So you talk. I'll do." Alan folded the check and crammed it into Johnson's hand. "Give it to Ethel. God knows she'll need it for other things. The house is my baby, and I don't want any help, not from you or anybody else."

"But why not?"

"Because it's something I want to do, that's all. And you goddamn outlanders can take your donations and do you-know-what with them." Alan thrust his half-finished Coca-Cola into a wire rack beside the door and slammed angrily into the store office.

Celia's face was crimson, her mouth tightly pursed.

Thomas appeared in the warehouse door. Stripped to the waist, his black torso materialized from black shadow, outlined by the satiny gleam of sweat covering his body. He returned George's greeting and stepped into the sunshine. The heavy carton he was carrying slipped in his moist grasp and he lowered it to the ground, leaning against it and panting heavily. His face was drawn and tired, with deep circles beneath his eyes. "You been sick?" George asked.

"Just working, for a change." Thomas wiped his hands on a rag tied to his belt. "Mr. Alan's been like a crazy man, trying to finish up Miss Ethel's house." He bent over the carton, and George moved to help him. "That's all right, Major. I got it." He scooped up the carton, moved unevenly up the steps to the loading platform, and disappeared into the store.

Johnson lit a cigarette, carefully contemplating the thin stream of smoke. "What's gotten into Alan about that house, anyhow?"

"Damned if I know. He shifts direction so fast, I've given up trying to keep track."

George waited until late that evening to ask Evelyn for her

opinion. It was the final hour of the day they both enjoyed, when they were dressed for bed and shut away in the quiet of their spacious bedroom. Before he could say anything about Alan, there was a shrill scream from Celia's room, ending in a sob. They ran down the hall to find Celia on her feet at the bedroom window, her eyes blanked by moonlight and sleep. Evelyn put one arm around Celia's shoulder and led her gently back to bed. Sitting beside her, she talked quietly, soothingly, leading Celia out of her nightmare into wakefulness. ". . . oh, Mother . . ." Celia flung her arms around Evelyn. "It was terrible. We went into Ethel's house, but when we got upstairs it wasn't Ethel at all, it was Martha lying there and—and—she said she wouldn't give me any more pound cake, and . . . it . . . it was awful . . ."

Evelyn stroked her hair. "It was a crazy nightmare, that's all. Just a nightmare."

Later, when Celia went back to sleep and the house was quiet again, George mixed two drinks and took one in to Evelyn. "What else can you expect?" she said to his questions about Celia's dream. "All we talk about is Ethel and that poor cat and that wrecked house. Who said what, who did what."

"True," George agreed. He sipped his drink, staring at the soft lamplight streaming across the lace of Evelyn's pink gown and her plump, paler pink arms. For days, he had thought of nothing but Ethel's brutal attack. And Celia came home from school to spend her afternoons slumped in a chair trying to read. How long had it been since Jim and Cynthia had come shrieking up the back steps? Not since Ethel had been put in the guest room. He would take them on a picnic, or something. Some place in the boat—get them out in the fresh air. Then he remembered he had never taken them on the promised trip into the field with Bertram-Down-Girl. Hunting season was closed, but he could take his camera and get some field photos. He'd ask Thomas to come along and handle the dog. He could use some relaxation, too.

George phoned Thomas at the store next morning, but

Thomas flatly refused to leave Alan alone to work in Ethel's house. "Sunday we're painting the bedroom," he explained, and then as an afterthought, "Tell you what, Major. How about trying out that fool dog on 'coon one evening? My Uncle Morgan says the new barn is full of them, and he's been trying to get rid of a few."

"Morgan? You mean the caretaker out at 'Harlan's Headache'?"

"Yes."

"I didn't know you two were related."

Thomas chuckled. "Guess I'm related to just about everybody in town, one way or another."

They agreed to go on the following weekend, when the full moon would give the cousins light enough for their first experience in tracking raccoons. George immediately felt better with something pleasant to anticipate. And to his delight, Celia hugged him with a happy giggle of excitement before running across the yard to invite Jim and Cynthia. It was the first time in days he'd heard their laughing chatter on the lawn.

The night of the hunt was chilly and clear, with damp wind smelling of a distant thundershower. George slowed the car and turned into the dirt road beside the high wire fence of "Harlan's Headache." "Looks like a car graveyard," he said, indicating the cluster of automobiles jammed helter-skelter across the shoulder of the road.

"Hunh," Thomas commented. "Baseball season, I guess. There's a field over there someplace."

Neither man noticed the dark and deserted playing field on the other side of the cars, and in the darkness they were unable to see the freshly cleared pathway that entered Harlan's farm at the end of the fence. Honeysuckle vines and brambles had been hacked out of the path and it snaked deep into the woods, following the clear edges of the marsh.

George turned into the driveway, easing the car over the cattle guard. The metal sign reading "Harlan's Headache" creaked violently, rattling in the wind. George touched the horn, signaling to Morgan that they were family. Thomas indicated the road to the new barn, and the car bumped down a gentle slope to the sprawling building beside a muddy duck pond. Painted garish yellow, the barn dwarfed Morgan's ramshackle little house. George stopped the car beside a hayrack and they tumbled out, shivering from a combination of excitement and the cold dew on their bare ankles. Bertram-Down-Girl whined restlessly.

Thomas looked back at the shack. It was dark, and sagging green shutters were closed across each window. "That's funny." He unhooked the barn door and tugged it open. A dilapidated truck stood just inside, leaning over badly broken springs on the driver's side. "He must be home. The truck's here." He shut the door and latched it. "Mind if I run up to the house a minute?"

"Go ahead." George rested against the car fender and began loading the .22, taking the shells from Jim's eager hands, while Celia and Cynthia amused themselves dancing with their spindly shadows in the moonlight.

"Look, Daddy!" Celia called. "My shadow isn't black."

Jim shut the shell box and slid it back into George's hunting pouch. "How can it be a shadow if it's not black?" he asked derisively.

"Well, it's not!" Cynthia insisted.

"Girls," Jim muttered confidentially to George.

George checked the safety catch before examining his own shadow. It wasn't black, he noted in surprise. Not black at all. More of a silver gray, or the shadow of a shadow. And in the moonlight, Bertram-Down-Girl's fur was washed to the tone of old pewter.

Thomas had circled the shack, knocking on the front and back doors. "Uncle Morgan—it's me, Thomas. I'm with Major and some of the kids." Thumbs hooked in his jeans pockets, Thomas came slowly back to the barn.

"Maybe he's gone visiting," George suggested.

"He doesn't usually lock up. And I can hear old Peaches whining in the kitchen. He never leaves without her." Like Bertram-Down-Girl and the shadows, Thomas's features were pale and gray in the ghostly light. Bertram-Down-Girl whimpered and nuzzled his hand, then shook herself with her ears flapping in machine-gun precision. Thomas laughed and shook himself in imitation. "This here lady is ready to go!"

"Me too!" shouted Celia, echoed by Cynthia and Jim.

"C'mon." Thomas took hold of Bertram-Down-Girl's collar. "I'll check on Uncle Morgan when we get back." He flung open the loading doors of the barn and led Bertram-Down-Girl inside. A cow mooed in protest at the disturbance, and a chicken squawked as Thomas inadvertently knocked it from its roost. Something darted from the barn, a small silver-furred shadow that scurried into the drainage ditch beside the barn. The two girls let out piercing squeals, and Jim shouted, "There goes one, Uncle George!"

Bertram-Down-Girl threw back her head in a full-throated, howling bay and galloped into the ditch in pursuit, almost knocking George down as she passed. Thomas ran after the dog, pulling Jim's arm. "C'mon!" Celia jumped into the ditch behind them, and Cynthia panted along with her. They ran ahead of George, shrieking, giggling, pommeling one another, slipping in dew-slick growth to rise with fresh shrieks and run again in affirmation of joy in the cool night air. George shouldered his hunting pouch and, cradling the gun, walked slowly along the edge of the ditch. His spirit ran freely with them; his body followed cautiously, his own joy centering on the release from winter's sharp pain in his shoulders. The raccoon scurried from the ditch with Bertram-Down-Girl and Thomas close behind. Jim and the girls scrambled up onto the field and zigzagged after them.

Celia flung her arms wide and leapt high over imaginary hurdles. She had no sensation of her feet touching ground, but gave herself over to a drunken ecstasy of moonlight and the heady smell of honeysuckle. She felt she could go on forever and forever and forever, running through the moonlight. She was as invincible as an Amazon; as swift and graceful as Diana.

"Wait for me," Cynthia puffed, but Celia shook her head and ran harder.

George chuckled, watching their chubby legs pounding along, their stocky behinds waddling in toddler-baby fashion. If they kept that up, they wouldn't last for more than one raccoon. He was tempted to stop them, but changed his mind. Let 'em run. Maybe it'll knock some of that weight off. He stopped and lit his pipe. The full moon was already past its highest point, beginning to sink toward the pine-speared horizon. Darkness never fell on such a night. Instead, twilight intensified, gathered up in flooding quicksilver that finally gave way to dawn. George hoped the kids could last the night. He had an overpoweringly deep yearning to watch starlight disappear into sunrise.

Celia and Cynthia vanished into the woods at the edge of the field, and he could hear them, running slower now, caught in the thick underbrush. There was an old logging road to the left side of their trail of noise, and he headed for that. No sense getting torn up with briars until the raccoon came to rest. He smelled smoke. Picnic, he thought, but his nostrils wrinkled in distaste. There was a caustic bite to the odor. Not rubber. More of a trash-pile stench. Smudge fire, probably. Some poor devil trying to escape a swarm of gnats. He plunged into the darkness of the woods and halted, letting his eyes get accustomed to the deep shadows. The two pale tracks of roadbed curved off to his right, lit by patches of moonlight. He sauntered along, following the racket Bertram-Down-Girl was making. "Owwwww, dammit." He recognized Celia's voice and smiled at her indignation. Briars, most likely.

Once into the underbrush, Jim and Thomas quickly outdistanced the two girls. Celia and Cynthia were stumbling along hand in hand, a little fearful of the trees enclosing them and the thorny vines slashing across their shins. Celia ran into a spider web and shrieked as she felt sticky threads glued to her face and hair. She brushed at the strands in terror. "Get it off! Get it off me!"

"Well, stand still, then." Cynthia rubbed at Celia's face with her sleeve.

"Get it off—get it off! It's all over me!"

"Celia?"

She gasped with relief at the sound of her father's voice immediately to her left. "Daddy—I'm covered with spiders—they're all over me . . ."

"Take it easy." She could hear him fumbling in the hunting pouch. His flashlight clicked on, beamed down at the ground to avoid blinding them. "Come this way. There's a road over here."

They picked their way to his side, and with the aid of the light George and Cynthia wiped away the remains of the spider web, assuring Celia there were no spiders on her clothing or hair.

Bertram-Down-Girl was heading back toward them in a curving line. Twenty-five feet ahead of them, the raccoon dashed from the underbrush and scuttled around a sharp bend of the road. With a violent snapping of branches, Thomas and Bertram-Down-Girl followed in hot pursuit, running side by side around the curve. Jim fell to his knees over a pine root, swore lustily, and pelted along after Thomas.

"That's not fair!" Celia whimpered. "Why don't they wait for us?"

"Honey, when a man is hunting, he doesn't—" George was stopped by the swift change in Celia's expression. Her eyes widened and her head came up, nostrils flaring as she sniffed at a gust of wind. A second gust scooped down from the pine tops and stirred the weeds at their feet.

Bertram-Down-Girl's baying halted abruptly, cut off in the midst of one of her mournful trumpetings. The woods were suddenly filled with rancid smoke and the wistful soughing of wind through pine needles. George felt cold sweat on his forehead. "Stay close behind me!" He walked swiftly along the road. "Thomas . . . Jim? . . . Thomas!" There was only the sound of the wind, and George broke into an uneasy dogtrot.

The curve in the road was a sharp turn to the left, hacked through an impenetrable maze of honeysuckle. For Celia, it seemed that they ran for all eternity, gasping for a breath of fresh air in the smoky night. Ten feet beyond the curve of the road, without warning, there was another sharp bend to the right that catapulted them onto the edge of a weed-choked pasture cut from the very heart of the forest. They stopped, momentarily blinded by the fierce glare of a twenty-foot-high burning cross. Wind swirled across the open field and flames roared higher, spreading orange light over a tight cluster of white-robed, masked figures. From news clippings, Celia recognized the caricatured dunce caps of the KKK, and her stomach tightened, her throat constricted. She tasted terror, and it left her helpless, silent. Beside her, Cynthia blinked stupidly, disbelieving what they had encountered. Shoulder to shoulder, the group of white robes erased individual forms. They were a bank of white upon white, punctuated by fire-lit eyes gleaming hatefully through narrow slits in their masks. Thomas stood almost squarely in their midst, keeping a firm clutch on Bertram-Down-Girl's collar. Black man and black dog, their color restored by the firelight, they made a brilliant etching against the white robes. Jim was behind them, obscured in their shadow, a forlorn and terrified boy.

George was equally terrified, but intuitively began analyzing their situation. The girls were at the end of the road, and he prayed silently that they'd have sense enough to run away. About two dozen men, he figured quickly. Heavy odds, with only a single .22 between him and Thomas. And God knows how many of them had guns, clubs, knives, what-have-you. He had to admire their choice of a meeting place. A good two miles from the highway, the heavy underbrush afforded total seclusion. And certainly no one in the scattered community of Negro farmers would question their activities. George grimaced, understanding now the locked shutters at Morgan's little house, the cluster of parked cars outside the gate.

With a loud snap, a heavy spark fell from the cross, and Bertram-Down-Girl whimpered uneasily. A bulky figure in a dirt-stained robe detached himself from the others and took several steps toward Thomas. Thomas backed away, wary and crouched for flight. "Well, well, well," the figure said. "What do you know? The Lord done sent us that high-falutin' nigger boy."

George recognized the surly voice. The safety catch of his .22 made an ominous click as he swung the gun into firing position. "Hold it, Brown." The figure halted. "Thomas. Jim. Get back here with me."

Without taking their eyes from the Klansmen, Thomas and Jim eased backwards towards George's voice. Bertram-Down-Girl pawed the air, howling in protest at being pulled away from the raccoon's trail.

Brown lifted his arms to the white-robed group. "Come on, you all. Let's get that nigger bastard." A few figures stirred, started forward. Encouraged, Brown let out a triumphant shout. "That's the way! Come on, Bert! Let's—"

Bertram-Down-Girl mistook the name for her own. Already jittery and high-strung by the excitement of the hunt, the mammoth dog let out a wild series of yelps. Tearing free from Thomas's hold, she flung herself full tilt on the startled Brown. He was knocked to his back at the foot of the cross and went down babbling in terror. "Help! Help, Bert . . . it's trying to kill me . . . Bert! . . ."

The repetition of the name further excited the dog. With her tail lashing joyously, she licked at the mask, dislodging the cap and blinding Brown in the folds of his robe. "Bert!"

A second tall, heavyset figure moved forward, swinging a long flashlight over his head to strike Bertram-Down-Girl. At that instant, Brown rolled to one side with Bertram-Down-Girl on top of him and the flashlight missed its target, striking the ground and shattering. Bent double by the force of the misplaced blow, the heavy man staggered back. His rump collided squarely with the flaming cross, and his billowing robe ignited with a sharp whoosh. His panic-stricken screams were added to Brown's. Dancing in a circle, he tore off his mask and ripped at the burning robes. Flames billowed from his rear, fiery peacock plumes fanned higher by his running. Several figures threw him to the ground and ripped the burning robe from his body. It was Albert Thatcher, foreman of the bridge crew. "I'm on fire!" he screamed. "I'm on fire!"

220

"Easy, Bert ... it's out now ..." George recognized Len Finch's voice. "Easy, Bert!"

Delighted that someone else wanted to join in the game, Bertram-Down-Girl leaped over Brown's prostrate form and galloped to the two Klansmen crouching over Thatcher. "Shut up, Len! Look out for the damned dog!" the second one yelled, rising to run. Seeing his quick movement, Bertram-Down-Girl's attention was diverted from Len Finch. With a joyful bark, the dog gave a long lunge and her forepaws caught the running man between his shoulders with the full force of her leap. He stumbled and fell, shouting as he hit the trampled earth, "Bertram-*Down*-Girl!" His masked hat had been knocked from his head by the impact of the dog, and Bertram-Down-Girl sat on it, settling back on her haunches and wagging her great black tail. The man sat up, searching frantically for his mask. Sheepish and embarrassed, Alan's red and sweating face was framed sharply by the neckline of his white robe.

"Mr. Alan!" Thomas cried out in anguish.

George's head felt constricted by sharp pangs of sorrow, and he could hear blood pounding in his temples. He stared contemptuously at the silent group of Klansmen. Alan, Len Finch, Albert Thatcher, and Brown sat clumsily on the ground, paralyzed by the knowledge of their exposure. George spat at their feet and turned his back on the masked ring of Klansmen behind them. "Come on, kids. Let's go home." Putting an arm around Thomas's shoulder, he led them from the field.

There were angry shouts and a surge of movement behind them as they reached the road. "No!" they heard Alan shout. "Let them go; for God's sake, let them go."

13

THE RIDE HOME was made in total, abject silence. George's rage had given way to nauseous relief, and he clenched his teeth against wave after wave of nervous indigestion. Thomas slouched deep in the seat, his forehead against the cold window glass, his face cupped in his hands. In the back seat, Jim chewed his lower lip and stared unseeing at the moonlit landscape. Cynthia pressed against him, her clammy hands clamped between trembling knees.

Celia slid forward on the seat with Bertram-Down-Girl and rested her hands on George's shoulders. He gave her arm a brief, reassuring squeeze. She was proud to be able merely to touch him, to feel the strength in him that was far deeper than bone and muscle. She shut her eyes, reliving the picture of his stocky form facing the ring of white robes. He seemed a giant in retrospect, outlined against the foolish Halloween robes of the Klansmen. And yet, funny as they looked, those silly men had done those terrible things to Ethel. And Uncle Alan was one of them. Had he gone with them? Laughing, teasing Uncle Alan?

They reached the town limits, and Thomas sat up with a deep, shuddering breath. "Major, would you please drop me off at the store?"

"I'd be glad to drive you home, Thomas."

"No, thank you. There—there are some things I need to take care of."

The bank clock chimed midnight, with heavy metallic gongs.

Main Street was deserted, store windows blank and impassive. George stopped the car in front of Villiers Hardware Store, and Thomas fumbled to open the door. He stepped out, looking up at the painted sign. The window display of toasters and percolators twinkled under the street lamp, aluminum lures for placards bearing a vague promise of "The Better Life." Turning, Thomas leaned into the open car door and reached across the seat to tousle Jim's hair. "You kids behave yourselves, you hear me? And, Major, I . . . God bless you. Always." They exchanged a warm handclasp. Slamming the front door, Thomas walked swiftly down the alley.

Jim only then understood that they were saying good-bye. "Thomas!" He ran after him to throw his arms around Thomas's waist and bury his blond head against his chest. Thomas rocked him in a tight bear hug, then pulled free and ran to the back of the store.

Lights burned all night long in the three family homes.

Jim and Cynthia had left the garage and gone hand in hand to awaken Fred and Agnes and tell them the night's events, moment by moment. They huddled together in the center of the rug and gave a halting, mumbled account of the evening. At the edge of the bed, Fred leaned on one elbow, listening, his thin form lost in white pajamas. Agnes struggled into a sitting position and pursed her thin lips. "If you've wakened us up in the middle of the night with one of your practical jokes, I'll—"

Fred threw back the covers. "They're not joking, Agnes."

Jim warmed to his father's immediate trust. "We saw them, and Uncle Alan was with them."

"In a costume," Cynthia added.

Fred got out of bed and sat down gingerly on the vanity bench, drawing Jim and Cynthia close with an arm around each one. "All right. I'm good and awake now, so start over again. Back at the beginning."

They repeated their story three times for him, until he was satisfied he understood every detail. Relieved of their terrible burden of knowledge, Jim and Cynthia went off to an exhausted sleep, leaving Fred and Agnes to pace the floor in consternated discussion of what, if anything, they should do. Or, as Fred cautiously pointed out, could do. "I can't believe it!" Agnes kept saying. "Not Alan. Not a member of our family!"

"Now, please, Agnes, don't get one of your migraines."

"I'm not about to!" she snapped. "There's too much we have to consider."

George and Celia stored away the .22 and the hunting equipment and eased upstairs to the living room, leaving Sallie and Evelyn to sleep one more night in peaceful unawareness. George sent Celia to her bedroom and went at once to his desk, taking out an envelope with his photos of Ethel's wrecked house. He knew now what it was about the lettering along the stairwell that had caught his attention. After a long search through his files, he found Brown's receipt for the setter, the bill of sale he had signed and underscored with a vicious swirl. George laid the marred sheet of paper on the desk, side by side with enlarged close-ups of the stairwell. The two swirls were identical. Even the letters of the receipt and those on the stairwell were formed alike. George studied them with rising excitement, fingering through the photos. "Nigger-Lover's Nigger" Brown had painted along the wall, and George remembered his sneering farewell when he left the setter: "So long, Mister Nigger Lover."

"Daddy ..."

He jumped, startled to find Celia standing at his shoulder. She had changed into her pajamas, but her eyes were brilliant, teeming with unanswerable questions. For once, he had no inclination to encourage her curiosity, longing to be left alone with his own. His head hurt and his indigestion bothered him. But he was thrown completely off guard by the one thing she asked.

"Daddy, were you scared?"

He was tempted to lie, to use the opportunity for telling her that he knew he had been facing cowards, because only cowards could dress up in anonymous masquerade for the purpose of terrorizing helpless victims. "Why, I—I felt—"

224

"Were you?"

He took her hands in his. "You're damn right I was. Scared stiff."

"You were just—just great." She smiled with a warmth that reminded him of Evelyn. It was a glimpse of the emerging woman, and he turned back to the photographs, hiding quick tears.

They heard Alan's car stop in his driveway and went to the window to watch him going into his kitchen. Even that simple act was altered now, overcast with implications. George rubbed his chin absentmindedly. Where was his white robe? Locked in the trunk of the car? Stored at some hunting lodge? Alan walked along the driveway, his face lifted toward their window. He must have been able to see them clearly, judging from the way he ran onto the porch and into the house. The kitchen light went on. Moments later the living room blazed with light. Poor bastard would probably drink all night, George guessed.

Celia leaned against his shoulder. "Know something funny? I feel sorry for him." George sat down at his desk, and Celia felt his withdrawal. "Daddy, could I just sit in here with you? I mean, I won't talk or anything."

"Sure. I don't want to be by myself tonight, either." His blue eyes were sad and wise; his gray hair gleamed silver in the lamplight. For no reason she could analyze, Celia felt it was another one of her "glory moments." But that was silly. There was nothing special about sitting together smack in the middle of their own living room. She settled herself on the couch with a pile of *National Geographics*, determined to respect his privacy, and they spent the rest of the night in restless, silent companionship. George mixed himself some bicarbonate of soda for his upset stomach. When that didn't help, he allowed himself a single scotch and soda, and the drink finally relaxed the sharp pains. Nerves, that's what it was. He longed for a second drink, but put the bottle away. He didn't want his senses fuddled, not tomorrow of all days. He would have to tell Sallie and Evelyn about Alan before he went to see Johnson. George paced the floor, trying to frame what he would say.

225

Midway through an article on African tattooing practices, Celia dropped the magazine into her lap. How could she sit there reading? But she had actually been reading, with avid interest. She chewed a fingernail and attempted to sort out her thoughts, only to discover that she had none. She scowled, trying to force herself to come to some important conclusion, worrying her mind like a puppy chewing on a meatless bone. Her efforts were useless. She was unable to connect what had happened with what it might mean. After a few minutes she gave up searching for profundities and went back to her magazine.

In the morning, George had no chance to give Sallie and Evelyn his carefully worded analysis. He followed them into the kitchen, silent beneath their teasing barrage of banter about the hunt. Celia edged into the room with them and slid onto the red mixing stool.

"Why, you both look like the raccoon was chasing you all night!" Sallie exclaimed. "And even Bertram-Down-Girl is a little—"

The back door opened with a crash and Alan lurched into the kitchen. His dew-dampened shoes slid on the waxed linoleum and he skidded heavily against the wooden mixing table. Fred and Jim appeared silently in the doorway behind him.

"Why, Alan! What's the matter?" Evelyn reached for his arm to steady him, but he yanked free, pulling himself defiantly upright.

"All right, all right. So I am a member of the KKK. So what!"

With a metallic clatter, the percolator slipped from Sallie's hands, the top rolling across the floor, settling at last beneath the sink with a long, hollow circling. "What are you saying, Alan? Did I hear you right?"

"You—you must be joking." Evelyn tried to laugh.

George shook his head. "Alan—I haven't told them yet about last night."

"Oh."

Bright sunlight streamed in the windows, brushing each of them with a sense of unreality that they could stand confronting

226

each other, discussing life-and-death affairs in the midst of an immaculate kitchen, the warm, pulsing heart of the house. But with one sentence, Alan had destroyed the comfort of their neatly-ordered existence as surely as if he had taken an ax and shattered the room into a semblance of Ethel's little house. Sallie sat down in a straight chair, covering her eyes with her hand. Evelyn leaned against the refrigerator and dug her shoulders against the strength of cold steel. Despite the wood stove's warmth, Jim was shivering and edged closer to Fred. The kitchen clock ticked merrily away from the top of the stove, every fourth tick a soft clank. Celia began counting the clanks.

George waited, curious as to what Alan intended to say. "Pixie," Evelyn always described Alan, "an overgrown pixie." He didn't look so damn pixieish this morning. Alan's eyes were red-rimmed, and a heavy stubble of beard showed on his cheeks. He was fingering an object he held in his clenched fist. Finally, he dropped it on the table, Thomas's heavy key ring with forty-one keys of all sizes and shapes. They landed in a pathetic sprawl of metal. "Thomas has gone."

George was astounded to see tears in Alan's eyes. "You didn't honestly think he could ever come back!"

"He left these." Alan poked at the keys with a grubby forefinger, drawing George's attention to his dirty hands. Probably soot from that damned cross. Alan's hoarse voice rambled on. "...car key...boat lock...store keys...all my house keys... there wasn't anything I wouldn't give that boy. Nothing. He might have been my own flesh and blood—and he didn't even say good-bye. No note. Nothing. Just took all his things and left these on my desk." Alan swept the key ring from the table, squeezing it hard in his clenched fist. "You'd think he'd at least have given me a chance to explain."

"How in God's name could you possibly explain?"

"It—was only supposed to be a—a sort of club, George. Just a club."

"Yes? Well, would you mind stepping into the guest room and—explaining—that to Ethel?" George felt waves of anger returning, twisting his stomach tighter.

227

"It wasn't meant to be rough that way, George. I swear to God it wasn't! We started—" Alan lifted one hand pleadingly. "—we started—well, just helping Harlan out from time to time. You know? Just helping out, where the law doesn't reach. And it was a big help to him. He always said so. He—"

Harlan too. George grimaced. So that was why he had quit; why the Klan met at his farm. George was reminded sharply of the local ghost stories about the farm and its high wire fence. Alan was still talking, giving random instances of their actions.

". . . like there was this drunk beating on his wife and she was scared to complain. We just paid him a little visit, that was all."

"And used a burning cross for your calling card?"

Alan's wheedling tone rose in anger. "Yes, in a way. That same drunk knew he was being watched, and he quit mussing up his wife and kids after that. Hell, George, you weren't even here. But you remember, Fred?"

"Yes." Fred's voice was deceptively gentle, and Jim looked anxiously at his father's impassive face. "I remember he died of a heart attack the very next week."

"Well, that wasn't our doing."

"Of course not. You were just being helpful to Harlan." George folded his arms, but Alan missed his scathing tone and went on eagerly.

"Yes. It was just to help keep law and order, that was all."

"Uh-hunh. Like you said, sort of a club."

"Well—yes. Vigilantes, you know?"

"Oh! A vigilante club. Vigilant when Ethel was half-murdered, vigilant when old Donald was chased into an oyster bank, vigilant—"

"Now hold on, George." Alan struck the table top. "Jus' a—a—damn minute. We didn't do any of that. That wasn't *us*. That was them outlander bastards from the bridge. Only the outlanders."

"But you must have known ahead of time they were going to Ethel's, didn't you? Didn't you!"

"We—they were—" Alan faltered, choking. "They were only

228

supposed to—to scare her a little bit. But the boys got liquored up, and—"

"Oh, for Christ's sake, you did know." George's knuckles went white as his hands clutched the counter. "You might as well have gone along with them and hit her yourself."

"She shouldn't have made them mad. It was her fault. It was! She got uppity with them about that derned fool red coat of hers and— Hell, George. Ethel's like family to me too. I've known her lots longer than you have, and I love her, but—"

"Love her? Then, Jesus—I sure hope you don't love Evelyn, and Celia, and Sallie. Or Fred and Jim. I sure hope you don't, Alan." George made a move to leave the kitchen and Alan stepped hastily in front of him.

"No, lissen a minute. See, we understand Ethel. But strangers around town have been complaining. They have. Tha's the truth, George—ask Harlan. She's been uppity as all hell to some outlanders. They think she's dangerous crazy, and they want her locked up, because she runs around claiming she talks to God and all."

"When did she ever say that? When? She says she talks to Spirits. And what's more, I think she does. Do you want to beat me up, too, for believing her?"

"It's not me, George! It's outlanders in town. And that's what they think, that she talks back and forth to God."

"And they don't?"

" 'Course not. Who'd ever claim a fool thing like that?"

George intoned softly, barely above a whisper: " 'Our Father, Who art in Heaven . . .' "

Alan crumpled, stumbling backwards against the table. "They swore to me they weren't going to touch her—jus' mess up the house a little bit. She shouldn't have gotten uppity with them . . . she shouldn't have . . ."

"Just tell me one thing, Alan. Last night, would you have stopped them from going after Thomas?"

"I . . ." Alan wiped his mouth with the back of his hand. "Yes. I think I would."

"You *think*?"

"Yes. I like to think I would."

"But you don't know? There was a long time there when you could have said something. But I didn't hear a word from you, not a whisper."

"I...I..."

"God help you."

"It was only supposed to be a club. And now—I—I'm stuck with it. Once you belong, you— Well, I can't drop out. It'd wreck the business. And I got my family to think about." Alan turned to Sallie. "You understand, don't you?" Alan extended a hand, begging for help. "Don't you?"

She turned away from him with the slightest shake of her head.

"Look, they'll be gone soon, all those outlanders. Then things will quiet down again, like they used to be." Alan turned back to George. "But meantime, we got to keep this in the family, because—"

"No."

"But, George, some people might—I mean—it might hurt the business. Hell. Nothing happened last night. You think telling about one little harmless rally is going to stop anything as big as the Klan?"

"I'm not that stupid."

"Then what's the point? Why make trouble?"

George pried Alan's fingers loose from his arm and stepped around him, walking swiftly through the swinging door into the house.

"George...wait...please."

The door rattled loosely as Sallie and Evelyn left the kitchen behind George. Alan dropped his hands to his side. He smiled hopefully at Celia, but she was fingering the pocket of her bathrobe. "How about it, Celia? You know all about clubs, don't you? You know how much fun you, Jim, and Cynthia have when I let you meet in my garage. You know how important it is to keep a secret. And—" His voice droned on, as drunkenly aimless as his nervous pacing around the kitchen. Wide-eyed and silent, Celia sat kicking at the rungs of the stool and staring at Alan. Was that the way they walked when they went to a secret Klan meeting? Did they always get drunk? What did they talk about? How do you say to somebody else you're going to beat up a—a— She couldn't use the word, even to herself.

Alan rounded the table and was abruptly silenced by Celia's steady gaze. "Ah, shit," he mumbled, turning away from her unspoken disdain.

Groggy and exhausted, Celia was relieved when he said nothing more. She stepped swiftly through the door and went upstairs to bed.

For a moment, the ticking clock was the only sound in the kitchen. Alan licked his lips and grinned unsteadily at Jim. "Women! Who needs 'em, eh, Jim?" He tucked his dirty shirt into his rumpled trousers, going around his belt four times. But Jim remained silent, his eyes averted as he chewed a hangnail on his thumb. "You and me are still friends, aren't we, Jim? . . . Eh? . . . What say, bucko? Want to go fishing? I'll let you run the boat and we could—" Jim dodged away from his hand, stepping behind Fred. Alan thrust his hands in his pockets, brushed clumsily against them, and left without looking back.

Fred laid a tentative hand on Jim's shoulder, relieved when he did not pull away. So Thomas had quit. What would the store be like now, without his eager, cheerful presence? And what was he, Fred Mark, going to say to Alan whey they met again? He knew already that he was going to quit too. Quickly, before the old fears had a chance to set in. He had no idea where he could find work, but he knew for sure he could not work with Alan. Never again would he take Alan's insults, veiled as rough humor. Fred squared his thin shoulders and gave Jim a brisk pat. "Son, how about giving me a hand at the store this morning?"

"Sure." The answer was immediate, but Jim's tone was reluctant.

"I don't like to take up your free time, but I don't think I can carry all my things home by myself."

"Your—things?"

"Yes. I—uh—" Fred hesitated, knowing if he once said it aloud, he had committed himself; then, with a breathy gasp, he did. "I'm going to have to find another job and it may be rough going for a time, you know, financially and all, but—"

"I'll help!" Jim interrupted. "I'll get a part-time job. And Cynthia can babysit. And—" He stopped, lost for words. Doubling up his fist, he swung a make-believe blow at Fred's stomach, and this time Fred remembered to double up with pretended pain, his hands clutching his waist. Jim grinned. "We'll do O.K., Pop. We'll do just fine."

Upstairs, George was at his desk, meticulously emptying his good pipe into a deep ashtray. Evelyn stood quietly, watching him tap out the ashes.

"George, do you think Alan had anything to do with our shed burning down?"

"No. I can't prove it, but my guess would be Brown." He showed her the photos and the receipt for the setter.

"Oh, good lord. He's probably had it in for you ever since then."

"Yes. I'm afraid so."

"Alan might have helped him."

"No. He wouldn't harm any of us, Evelyn, you know that. He's not a vicious man. Stupid, maybe. But not vicious. Not by himself, that is. I think Alan was telling us the truth, that he drifted into the Klan and now he's scared to get out. And who can blame him?" George fingered the burned tobacco in the ashtray, pushing it into a tight pile, pensively studying the black smears on his hand.

"George? . . . Are you all right?"

"Oh, sure." He dusted off his hands. "I'm fine. Just tired. Feel like I could sleep a month."

"Why don't you get a nap before you go to Johnson?"

"No. I want to give him the details of the rally while they're still fresh in my mind. The 'specifics' he wanted, you know?" He slipped the receipt and the photographs into a brown envelope, tucked them into his pocket, and left the room with a heavy, uneven tread.

Evelyn sat down on the couch and laid her palms on the glossy surface of the coffee table. There had been rioting in the streets of Shanghai the day they bought the table, but she had been soothed by the thought that when they would finally be able to use it, they would be back in the gentle safety of Beldon. Safety. She wanted to stand in the middle of the living room and scream her lungs out. Instead, she went to her room and dressed for the day. George would be hungry when he got back. She went through their golden sunporch into the kitchen and began fixing his favorite combination of ham biscuits and coleslaw. It troubled her that she could see Alan's garage from the side window; and it troubled her even more that she couldn't keep her eyes away from the window. Finally, disregarding the flour all over her hands, she went over and yanked down the shade.

It was past noon when George came home from Johnson's house, but he refused to eat anything. "Later, maybe. Right now I just want to go to bed."

They went into the bedroom and George undressed slowly, telling Evelyn about the rally the night before. She listened without comment, more concerned about George's haggard face and his slurred speech. She interrupted an involved comment about Alan, a comment he had already made twice before. "Can't I bring you a cup of soup, at least? You haven't eaten a thing all day."

"No ..." He sat down on the edge of the bed, holding his left arm. "Tell you the truth, I think you'd better call the doctor. I—I don't feel so good. My—" A harsh pain slammed through him, tearing the breath from his lungs and knocking him back heavily across the pillows. Not indigestion, he knew, not this time.

"George? ... Oh, my God—George!" He was unconscious when she reached his side, and she called down the steps frantically. "Mother! Come quickly! It's George." Evelyn loosened his pajama belt and began patting George's face, rubbing his wrist.

233

Sallie ran up the steps and came into the room.

"Oh, Mother . . . he was talking to me, and he just blacked out."

Sallie looked down at George's face. His lips drooped at the left side, his breath came in shallow gasps. It might have been the face of her own husband, twenty years before. "It's his heart," she said quietly.

Together, they swung his feet to the bed and settled him beneath the sheet. Sallie left Evelyn by his side and went downstairs to phone for the doctor. She could hear Ethel's gutteral muttering from the guestroom. Ethel knew. Somehow. With her uncanny perception, she already knew. "Pray for us all," Sallie whispered. "For every one of us."

Dr. Phelps was making a round of calls out in the country, Miss Effie explained at once, but she would track him down as soon as she could. Sallie went back upstairs and sat down in Evelyn's wicker chair. With folded hands, the two women took up their watch. Through the long afternoon, George drifted in and out of consciousness, making mumbled comments from other times and other years. In desperation at her helplessness, Evelyn bathed his forehead with a warm cloth, or moistened his lips with water. She answered everything he said, not knowing whether he could hear her or not, but holding tight to his hand as if she could physically drag him back to the present. Late in the afternoon, George opened his eyes, staring at her with surprise. He stirred restlessly, trying to shift his weight, irritable when he could not. Evelyn saw that his left arm was paralyzed. She freed his useless hand from beneath his hip and laid it gently across his chest.

". . . Evelyn . . . wha' happen . . ."

She could barely understand his words. "It's all right now, darling. You—you fainted." She caressed his face. "Dr. Phelps is on his way. He'll be here soon now." Please, God, make it soon.

He lifted his right hand and pressed her cool palm against his forehead. ". . . feels good . . ." He went peacefully to sleep, and

234

rather than risk waking him by withdrawing her hand, Evelyn laid her head on the pillow beside him and waited.

The grandfather clock struck five. The notes reverberated in the empty hallway, seeming to hang in the air with the prismatic colorings of a brilliant sunset.

In her room, Celia awoke with a mighty yawn and rolled to her back, listening to the pealing chimes. Five. She was momentarily confused. If it was only five in the morning, why was her room bathed in sunlight? Or was she in her room? Recollection came back. But if it was afternoon, why was the house so still and quiet? . . . She was at once wide awake and jumped from bed. It was not the silence of an empty house. Something was wrong. She padded barefooted to the door and cocked her head, listening. Sallie and Evelyn were talking in low, muted voices. The fact that her grandmother was in her parents' bedroom was in itself unusual, and Celia slipped along the hall to the open door at the head of the steps. At first she thought her father was asleep, lying on his back making funny little snoring sounds. But it was even more peculiar that her mother and grandmother should stay in the room if he was asleep, with her mother sitting by him in that uncomfortable position. "Mother?" she whispered.

Evelyn's head came up from the pillow and she put her fingers to her lips. "Shhhh, honey. Daddy's sick."

"Sick?" Celia tiptoed to the bedside, standing beside George's left arm. "What's the matter with him?"

"He's had a—an attack of some sort. We're waiting for Dr. Phelps."

George awoke at the sound of their voices to see Celia's worried face. He smiled, a lopsided grotesque grin. ". . .'s O.K. . . . hon . . . O.K." There was a weight on his chest and he could dimly discern a hand. Believing it to be Celia's, he reached down and began stroking it consolingly ". . .'s . . . O.K. . . . don' . . . worry . . ." Gentle, comforting strokes along his own lifeless fingers. Horrified, Celia clapped her hands over her mouth and

Evelyn thrust her roughly aside. Before George could be aware of his mistake, Evelyn took his good right hand in hers and lowered his paralyzed arm to the mattress. "Celia. Go get dressed, dear. I want you to go to the store for me."

Celia backed away, staring at George's drooping lips. Moments later they heard her bedroom door slam shut against her muffled weeping.

Evelyn bent closer to George, pressing his hand between hers. "Can I get you anything, darling?"

He nodded. "Wah-er . . ."

"What?"

". . . wah-er . . ." he repeated peevishly.

"I'll get it." Sallie pushed herself to her feet, hurrying briskly into the upstairs kitchen to wipe away her own tears. She had finished making a pot of tea when she heard a car stop in front of the house. She took the tray in to Evelyn and set it on the dresser. "Some tea," she whispered. "I'll be right back. I think that's Dr. Phelps driving up."

"I hope so!" George had drifted back to sleep again. Evelyn gently freed her hand and went to the door, peering down the steps after Sallie.

"It's him!" Sallie said. "He'll be right there."

"Oh, thank God!"

". . . Evelyn . . ." George twisted on the bed, searching for her hand.

"Yes, darling. I'm right here."

George was wracked with another heavy pain. ". . . and the doctor's here, now. He's on the way up," she was saying, her back to him. Turn to me, Evelyn. Oh, please turn to me and let me see your sweet face. He thought he called her name, but there was no sound of his voice in the shrouded room. George extended his arm to her, shaking violently with the effort. She stood at the bureau, mixing something in a cup. For him, he knew. She was moving so cautiously to keep from disturbing him, easing a spoon around in the liquid. But I'm awake, Evelyn. Look at me. I want to see your face. He felt the final hurt beginning, and his mouth twisted with ironic agony. How can a man be in the same room with everything he holds dear in life, and yet be so very much alone? The last thing he saw was the nape of her neck; the soft, dimming outline of her cheek. His arm dropped to the mattress with a rustling sigh of the sheets. A fraction of a second too late, Evelyn turned her smiling face to the bed. "George! Oh, my George! . . ." It was a mourning shriek, as universal as death itself.

In her bedroom, Celia heard it and buried her answering shriek into her pillow.

Dr. Phelps heard it as he was running up the front porch steps. He paused and entered the house at a saddened, sedate walk.

Sallie heard it, in the act of opening the door for Dr. Phelps. She froze for an instant, then thrust the door open wide. Evelyn would need her now. There was time enough later on for tears —Evelyn would need her.

And, in the guestroom, immediately beneath the dead man's bed, Ethel heard it, and her muttering ceased. She riveted her eyes to the ceiling. "They hadn't oughta took him," she said to Thomas's mother. "They hadn't oughta."

14

A T EVELYN'S REQUEST, Fred made funeral arrangements through a Savannah mortuary. Celia had no memory of the day and a half before the funeral. They must have dressed; eaten; talked; slept. Her only recollection was sitting in the hushed house, whispering around the closed coffin resting so strangely in Sallie's living room, and praying for time to pass so that they might be freed from oppression. And somehow, eventually, time did pass.

The morning of the funeral was dim and misty, with gentle fog drifting in from the ocean. Celia watched Fred and Johnson and a group of silent men tenderly place the coffin in the yawning craw of an oversized gray hearse. You were supposed to cross your fingers when you saw a hearse go by, and she crossed hers now. But that was no strange ghostly creature riding in the black box; that was her father. She spread her fingers wide. Never again would she imitate that stupid gesture.

She and Evelyn rode with Sallie in a black limousine driven by the funeral director. Slowly they followed the hearse through town to the National Cemetery, where George was to be buried.

The solemnity of the occasion was broken by an angry oath from the funeral director. Slamming on the brakes, he halted the limousine and sprinted across several graves to the cemetery caretaker, who was standing beneath the canopy, awaiting them with piously folded hands. The two men began a heated discussion. Celia watched, idly curious at the soft carpet of blossoms that surrounded them in every direction. The limousine and the ugly gray hearse seemed to float on a sea of wildflowers.

"Oh, what is their problem?" Evelyn asked irritably, and rolled down the window. They could clearly hear the argument between the caretaker and the funeral director. It seemed that although George's account and condemnation of the Klan rally was not due to appear in the paper until the next day, word had already gotten out by word of mouth. From miles around, Negro families had arrived at the cemetery at dawn, each one bearing sprays of wildflowers. The stark canopy was laced with them, transformed to a bower of lavender wisteria and wild pink roses. When the canopy could hold no more, they had laid the blooms on the ground around the grave site. The freshly turned and raw mound of dirt was a hillock of primroses, violets, and jasmine. Soft, delicate color covered the harsh ground of nearly half the small cemetery.

". . . and how could I stop them?" the caretaker was grumbling. "It's a public cemetery, isn't it? They can bring flowers to anybody they want to."

"Dammit to hell, my canopy isn't public property. Help me get that mess off of there." He reached for a trailing spray of wisteria.

"No!" Evelyn's voice was hoarse. "Don't touch a single flower."

"But, ma'am!" He came back to the car, bowing and whispering again in his best funereal manner. "It's highly irregular. And—and look at how out of keeping they are beside all these expensive wreaths. It'll only take a minute to clear."

"I—said—no." How George would have loved them, she thought. Oh, how he would have loved them. Evelyn rolled up the window against the frantic man's continuing protests. Johnson appeared, and tugged him away. Scowling, the funeral director turned to the pall bearers, and the sad ceremony was at last permitted to begin.

Evelyn had longed for the moment when she could return to the house, go to her bedroom, and shut the door against the world. She would have a couple of good stiff drinks. Three, maybe. Or four. As many as it would take to give her a few hours of oblivion. But midway up the steps, tugging off her black veiled hat, she stopped and leaned against the banister. His clothes still hung in the closet, smelling of pipe tobacco; his after-shave lotion still permeated the bathroom. She couldn't go in there. Not just yet. And not to drink. Celia might want her. She dropped her hat on the banister post and went back to the porch to be with Sallie and Celia. Evelyn hesitated at the screen door, hearing Agnes and Annie talking. She would have preferred doing without them for a time. But before she could retreat to the steps, Annie saw her and hurried over to give her a tearful embrace. "The Lord giveth and the Lord taketh away," Annie sniffed, precisely as Evelyn had expected.

"Oh, Annie. For heaven's sake, let her sit down." Agnes pulled a rocker out for Evelyn and gave her a gentle pat on the hand. Evelyn nodded gratefully and settled herself in the chair with Agnes on one side and Annie on the other.

Annie dabbed her eyes with a handkerchief scented with lavender. "Oh, me. Many are the wonders He chooses to perform, but mysterious are His ways sometimes."

"Please, Annie. I've had enough sermons for a while, if you don't mind." Evelyn felt she was drowning in lavender scent.

To her relief, Sallie and Celia came out with a tray of iced tea, which nobody wanted, but which everybody drank, glad for some tangible object to focus on in the empty morning light.

The chairs rocked at random. Ice cubes clinked. In the back yard, Bertram-Down-Girl barked lustily, a long hollow racketing.

"I must say," Annie commented suddenly, "that Mrs. Beezely sending you pickles instead of a wreath was certainly—certainly —peculiar." She laughed an unpleasant noise.

"No it wasn't," Celia blurted. "She's my friend. There were

240

flowers enough forever—but she knows how much Daddy and I—how much I like pickles, and I think it was great."

"I still say it's peculiar. Like Mrs. Beezely, for that matter."

"She is not peculiar—she's my friend, and she's nice." Celia moved as far as possible away from Annie and perched on the banister rail.

"Heavens, Celia. You sound just like your daddy."

I hope so, Evelyn thought. Oh, I do hope so.

They all rocked again, a rumble of wood across wood.

Annie shifted in her chair, uneasy in the silence. "Alan sent his love, Evelyn. He said, 'Be sure to give Evelyn my love.' He was so sorry he couldn't come to the funeral, but he's sick. I think he has one of those flu bugs."

Agnes struck the arm of her chair, pursing her lips. "Annie, that is the fifth time today you've told us that stupid lie. The fifth time! Now we all know Alan's drunk as a lord, and has been for three days, so stop going on and on about it."

"He is not drunk, Agnes. He's had a hot toddy for his—his condition, but that's all."

Dear God. Evelyn leaned her head against the back of her chair and closed her eyes. Don't let them fight. Not today.

Annie held the lavender-saturated handkerchief to her mouth and spat out a lemon seed. "It was such a lovely service."

"Yes, it was," Sallie said quickly, hoping to silence her.

"Lovely. Really—lovely!" Annie insisted, as if they had disagreed. "And I know how much you're going to miss him, Evelyn. Believe me, I know. But it was the best thing for George. It was God's mercy, really."

"What?" Evelyn asked incredulously.

"Oh, Sis. You know perfectly well he wasn't happy. George had so many—sort of—peculiar ideas—he didn't fit in. And he never would. He was an outlander and always would have been."

"That's a lie—a lie—a lie!" Celia thrust herself from the banister, shrieking incoherently. "Just because he didn't go sneaking around behind people's backs like Uncle Alan ... he always said what he meant and he—my Daddy—he's—he *was* ..." Her head wrenched back in a spasm of sobbing. Slamming her glass on the tray, she bolted from Evelyn's reaching hands, ran down the steps, and disappeared around the house.

"Celia, honey—wait!"

Sallie stopped Evelyn at the screen door. "No. Let her go. Let the child meet her grief. Like most of us, she's just beginning to understand what she's lost."

Evelyn went swiftly into the house and up the steps.

Agnes chewed hard on an ice cube. "Annie, you are a classic old fool."

"But—I—I only meant—" What had she meant? It was supposed to be consoling. It had sounded consoling to her, when Alan said it, right after they heard George had—passed on.

Sallie leaned back in her chair with a sigh, twisting the ring on her right hand around on her finger. She was remembering the wild flowers in the cemetery. "I don't think George was the outlander. I think maybe we are."

"Mother! What's gotten into you?" In utter confusion, Annie rose and tugged her corset into place. "I think I'd best go home and check on Alan."

"Good idea," Agnes snapped. "You're no help around here."

With a virtuous sniff into her handkerchief, Annie was gone, trailing lavender as she waddled down the steps.

Sallie rocked gently. Yes, George was right. But now he was gone. Who would take up the burden he had left them? She glanced down at the ring she was twisting around and around on her finger. What could she do with these old and bony hands? Hands. Celia had wept for George's paralyzed hand. And only that morning, Sallie had awakened at first light, startled by what seemed to be a stranger's hand on the pillow. Dry and wrinkled; arthritic knuckles crooked under loose skin. What had happened to the years? She pushed the tiny pearl of the ring to the top of her finger, fondling it with her thumb. It was the first birthday gift Charles had given her. She would give it to Celia, she decided. Next birthday, while her hands were still young and pretty.

"... and Mother, I wish you could have seen Fred's face when I said I was proud that he quit. Do you know, he actually expected me to be mad? He's a sweet man, and a dear man, but I've never felt proud of him before. I never in this life thought he'd have the nerve to strike out on his own, and I am proud. So proud I could bust wide open."

Sallie was unhearing, her eyes distant.

"Mother?" Agnes watched anxiously. "Are you all right?"

"Yes." Sallie stopped twisting the ring. "I—I just feel so—old."

When Celia ran out of the house, she headed instinctively for the boat dock and the solace of open sky and cold salt water, the blessed privacy of space. Bertram-Down-Girl fell in beside her as she cut through the back yard, and she clutched the dog's collar, her fingers digging into warm black fur.

The tide was coming in. Heedless of lapping waves, girl and dog leaped off the seawall and waded through hip-deep water to scramble clumsily into the boat. Celia yanked loose the tie line, ripping a fingernail in her frenzy to get away. The engine would not start. After several angry attempts, she crawled to the hinged back seat and lifted it, searching through the tool chest for oar locks.

Celia took up the oars and rowed unevenly into the deep channel, swinging the boat away from town. But that was with the tidal current and the wind. "Always start out rowing against the tide," her father had told her. "That way, you'll have it with you on the way home, when you're tired." Three days ago she would have defied his caution. Today, it had already become legend, a loving dictum to be lovingly attended. She turned the boat around. Rather than row along Main Street, Celia headed for the maze of marshy islands across the channel, taking a diagonal course against the swifter deep-water currents. She rowed for an hour along empty inlets and white sandbars, pausing occasionally to watch one lone, circling gull. Celia reached the end of the marsh and stared across the wind-chopped bay, leaning on the oars. It was dangerous to go on without a motor, yet she could not face turning back. Where to go, and what to do? The boat coasted into a mudbank and was sharply spun around by the wind. So be it. She'd let it drift back toward town while she rested. She pulled in the oars and lay down on three life preserver cushions, with her head pillowed on Bertram-Down-Girl's back. Her eyes felt scratchy from crying and she let them close, lulled by the boat's gentle bobbing and the sound of wavelets slapping against the bow. She dozed lightly, to be awakened by a cold sense of blackness. Had a thundersquall blown up while she carelessly slept? Her eyes came open, but a cloudless sky still arched above her, brilliantly blue with sunlight and wind. Her bare legs and damp body lay sprawled in golden light. Then why was her face in shadow? Her head turned sharply, peering upside down at the bow of the boat. It had drifted into a narrow cove of the marsh, held against the mudbank by the wind. From where she lay, one tall sprig of marsh grass towered over her. She remained motionless, caught by the fact that one sprig of grass could split the sky, shatter the sunlight, spear the heavens. One slender sprig of grass. And the sky would never be wide again. Never arch above her without a slender, inherent shadow. It had never occurred to her that someone she loved could die. Could simply be snatched away. And now her father was lost to her. But Martha was lost to her too, and Martha wasn't dead. She might as well be. And so might Uncle Alan be dead, and Aunt Annie. And Thomas. They were all lost to her. Seizing an oar, Celia hastily thrust the boat away from the now ominous marsh grass.

There was a soft rippling sound, the noise of rushing wavelets. Celia turned her head to see riffles approaching her through the dead calm of the inlet. A porpoise abruptly surfaced, its head cutting the water to lead the long gliding arc of its body. Then another. And two more. Then countless more. A school of porpoises surrounded the boat, bumping it gently as they dived again and again, close enough for Celia to have touched their inquisitive faces. They seemed as curious about Celia as she was about them, apparently repeating their dives to peer into the boat. "They're smiling," she said aloud. And she began to laugh, leaning back against Bertram-Down-Girl and letting tears and laughter roll together. She rowed back into deep water and watched the porpoises swim away from her. No sign of the white one, but maybe one of them was the gray baby they'd rescued from the creek. Stiff with chill, Celia stood up and made her way to the stern. Standing tiptoe on the back seat, she watched the school of porpoises heading toward a bend of marsh and oyster banks. "Look at them!" she exclaimed. "Just look!"

Sensing her excitement, Bertram-Down-Girl lunged from her spot at the center of the boat. The small craft rocked heavily. Shrieking dismay, Celia was caught off balance and pitched head-first into the deep-dredged boat channel. She came up sputtering indignantly. "Damn you, Bertram!" she yelled, momentarily forgetting to add "Down-Girl." Barking ecstatically, Bertram-Down-Girl sprang into the water after her, swimming close to plant massive paws on Celia's shoulders and enthusiastically licking her face. Laughing and choking, Celia was again thrust underwater by the dog's heavy weight. She swam away a few strokes and came up yelling "Down-Girl!" The dog paddled contentedly around her, and the two floated easily along beside the drifting boat. Celia caught hold of the bow with one hand and Bertram-Down-Girl's collar with the other. "Silly dog. Don't you know I'm not ready yet for baptism?" She giggled, and rubbed her nose against the dog's. The icy water gave swift relief to Celia's tear-swollen eyes and eased the cramped feeling in her head. But she realized they were drifting into the boat lane, and she could hear a yacht approaching from behind the marsh. Reluctantly, Celia swung one leg over the port side and pulled herself into the boat. In deep water, she had to half lift, half drag Bertram-Down-Girl back into the boat, and almost fell overboard again in the process. Giggling foolishly, Celia collapsed against the life preservers with Bertram-Down-Girl licking her salty feet. The wind was blowing stronger now, and her wet clothing was cold paste on her body. Celia sat up and rubbed salt water from her eyes. She was laughing, she realized. Her father was dead, and she was laughing. She wondered about it, but felt no sense of shame. What was her mother doing, she suddenly thought. Certainly not laughing. She shouldn't have left her all alone like that, on that awful porch. And yet, she didn't want to go back. She dreaded facing people, dreaded the painful formalities of conversation. Slowly it occurred to her that perhaps her mother did, too. She should do something to help. But what?

The school of porpoises had shifted direction and were now swimming exuberantly in the wake of the yacht. Celia smiled, watching them. Vividly, she remembered her father standing in the slimy mud of the creek when they rescued the baby gray. "Take the first step," he had said. "That's the hardest one. After that, it's easy." Standing in the mud—standing before an ugly group of white-robed men. She wondered what his first step had been.

Celia slid the oars into place and began pensively rowing back to the dock. She would go and get her mother, and bring her back out in the boat. Maybe the porpoises would still be there. And then they would go by the store and thank Mrs. Beezely for the pickles—it was a long time since she had visited, and Mrs. Beezely surely must be lonesome. A boat ride; a visit. It wasn't much, Celia thought. But perhaps later she could think of something important to do. Or say. Even if she had to disagree with her cousins and her friends. "Marked," Ethel had said. Was that what it meant? The thought made her break into a cold sweat, remembering the first outcast days at school. Maybe. But, dear God, she prayed, please don't call on me to be marked too much too soon. She began rowing swiftly, exhilarated by the push of a freshening wind behind her and the swift cresting tide.

J
813.54
D 29

122045

LIVINGSTONE COLLEGE LIBRARY

3 7255 00004 5175

DATE DUE

DEMCO 38-297